BOOK 1

GHOST HUNTRESS
the awakening

MARLEY GIBSON

Houghton Mifflin Harcourt
Boston   New York   2009

ACKNOWLEDGMENTS

Thanks, first and foremost, to Deidre "Professor" Knight for her undying support of me and my writing career. The coach to my quarterback; the conductor to my orchestra; the seasoned batter to my deep-fried chicken. And for stepping off an airplane and planting the seed that eventually blossomed into the Ghost Huntress series.

Thanks to the incomparable Julia Richardson, who got exactly what I was trying to do with this series from the get-go. And to everyone at Houghton Mifflin for the wonderful support of Kendall and her pals.

Thanks to everyone at The Knight Agency, the TKA Sistahs, the Bunnies, the Sporkies, the Trackers, the Buzz Girls, NEC, CLWof TW, and the YARWA. Yes . . . all of those things mean something to the right people. A special shout-out, as always, to the WACs, Dr. Jessica Andersen and Charlene "Charmander" Glatkowski, for their daily support.

Thanks to my critique partners on this book: Wendy Toliver, Jenn Echols, and Diana Peterfreund.

Thanks to everyone at my day job who loaned—okay, begged me to use—their names for series characters. To my boss, Matt Raynor, for understanding what my writing means to me.

To my "spiritual" advisors on this whole project: the folks at the New England Ghost Project. Thanks to Ron Kolek, Maureen Wood, Jim Stoner, and Clay and Janet Rucker for all the fun on the ghost investigations.

To the experts in the paranormal community for supporting me: Jason Hawes, Grant Wilson, Chip Coffey, Chris Fleming, Michael and Marti Parry, "Darkness" Dave Schrader, and Patrick "Captain Knots" Burns.

Thanks to Comcast for bringing me hours of *Ghost Hunters, Ghost Whisperer, Lisa Williams, Most Haunted, Dead Famous, Haunting Evidence, Psychic Kids, Paranormal State,* and *Darkness Radio.com,* and all the other shows I absorbed while researching Ghost Huntress.

Thanks to Joe and Lizanne Harbuck, the parentals; to my sister's family, Jennifer, Dave, Sarah, Josh, and Stephanie Keller; and to my brother, Jeff Harbuck, for all of their love and support.

Finally, thanks to Mike and The Team, as always, for putting up with the *clickety-clack* of the keyboard when I'm in the writing blood fever. Thanks for doing the dishes and taking out the trash and designing my website and buying ghost-hunting equipment and accompanying me on all of these research trips. I couldn't have done this alone . . . nor would I have wanted to.

To the other two members of The Unholy Triumvirate,
Maureen Wood and Deidre Knight.
I couldn't have written this book without two such strong,
positive women in my life.

Luv, hugs, and light!

FOREWORD

I met Marley Gibson at one of the many paranormal conferences I regularly attend, and an instant friendship was born between us.

When I found out Marley was writing a Ghost Huntress book series, I was excited for her and offered to write the foreword for the first novel. Because the book is about a teenage ghost hunter, I had to seize the moment. I knew I had a unique opportunity to speak to the next generation of ghost hunters.

Reading Marley's book, I found many parallels to how I work in real life and what actual paranormal investigations are like. I read about investigations during which nothing "paranormal" happens—true to life. I read about an investigator going through a spiritual awakening—another thing that happens to many investigators. I was impressed to read such an accurate account of many facets of paranormal investigation, because so much of our work in this field is distorted by the very eyes and ears we experience it through. This genuine edge to Marley's work stems from her firsthand insight into how paranormal investigators really operate, as she is one herself.

While we are all entertained watching ghost hunting and paranormal investigation on television, it's important to remember it is just that—entertainment. To the new generation of ghost hunters, I urge you to take media accounts of paranormal activity with a grain of salt. No, that investigation was not really conducted and concluded in thirty minutes! What you see on television is almost always distorted in the editing room. No, you're not going to experience a paranormal event on every investigation. The harsh reality is that ninety-nine percent of the time spent on an investigation is waiting for something to occur—if it occurs at all. This is clearly not a pastime for the impatient or the hyperactive.

Neither should it be construed that what is presented on television is the final, irrefutable word. We are all still learning in a field that is almost entirely hypothetical in nature. Investigators can (and do) make mistakes and errors in assessing the evidence they collect. As such, I believe paranormal evidence is always inconclusive. We have no smoking gun pointing toward the existence of paranormal phenomena. Data collected at the present time cannot withstand the scrutiny of science. So we are left to speculate and hypothesize on the phenomena we observe and document. While it's fun to entertain the notion of the existence of ghosts, it's still inconclusive at the end of every investigation.

I'm often asked what is the most important piece of equipment to bring on a paranormal investigation. The answer to that inquiry is simple: an open, objective mind. I have seen many promising investigators (and even a few seasoned veterans) get themselves swept up in the thrill of the hunt. No foul on their part—the adrenaline rush we experience while poking around in a historic building in the middle of the night or being on a battlefield where thousands of soldiers lost their lives can and does distort our perception of reality. Eager to find that incredible photograph or mysterious voice on an audio recording, our minds let objectivity take a back seat. This is why re-reviewing your evidence the following day, after the adrenaline rush has worn off, is vital. Oftentimes a good night's rest and a fresh look the next day can point out errors missed the night before.

I could go on about this topic for many pages, but I won't. Instead, I will leave you with one parting thought. If you are serious about becoming an investigator, please do yourself and others dedicated to our field a favor and work alongside a reputable group or investigator before striking out on your own. Do this for at least two years to make certain it is something you are dedicated to doing. There are far too many "rogue" groups that set up shop with little to no experience conducting investigations. When an investigation goes bad, they end up giving the established and dedicated groups a black eye. Or they become disenchanted when it isn't exactly what they see on TV and fold the group, leaving their members and clients hanging.

There certainly is much more to being a paranormal investigator than watching a few TV shows and taking photos with a digital camera. To the dedicated and enlightened investigator, however, it is a true spiritual awakening to learn that death is not the end for us.

Patrick Burns
August 2008

Patrick Burns has been a paranormal investigator for almost twenty years. He is the founder of the Ghost Hounds group out of Atlanta and is the star of Tru TV's (formerly Court TV) Haunting Evidence. He is also the organizer and director of the GhoStock conferences, held twice yearly. For more information, visit Patrick at www.myspace.com/patrickburns or at www.patrick-burns.com.

CHAPTER ONE

IT'S TOO FREAKING QUIET HERE!

I can't sleep. Not a wink.

This is the third night in a row this has happened. Ever since we moved from my beloved twenty-two-hundred-square-foot high-rise condo on the Gold Coast of Chicago to this creaky old Victorian house here in Radisson, Georgia—i.e., out where God lost his shoes—I haven't had a decent night's sleep.

A teenager like me needs the proper amount of rest or else her growth will be stunted. It's bad enough I'm not blessed in the boobage department, like my *thirteen*-year-old sister, Kaitlin. Aren't older sisters supposed to develop faster? Now this whole insomnia prob. Oh, like dark circles under my eyes are going to make me even *more* popular when I start my new school tomorrow.

I roll onto my side and hang off the bed, peering over at the North American Van Lines cardboard box marked "Moorehead—Kendall's Bedroom." I wonder if there's any Tylenol PM in there from when I couldn't sleep last summer because I was working part-time at Intelligentsia Coffee on North Broadway and had a caffeine contact high. Hmm, probably not. I shouldn't take that anyway, especially since I turned down Mom's offer of a sleeping pill sample she got from the pharm rep—she's a nurse—that she occasionally takes. Course, my sleep disorder isn't related to hot flashes, like hers is. Mine's because of this freaking silence!

I mean, living in downtown Chicago since my birth, I got used to the noise of a city: The cacophony of cars, taxis, and delivery trucks. The hustle and bustle of tourists and townies alike trekking around the Windy City. The El with its metallic symphony along the rails. The planes from O'Hare and Midway coasting through the sky, like you could reach up, grab them, and hang on. To me, it's a harmonious concerto of urban life. Not this unbelievably earsplitting silence of Main Street in Radisson, Georgia.

I'm seriously not kidding about this deafening quiet. I'm almost on a first-name basis with the crickets and chirping cicadas that live in our backyard. I have to crack the window to let air in—I have a ceiling fan, but it's not helping with the night warmth—and the outdoor insects serenade me with their nightly opera while I lie here staring up at the crown molding on my bedroom ceiling. As my Grandma Ethel used to say, "It's so quiet you can hear the dead thinking."

Yeah, like that's what I want.

What I want is to see the inside of my eyelids and some

colorful, vivid dreams of the Justin Timberlake or Channing Tatum variety. That's what I'm talking about.

Flipping to the middle of the bed, I wipe the back of my hand across my forehead, mopping up the sweat from the September heat. At home in Chicago, I'd have my favorite Patagonia Synchilla blanket between the sheet and comforter to keep me warm. I hardly think I'll need it anytime soon here in Radisson. Which just ain't right. Nothing's right. Not anymore.

I don't want to be an angst-ridden, sulky sixteen-year-old, but this relocation *will* take some adjustment. Honestly, I haven't felt like myself since I moved into this house and started unpacking my things. I've had a killer headache for the past three days (behind my right eye), and no amount of ibuprofen can battle it. Maybe the pain's purely psychosomatic due to the whole moving away from everyone and everything I've known my *entire* life to a town no bigger than the Lincoln Park section of Chicago.

I roll around underneath the covers and rub my fists into my eye sockets to try and dig at the source of the headache. If I can just go to sleep, I'll be okay. A deep, deep sigh escapes my chest, blending into the whir of the ceiling fan. At first, I thought this not-so-Kendall feeling was allergies or something like dust mites from this musty hundred-year-old house. But I'm not sneezing or anything obvious like that. The symptoms border on weirdness more than anything else.

Like yesterday . . . I was hanging my whatnot shelf (you know, for all those trinkets your grandparents give you over the years from their travels) and my fingers got all tingly to the point where I couldn't hold the hammer anymore. Not like "oh shit, I'm having a heart attack" tingly. More like when your arm falls asleep and it feels like there are ten thousand ants marching underneath your skin. Yeah, like that.

Then when I was helping Mom set up the picnic table and hammock in the backyard, I literally burst into tears like I do whenever I watch *The Notebook*. Except I had no reason to cry. None. Whatsoever. Mom thought it was because I was depressed about being away from Chicago, which probably had a little to do with it, but it really made no sense. I told her I was PMSing so she wouldn't worry or try to cram some drug samples from her stash into me. The "that time of the month" answer seemed to satisfy her.

The most bizarre thing so far, besides gearing up to be a somnambulist (What? I listen to DJ Brian Transeau's music . . . he rocks!), happened when I was playing solitaire on my bed last night. I'm not talking computer Klondike, but honest-to-goodness playing cards—how old-fashioned of me!—because the cable and Internet connection isn't hooked up yet in the house. How does anyone expect me to exist and contact the outside world if I don't have my Comcast?

So, while I'm playing solitaire and shuffling the deck, the queen of hearts—that tarty wench—kept flying out. No matter how I shuffled or laid out the cards, that stupid woman with the bags under her eyes and the pissed-off look on her face found her way out of the deck. It was like the card had a mind of its own, and it massively creeped me out. As soon as the computer's connected, I'm totally Googling that damn card to see what that's all about. I'd heard from my friend Marjorie, back home—yes, Chicago is still home—that some people do tarot-like readings with ordinary playing cards. Not that I'm into that stuff or anything. Maybe I'll find a book on it and get an explanation. Or maybe I'll just go insane first.

Another deep groan from me as the wind catches the ivory-colored curtain next to my bed. The sheer linen drapery does a bit of a pole dance around one of the four bedposts. It's only nine thirty, but I thought if I went to bed earlier tonight—in anticipation of my first day of school tomorrow—I might fall asleep faster. No. Such. Luck.

My bedroom door opens with a squeak.

"Kendall? Are you awake, sweetie?"

"Of course," I say bitterly and kick off the thin comforter and sheet. "Sorry," I add.

"That's okay. I understand." Mom pushes into my room and snaps on the light. She's taken to wearing her shoulder-length brown hair up in a messy bun, making her look younger than her forty-eight years. I sit up, squint, and see that she's carrying a large box. "Your dad just got back from Mega-Mart—"

I interrupt her with a harrumph. "They actually have a Mega-Mart here?" Go figure.

She scowls at me a bit. "Now, Kendall, you haven't fallen off the edge of the earth. Sure, it's not downtown Chicago, but Atlanta is only an hour away and we have all the necessities of life right here in Radisson."

I blow a strand of brown hair off my cheek and swing my feet off the bed. Why Dad couldn't have gotten a job in the ATL is beyond me. I know he's, like, the best at what he does —he's a city planner—and Radisson's doing all of these improvements and renovations to make the town more appealing to families and industry, but it would've been nice to go from one urban area to another. I mean, during the Civil War, Radisson wasn't even important enough for General Sherman to burn it on his famous March to the Sea. How is it going to be the town for me?

Mom sets the box on the edge of my bed. "As I was saying, Dad bought this thinking it might help your little . . . problem."

Unless it's a cast-iron frying pan to bash me over the head with for a concussion-induced good night's sleep, I'm not interested. Ooo, maybe it's a wall-unit air conditioner, like Dad said he'll put in every room in this ultra-old house. *Scaaaaa-ore!*

"Look at this!" Mom tugs out a large, white speakerlike device that's about as big as a bathroom scale. "This will help you sleep."

I lower my brows as I read the box. "LifeSounds 440?"

Mom unfurls the long cord and stretches it over to the nearest electrical outlet. The machine buzzes to life, and the soft sound of static reverbs through my room. "It's a white-noise machine. They're supposed to be very useful for sleep problems."

"Aren't those for babies?" I ask, not convinced this is actually going to work.

Waving me off with a flick of her hand, Mom says, "Babies, adults, anyone who needs help with somnipathy." There she goes, getting all medical on my ass.

"Huh?"

"Sleep disorders."

"Mom, I don't think I have—" I bite my tongue because I don't *know* what I think I have.

She places the speaker on my nightstand and then reaches for the pamphlet that came with it. "Ooo, listen to this. 'The sounds of the LifeSounds 440 white-noise machine include a womb, heartbeat, and lullaby section. These natural sounds are peaceful and comforting to infants, providing a secure and calm feeling.' And look, Kendall, it has a one-hour timer, adjustable volume, and you can take it with you when you travel."

Right, because every girl wants to take a flipping baby monitor with her to a slumber party! "I don't think womb sounds are going to help at my age."

The light in Mom's eyes dims, spelling out her disappointment. I have to realize this move has been hard for her too. She had to give up her job in the neonatal ICU at Northwestern Memorial to take a staff-nurse position with the town's one (well, okay, maybe not *one*) doctor. I need to cut her some slack.

I swallow my annoyance at the entire sitch and smile. "I'm sorry. Thanks for getting this. I'll give it a try." Why not? Can't hurt.

She leans over and tucks me into the bed like she's been doing for as long as I can remember. The woman is a pro at hospital corners and literally traps me in the straight covers. She kisses me on the head. "Try to get some sleep, sweetie. Tomorrow's a big day."

"I know, Mom."

"You'll make lots of new friends and fit in . . . you'll see."

"I hope so." Although I have plenty of friends back in Chicago. "I just want to blend in, not be too different or anything." At least that's what I tell myself as I picture walking into a building full of strangers in a matter of hours.

"Deep, cleansing breaths, Kendall. Say a prayer and just relax," Mom says. "I believe your sleep issues are merely stress-related, and once you start school, everything will be back to normal." She moves toward the door.

"Thanks, Mom." Although what's normal now? No more Cubs games. Or Bears, or Blackhawks, or Bulls. (Sorry, not a White Sox fan.) No more movies at Century Landmark or hot dogs from Weiner Circle. No more St. Paddy's Day parades with the dyed-green river. No more treks to the Sears Tower to check out the views. No more ditching one day of school to go to an *Oprah* taping. No more Chicago Chop House with *the best* steaks on the planet. No more Marjorie. No more . . .

Mom turns back to me. "If you don't start getting regular sleep, I'm taking you to the doctor and we're putting you on some medication." She's not saying it as a threat, more as a point of information.

Bleck . . . I don't want to be one of those messed-up kids on seven different medications for all sorts of afflictions. I want to be a normal teenager who goes to school, has friends, watches too much TV, talks on the cell incessantly, and plans for her future. Not too much to ask, right?

Mom nods her head at me. "Try to get some sleep, sweetie. And remember to say your prayers." She flicks off the light and closes the door behind her.

"I always do." Mom's big on religion. Not in an "in tents for Jesus" sort of way, but as an important part of the fabric of the Moorehead household. I respect—and go along with—that.

I wrestle with the locked-down covers until the sheets are free from their mattress prison, and so am I. The white-noise machine churns away with a staticky rhythm on my right. It's a lulling kind of *whoosh, whoosh, whooshhhhhh*. I'll admit it is sort of calming. Maybe this will work. I turn onto my stomach and get in my preferred falling-asleep position, one hand under the pillow and the other on top, cuddling it. Eyes closed, I take one of those deep, cleansing breaths Mom talks about. *Breathe in through the nose, out through the mouth*. That's what I learned in the class Marjorie and I took at the Nature Yoga Sanctuary in Chicago last summer. *Breathe in through the nose, out through the mouth.* Lather. Rinse. Repeat.

After a good long while of deep breathing, I feel myself teetering on the edge of consciousness. Ahh, yes . . . "To sleep: perchance to dream: ay, there's the rub." (I love Shakespeare, what can I say?) I'm settling into my fluffy pillows, spiraling down into the lovely world of desperately needed REM, when I swear on a stack of Bibles that I hear a whisper.

"I'm heeeerrrrre."

I peel one eye open. "Who's there?"

"I'm heeeerrrrrre."

"Kaitlin, if that's you, I'm going to beat the shit out of you," I snap, thinking my brat of a little sister is being, well, a brat. "Is that you?"

"Nooooooo . . ."

Okay, what the . . . ? The hairs on my arms rise, as does my anxiety level. I sit up. "Who's there?" I repeat more firmly.

Nothing. Silence. Except for the white-noise machine.

After a minute, my heart rate returns to some semblance of normal. I lie back down, ridiculously annoyed. I'm sure it was Kaitlin totally screwing with me. She's such a PITA. (Do I need to explain what that stands for? Rhymes with Pain in the Glass.)

Settling into the pillow again, I restart with the *breathe in through the nose, out through the mouth* when I hear the whisper once more.

"I'm heeeerrrrrrre."

Bolting up, I jerk on the lamp cord. "Look! You're pissing me off!"

I glance around the room, and there's no one there. No Kaitlin. No Mom. Just my large brown Gund teddy bear, Sonoma, sitting on the rocking chair next to my bed, looking at me like I've lost my marbles. The white-noise machine continues to *whoosh* beside me. Maybe if I turn the volume up, it'll block out whatever it is—probably the television from Mom and Dad's room—that I'm hearing.

Just when I lift the volume level, I hear it again.

"Are you hearing meeeeeeee?"

I fling off the covers and sit up stiff-straight. Chill bumps dance across my skin, making tiny mountains in my sweaty flesh. The hairs on the back of my neck are at complete military attention. I swallow hard but find a massive lump of unease in my esophagus that isn't budging.

Holy Mother of Christmas Past! The whispering voice is coming from the white-noise machine! Are you effing kidding me?

You're here? Well, I'm *out* of here!

CHAPTER TWO

"YOU DIDN'T HAVE TO DRIVE ME, Mom," I say the next morning. I squint behind my super-trendy (at least they were in
Chi-Town) black Coach sunglasses that hide my sleep-de-
prived eyes from the blaring Georgia sunshine.

Our Toyota Sienna is parked in front of this extremely aged,
brick building with *Radisson High School* chiseled in the top
cement in a very Times New Roman way. It's a three-story
building that looks old as dirt. The American flag out front
flaps crazily in the strong breeze. To the left is a student parking lot full of pickup trucks, SUVs, and the random Jeep. I
wish I had my own car and didn't have to be carted in like . . .
well, Kaitlin. Sure, I expected Mom to drive her to school, but
a junior like me just should *not* be seen in the family minivan.
Especially when it still has Illinois plates that scream *Look at
me! Look at me!*

"I can walk from here," I say.

"But Kendall—"

Quickly, I unclick the seat belt and feel the kink in my

back from sleeping on the sectional sofa in the living room. There was no way in blue-blazing hell that I was going to sleep in my room—even if I could have—after that raspy-whispering-from-the-noise-machine incident that nearly made me have a frickin' embolism. My pulse was in overdrive, as was my imagination, apparently set on determining exactly what it was I'd heard. Somewhere in the middle of it all, curled on the couch in a protective fetal position, I managed to get a couple of hours of shuteye.

That's when I saw . . . him.

Well, not *saw* saw him. Dreamed of him. This goooooor-geous guy. Not any guy that I know—certainly no one from back home in Chicago. I swear, he had the most amazing Dasani-bottle-blue eyes I've ever seen in my life. It was like he knew me—dare I say?—soul deep.

After I woke up, I rubbed images of the gorgeous guy from my sleep-neglected eyes. I took the world's hottest shower and got dressed in the Blue Cult jeans that Marjorie gave me (don't tell me they're not stylish, because they make my hindquarters look fabulous) and a simple long-sleeved navy shirt that fits snugly over my 32As (don't poke fun!). Hmmm . . . blue seems to be my color of choice today. As much as I know I *will* stand out, I don't want to wear anything socially suicidal on my first day. I mean, jeans are universal for teens everywhere. Surely I won't muck it up too badly. Unless they say the brand is last season?

Mom unlatches her seat belt as well. "I'll come in with you."

I stop her with my hand. "No. I can do this myself. How hard can it be?"

"Well, Kendall, I went in with Kaitlin and—"

"Kaitlin's thirteen. I'll be okay, Mom. I swear."

"Don't swear, dear. It's not proper."

What is proper these days? Good thing Mom can't hear the wild pounding of my heart or the ringing in my ears. And that irritating headache from last night has returned. Only this time, it's in the back of my neck. *Thump, thump, thump,* like there's a tiny elf with an even tinier hammer beating on my cerebellum. Geez, Louise! I need to pop an Excedrin—or four—fast. The throbbing's probably stress from fitful sleep, starting a new school, and my overactive imagination that conjured up Dasani-Blue-Eyed Boy. Yeah, that's it.

I stretch across the console and plant a quick kiss on Mom's cheek. "Love ya! Mean it!" Before she can say another word, I hop out into the sea—okay, more like a gentle country river —of students headed into the hallowed halls of Radisson High. There are kids swooping in on bikes and skateboards. A Ford F-150 with about six guys in the back drives by and squeals into a parking space. There's a scary-looking guy in leather on a rather impressive red and yellow crotch rocket, and even one tall girl on a Segway. Who knew you could get one of those around here?

Taking a deep breath and mentally begging the head pain to go away, I put one Reebok'd foot in front of the other and slowly walk the brick path toward the front door of RHS.

Here goes nothing.

"I'm Kendall Moorehead," I say to the woman behind the counter in the school's office. "I was told to check in here because I'm new."

The frazzled lady takes a pencil from behind her ear and places it between her teeth. "Evvwyonez sorrrda nooo tahdahy."

"Excuse me?"

She removes the pencil. "Sorry, it's just that everyone's sort of new today, sugah, with it being the first day of school and all and everyone getting settled." She thumbs through a stack of cards and pulls one out. "Here you are. Moorehead, Kendall. Your first class is Mrs. Johnston's. Round yonder, hit the stairs, third floor, room three thirty-three."

I stare at the card in my hand, trying not to be hypnotized by her singsongy Southern accent. Guess I'll have to get used to that, now that I'm living in the South. Hmm . . . calculus, physiology, English literature, history, Spanish I, and computer lab. I see my classes have already been picked, probably by my mom. Fine. Whatever. It's all core stuff I need anyway.

The pencil-chewing woman stares at me. "Now scoot! You don't want to be late. First impressions are everything."

She's telling me this? At least I styled my hair this morning with something other than number-two lead and yellow paint and I managed to get my cereal inside of me instead of on the front of my shirt, like her. Frowning, I mentally scold myself for being so judgmental, particularly when I'm about to hop on the stage in three seconds and be judged by Randy, Paula, Simon . . . and all of Radisson High. Sure, I've seen all those teen movies where the heroine is a fish out of water and soon takes over the school and wins the heart of the popular-quarterback-who's-really-a-sensitive-headed-for-an-Ivy guy. This is not a movie. This is my life. I've never been the new girl. In my sixteen years, I've been educated solely by the Chicago public school system. I don't know if I'm ready for how they do it here.

Instead of heading straight up to Mrs. Johnston's homeroom class, I leave the office and weave through a maze of probing eyes—why can I feel each individual scan?—and not-so-faint whispers to find the ladies'. I push into the bathroom, and it seems that every girl in there turns to check me out. I might as well be holding up a sign that reads I'm Not from Round Here.

Really, there's not much for them to see other than an ordinary Midwesterner with long, ever-so-slightly wavy brown hair, very little makeup—some eyeliner and mascara—and a nose full of freckles. Okay, so Marjorie thinks I'm a little on the Amanda Bynes end of the scale, which is fine with me. She's a fave of mine, so I'll take it as a compliment. I lower my eyes (hazel, BTW) and look at my feet as I walk to the sink. All around, I hear girls grab their books and bags and rush out, obviously hurrying to class. Which is what I should do, instead of dawdling.

I think of splashing some cold water onto my face, but I'm not a hundred percent sure that my mascara is waterproof. Since there's no major mall here in Radisson, I had to settle for a pink container of some Maybelline, L'Oréal, or what have you from Mega-Mart in lieu of my regular waterproof Clinique that I can't find anywhere in my makeup bag— Kaitlin probably boosted it without my permission. Instead, I turn on the hot and cold water and wash my hands with the generic, detergenty-smelling soap.

All of a sudden, my stomach cramps up. A burning pain that sears me right in the middle, like I've been slashed with Darth Vader's light saber. It really hurts. Like, bad. Like I want to throw up. The nausea is rising up into the back of my throat and there's a wicked acid sensation. I move toward the stalls, thinking I'm gonna get sick all over the place, when I hear the sounds of someone *actually* retching. *Ewww* . . . now I'm really gonna blow chunks. I so can't deal with hearing someone else barfing. I nearly double over from the tenderness in my throat and the ache in my abdomen. It's almost as if I'm feeling *her* throwing up.

That's just goofy as hell, though.

At the sink, I jerk the faucet back on and scoop a handful of cold water into my mouth, trying to wash away the yucky sensation. A toilet flushes down on the end of the row. More retching sound amplifies inside my headache. Jesus . . . what's going on with me?

A stall door opens and out walks the tall girl I'd seen outside in the parking lot on a Segway. Is she the one who was sick? No, for some reason I know she's not. Plus, she kind of screws up her nose when the gagging sound continues. She stands next to me at the sinks and looks me over. Lowering her brows, she asks, "Are you okay?"

I nod and then dab my mouth with the coarse, industrial paper towel. "Yeah. I'm just sensitive to hearing other people . . . you know, puking like that."

The girl waves her hand in the air dismissively and then goes to wash her hands. "Don't pay any attention to it. It's just RHS's own after-school special."

"Excuse me?"

She lowers her voice and points behind us. "Courtney Langdon. Cheerleader. Does it all the time when she's trying to keep her size-zero figure for football season."

"I think that's called a disease."

The tall girl shrugs. "Try telling *her* that. Splurge and purge. That's her lifestyle."

I bend to look under the stall and see this Courtney girl still on her knees. "Shouldn't someone do, like, an intervention or something? Tell the school nurse? Advise her parents of what she's doing?"

"Nah," the girl whispers. "She'd scratch your eyes out for

doing that. She's a certified bitch. We're all used to it. You'll get used to it too."

Well, who am I to take on the school bitch on my first day?

I doubt I'll get used to it, though. Especially if it causes horrific suffering of my own, like I'm currently experiencing. "I, umm, suppose so." I just hope the "bitch" doesn't hear us talking about her.

The tall girl smiles at me like she's sizing me up. I do the same to her. She's lanky and slightly geeky, wearing a graphic T-shirt that reads "More Cowbell" half tucked into a pair of dark, worn Levi's. And she's as flat-chested as I am. Thank God for small miracles! (No pun intended.) It's apparent from her relaxed look that she's not too worried about fashion. Or maybe she's just comfortable in her own skin. Her hair is messy, black, and in a bob that fits her smiling face well.

The toilet flushes and I hear Courtney, of tossed-cookie fame, gather her things and bang out of the stall. I stare at her mane of golden blond hair and her thick, thick makeup that you could almost carve your name in with a fingernail.

Courtney sneers at me. "What are *you* looking at?"

I shift my eyes down to the floor. "Nothing. Sorry."

"Damn right." She whips the tip of a berry-colored lipstick over her mouth and then nods at the tall girl in the mirror. "Junior year and I see you're still a fashion disaster." Then she turns and leaves.

When the door shuts, I can't stop myself from saying, "What a beeyotch."

The tall girl shrugs. "Told ya."

The bell rings and I feel my nausea dissipate just as quickly as it started.

Huh . . . that's weird. All that pain must have been from first-day nerves. I'd like to talk to this girl more, but I don't want to be late for homeroom. "Crap! I better run to class," I say.

"Hope to see you later," she shouts after me.

"Yeah, me too!"

I take the stairs two at a time to get up to Mrs. Johnston's class. Talk about a workout! When I finally reach the top, a little more winded than I'd like to be, I see that room 333 is bright and airy. Mrs. Johnston has the windows open, and I can hear birds chirping away like a Disney soundtrack gone bad. It's as if the birds are sitting here on the desk in front of me. Do I have some sort of bionic ear all of a sudden? I feel like I'm ear-jacking the birds' feathery conversation. Or maybe it's just that the stillness of a small town makes any sound more amplified.

There's a seat in the next to the last row by the window, so I swerve through the backpacks and stretched-out legs of my fellow classmates and plop down. The students look . . . normal. Girls in jeans and cute tops and guys in khakis and NFL gear. They have hairstyles that look the same as we have in Chicago, with the exception of some of the boys who sport 'Bama Bangs like the gang from MTV's *Two-a-Days*.

One really pretty girl with long, flowing gold-blond hair— all glossy and perfect, resembling a Pantene commercial—

smiles warmly at me. I bet she's one of the popular kids, with a face like that. She's probably best friends with that Courtney Langdon chick too. I can see it now: they're the heads of some high school sorority that you can join only if you can trace your family tree back to Scarlett O'Hara. They'll laugh at me as I walk through the lunch cafeteria, for eating the wrong food or what have you.

However, Pretty Girl smiles again and waves at me in welcome.

I snicker to myself. *Geez . . . paranoid much, Kendall?* I can't help it, though. This is all so new to me. I can't assume that I'm going to fit in. My accent is different from everyone else's. That alone is bound to get me a mass inspection. Then again, maybe Pretty Girl will invite me to sit with her and her friends and introduce me around, then include me in the Scarlett O'Hara–ish secret sorority. I can't be so negative. I've got to be optimistic. What other choice do I have?

As I'm pulling my notebook and my favorite blue (again with the blue!) Uni-ball pen out of my bag, I get this intense, shooting pain in my left leg. It's not like the tingly, fallen-asleep feeling my hands have been experiencing the past few days. This freakin' hurts! If I didn't know any better, I would think my tibia had cracked right below my kneecap. Huh? How do I know that? Am I suddenly an intern at Seattle Grace, or what? Sweat dots my upper lip, and the underside of my hair dampens. My breathing increases, like when I'm on an airplane and we're about to take off. I do *not* like to fly, so my dad always tells me to stare out at the horizon. Only right now, the horizon for me is the lush, green schoolyard of Radisson High, and it is so not helping.

I sense fresh, hot tears pooling in my eyes from the severe throbbing in my leg, and I try to pinpoint what's happening to me. Rubbing hard on my left calf muscle, I literally feel the warm anguish of a break. I broke my arm when I was nine years old, so I know what the sensation is like. Holy crap! Seriously, did I dislocate some ligaments or jar something loose when I was barreling up the stairs? Is this some sort of inherited degenerative bone disorder no one in the family warned me about? I certainly don't remember knocking into anything in the last few minutes. Folks, I'm on full freak-out mode inside my head.

I have to do something about this. Like, now.

I'm about to raise my hand and ask for some help getting down to the school nurse's office when I see a large guy come into the classroom.

"Okra!" a guy shouts out at him.

"Hey, it's Okra!"

This kid's name is Okra? Like the vegetable?

"What up, dawwwwwwgs?" he calls out.

Mrs. Johnston rises from behind her desk and removes her reading glasses. "Why, Sean Carmickle. I didn't think we'd see you today. I heard that was a nasty fall you took off your father's tractor, young man."

"Yes, ma'am," he says. "Fixed myself up real good. Doctor said no football for me this year, but I might be able to play roundball if it heals up okay by January."

"You poor thing. We'll certainly miss you at wide receiver."

"You know it!" his friend—more than likely a teammate—shouts out.

Mrs. Johnston nods. "Sean, you just go take a seat over there so you can stretch yourself out."

Curiosity is totally killing the Kendall-Cat.

I tuck my foot underneath myself to get a few extra inches of height so I can see over the kids in front of me. The searing pain in my leg continues to thud and I feel my eyes grow wide as I look at Sean "Okra" Carmickle hobble on his crutches across the room to take a seat. When I finally get a full view of him, I nearly choke on my intake of breath. His left leg is encased up to his thigh with a thick white plaster cast, obviously surrounding his broken bone.

Hold the phone!

Okra's left leg. My left leg.

My mind is reeling. Spinning, even, as I think of the ridiculous chances.

Courtney getting sick. Me feeling sick.

Then it hits me like Brian Urlacher sacking Tom Brady on fourth and long . . .

Jesus in the garden! Am I feeling *other people's* pain?

How is that even possible?

CHAPTER THREE

"KAITLIN, I'M GONNA TAKE A NAP, so don't get into any trouble, understand?"

"Kiss my butt, Kendall." She sticks her tongue out at me. "You're not my mother."

Why does Kaitlin love to push my buttons so much? "No, I'm your big sister." I swear, I can't believe we came from the same parents. "When Mom and Dad are at work, I'm in charge."

"In your dreams." She plops down in front of the television and cranks up Halo 3 on the Xbox. I'll never understand why my parents let her play shit like that, which only serves to warp her already demented mind. Whatever.

"Well, I'm going upstairs and putting my headphones on." What's the point? She's not even listening to me. "Unless you've severed an artery and are bleeding to death, it would behoove you not to disturb me, okay?"

She blinks twice at me. "*Behoove*'s not a word. You made that up."

I roll my eyes. "Look it up in the dictionary, brainiac."

With that, I pound upstairs to my room, the second bed-room on the right. It's in the front of the house, overlooking Main Street, with a nice bay window and a cushiony seating area. I wish I'd gotten the back bedroom, but Kaitlin snagged it when we first walked into the house. Mom told me to "be the bigger person" and let her have it. Her room has a huge walk-in closet and its own bathroom. I have to use the one in the hallway with the antique claw-foot tub and added-on showerhead. Fine. At least all of Kaitlin's wet towels and ridiculously large bras won't be in there, like when we lived in Chicago and had to share. Maybe there's a weird-ass voice in her room too to scare the crap out of her. *Mean Kendall.*

Peeling off my school clothes—an uneventful day at best, consisting of syllabuses (or is it *syllabi*?), welcome-backs, and fish sticks with mac and cheese for lunch—I grab my dad's Bobby Hull jersey (Chicago Blackhawks' Golden Jet from the '70s) and climb onto my four-poster bed. Exhaustion has overridden the panic from the happenings of last night. Besides, it's daylight, and I can see if anything freaky happens in the room. I want to get cuddly with my pillow. My MP3 player has been charging since this morning, so I should get at least four hours of tunes while I snooze away. Because I *am* going to get some sleep.

Queuing up a good old favorite Justin Timberlake CD, *FutureSex/LoveSounds*—Marjorie and I saw the concert when he played the Allstate Arena in Rosemont, IL—I squiggle the earbuds in tight so that nothing bothers me. I'll be damned if

I'm turning the noise machine on. Besides, the sexy falsetto of JT is enough to drown out the buzzing of the neighbor's lawn mower down below.

A few minutes later, I'm heading into the zone, where Justin and Timbaland are well on their way to bringing "SexyBack," when the MP3 player completely craps out.

Sitting up, I look at the digital display. "Are you kidding me?" The battery symbol is flashing, which means it's almost completely drained. Dead. "But I charged it all day." I hang off the side of my bed to get the cord, but it's not anywhere in sight. "It was just there!" I say to no one.

Back home, Kaitlin used to move my things around all the time. I swear, if she's messing with me, I'm going to ignore my parents' dictate to spare the rod and spoil the child. That is one majorly spoiled child as it is. She needs a good spanking, especially if she took my charger.

Bulling out of my room and down the staircase, I stop in my tracks when I see Kaitlin fully ensconced in her Halo 3 diversion. Whoa. She doesn't look like she's moved from there at all. No one else is here, so who took my cord? Did Mom hire a maid that I don't know about?

My fingers tiptoe over my forehead as if to touch the sharp pain that has returned. I press hard into my skin. It's no use, though. I give up. I'm doomed. Sixteen and living a hopeless life at the moment. I wish I could walk out to the end of Navy Pier—no, I don't want to drown myself or anything, just drink in the briny aroma of Lake Michigan. That always used to chill me out.

Since I can't do that, I head to the kitchen. I grab a bottle of water from the fridge and fish out the Cheetos from the over-the-sink cabinet. If I'm surrendering to whatever funk has overtaken me, I'm not going down hungry. Then I hop into a pair of shorts from my old school, which I dig out of the laundry basket by the door, and walk carefully over the rickety back porch and down the steps. Flinging myself into the hammock, I start stuffing the puffed treat into my mouth.

After several ounces and way too many Weight Watchers Points—my mom's all about the Points, and we all suffer through it with her—I set the half-eaten bag on the ground and wipe the Cheetos dust onto my shorts. The food has helped curb my headache a bit, but I still have this remarkably uneasy feeling about . . . everything.

"Am *I* doing this?" I ask, wondering when I started talking to myself. Well, I have no friends here, so who better to trust than *moi*. "The headaches, the hand tingling, the loss of sleep. Then there was that whole weird thing when that chick was barfing in the bathroom . . . and then that Okra guy with the broken leg. I totally felt it. I won't even think about the voice in my room last night."

"What voice?"

I nearly flip out of the hammock, but manage to right myself before eating a face full of the lawn. Looking up at the tall visitor I'd talked to earlier at school, I say, "Man, you scared hell and four dollars out of me."

The girl reaches into her pocket, digs out a five, and tosses it at me. "Keep the change," she says with a smile. I can't help but laugh. "Sorry I didn't introduce myself in the bathroom this morning . . . or in calculus class. You have Mr. Kline, right?" she asks. It had been nice to see a semifamiliar face in class. Of course, that puking Courtney chick is in my physiology class.

Standing up, I say, "Yeah, that was me in calculus." I stretch out my hand like my mom taught me. "I thought I saw you in the back, drawing in your notebook."

She shakes my hand firmly. "Yep. I'm Celia Nichols. I live over there." She points across our backyard toward the gigamonic white Tara–like mansion on the street behind us.

"You live *there?*" I manage. "Isn't it, like, historical and stuff?"

She shrugs, and her wavy bob moves in the September breeze. "Yeah, it's one of the town's original houses. Apparently, General Sherman had the hots for the woman who owned it way back when, so he didn't burn it during the Civil War. At least, that's what my parents found out when they moved in back in the late eighties. My parents are kind of older and had me late in life, you know? Of course, back then, real estate prices were inflated due to Reaganomics, and in smaller U.S. towns you could find real estate steals such as my house, which was protected because of its historical status. The main reason historical homes were selling low in the eighties was that no one yet understood the true intrinsic value—"

"You said your name's Celia?" I ask, interrupting her. Man, she could talk the ears off a billy goat, as my Grandma Ethel— she was from *southern* Illinois, close to the Kentucky border— used to say. I need to be nice, though. The girl may be somewhat awkward, a little geeky, and in need of a consultation with Tim Gunn and Heidi Klum, but she's making an effort to be neighborly. "I'm Kendall. Kendall Moorehead."

She squints her dark eyes at me. "I figured as much. Mama said y'all were from up north. Which is totally cool with me. I'm an equal-opportunity person and all of that."

Trying not to chuckle too hard, I say, "Well, I'm not from 'up north.' We moved here from Chicago. Not exactly a bastion of damn Yankees, but Illinois *is* a blue state."

"So, what voices were you talking about?" Celia asks.

I bite my bottom lip. "Oh, you heard me, huh?"

"Yeah, it's pretty quiet around here."

"You've got that right." Except when it comes to white-noise machines. A shudder creeps up my spine. Even the thought of that voice causes the hairs on my neck to electrify like they're being charged by the Van de Graaff generator I saw on my school's overnight field trip to the Ontario Science Centre. Oh, Canada . . . talk about needing a visit to the salon afterward.

"So . . . come on," Celia says. "It's better to talk to a real person than to talk to yourself, don't you think? Despite my diarrhea of the mouth—which my dad says I was born with —I can be a really good listener. You got any more of those Cheetos?"

Gross image aside, she's right. It is nice to have someone to talk to other than Kaitlin and her prepubescent brain. Like I could tell my little sister about last night. Not in a gazillion years. I reach down and pass the Cheetos to Celia and sit in the middle of the hammock. "Here you go. They're my favorite."

"Mine too!" Celia grabs a handful and pops two of them into her mouth. When she finally swallows, she says, "So, Kendall, as I see it, I am officially your first friend here in the great state of Georgia and the mighty town of Radisson."

Grinning, I say, "It would appear so."

"This means you have to confide all of your troubles, se-crets, and desires to me." Her mouth quirks into a crooked smile, and I can tell she's as hungry for a friend as I am. "This voice you speak of . . ."

"I speak of?" I fall backwards on the hammock. "You must read as much Shakespeare as I do."

Celia puts her hand to her chest. "'So wise so young, they say do never live long.'"

"Ahhh . . . *Richard III.*"

"You are very good, Lady Moorehead. Now, enough distractions. Out with it." Celia munches on an extra-long Cheeto and fixes her dark brown stare on me.

"Do you know anything about my house?" I ask with some trepidation. "Like, its history?"

"What? That it's haunted?"

Choking a bit on my gasp, I stare at her wide-eyed. Wow, she's so matter-of-fact. "Is that what you heard?"

She wipes her hand on the knee of her jeans. "This *is* a historic Civil War town. Almost everything in Radisson is allegedly haunted by something. The lady who lived here before y'all said the house was haunted, so that's why she had so many cats. To give her a heads-up whenever she had—shall we say —company of an otherworldly nature." Celia glances about. "I think a few of the cats are still around here. Natalie, Buckley, and one other. For what it's worth, I'm sure my house is haunted too. I've tried setting up my digital recorders, but Dad always tells me to take them down because I taped one to a windowsill and it crashed down in the middle of the night."

I'm confused as I try to process and digest everything. "What do you mean?"

Celia's eyes grow big again. "Haven't you ever watched the Sci-Fi channel?"

"We get the Sci-Fi channel this far out in the boonies?" Color me surprised.

Clicking her tongue, Celia says, "Radisson isn't some one-horse town, Kendall. We've got everything. It's the world headquarters of Mega-Mart!"

"For real?"

"Yeah, Radisson may be spread out, but we've got whatever you need. And you've got to watch the Sci-Fi channel. They have this show about these guys named Jason and Grant in Rhode Island who do paranormal investigations. They're plumbers by day and ghost hunters by night. Then on the Travel Channel there's this show from England called *Most Haunted,* and they do the same thing. There are psychic investigators and historians and a crew and—"

Holding my hand up, I stop her. "Wait! Are you saying you've tried ghost hunting?"

"Totally!" She shoves the Cheetos at me. "Here. BRB!" I watch as she bolts on gazelle-like legs through my yard and across the street to her house. She disappears behind the large front double doors.

I hope she comes back!

I can't believe we're talking so freely about ghosts and spirits and all that. Like it's a normal topic of conversation. More than likely, Celia Nichols was just humoring me before and now she's gone off to call the authorities to come throw a net over me. Hmm . . . maybe I don't want her to return.

Just then, a tabby cat wanders into the yard from the dividing bushes next door. The cat locks eyes with me and makes a beeline over. She—I can tell it's a she—rubs my leg and starts purring like we're long-lost friends. Her tag has a rabies-shot registration from a local Radisson vet. Okay, so there is more than one doctor in Radisson.

As I'm scratching the kitty behind the ear, Celia hustles back across the road. She's carrying some electronic equipment with her and wears the biggest grin on her face. Seems I've touched a nerve with the talk of ghosts in Radisson. But honestly, is that really what woke me up last night? Couldn't I have been hearing someone's conversation from next door or out on the street? Was a TV left on somewhere? Right. What TV says "I'm here"? I simply have no other explanation, so I prepare myself as Celia sits on the ground next to me and the kitty.

"Eleanor! That's the name I couldn't remember," she says, snapping her fingers at the feline.

The tabby gazes up at me like she can see into my soul. "Well, hey there, Eleanor."

Rarrrrrrahhhh . . .

"Natalie's the one you have to look out for," Celia notes.

"Why's that?"

"Solid black."

I snicker. "You don't believe that hooey about a black cat bringing bad luck, do you?"

"It's more than that." Celia twists her arms around and cracks her bones. "Mrs. Elliott, the woman y'all bought the house from, said Natalie knew when things were going to happen. She'd jump up on the bed and thump her tail like mad."

I furrow my brows. "What kind of things?"

Celia shrugs as she fidgets with the equipment she brought over. "I don't know. Bad things. The cat predicted that hurricane we got two falls ago, and a fire down at the Methodist church. Last time it happened, Mrs. Elliott's brother was in a car wreck an hour later over in Lumpkin, Georgia, so she up and moved away to be with him . . . and she left all of the cats behind."

I almost feel like growling. My hackles are up. Especially since I used to volunteer once a month at the downtown Chicago SPCA. "She *left* her pets? What a horrible woman! I'll take care of Natalie if she comes around." I look at the kitty next to me. "I'll take care of you too, Eleanor."

Celia bites her lip slightly. "Just be careful, Kendall."

Careful of a cat? Right.

I let out a sigh and then turn my attention to the electronics on the ground before me. "What's all this?"

"It's a mini-DVD recorder. I got it off eBay last October for a steal! The batteries are fully charged, but you have to know that entities from the other side like to suck the life out of batteries. It's a known fact. They use the energy to move things or be seen or heard."

"How . . . how do you know all of this?"

"TV. Well, TV and the Internet. You can learn more from Google and Wikipedia than you ever can in school," she says proudly.

I think about how my MP3 player just died after like five minutes when it had been charging all day. Could that be what happened to it? An "entity" sucked the energy out of it? Surely not.

I pick up something that looks like a remote control. "What's this?"

Celia's face lights up. "Oh! It's an EMF meter."

"A what?"

She takes the device and turns it over in her palm. "An electromagnetic-field meter. It's a scientific gadget for measuring electromagnetic radiation and energies." I can tell she's gearing up for another long speech. "See, there are lots of types of EMF meter, but the two largest categories are single-axis and tri-axis."

"Ummm . . . Celia . . ."

"Single-axis meters are cheaper than tri-axis meters, but they take longer to completely read energies because the meter only measures one field dimension. Single-axis instruments have to be tilted and turned on all three axes to get an accurate measurement. A tri-axis meter measures all three axes at the same time, but they're usually tons more expensive. Most meters measure the electromagnetic-radiation flux density, which is the amplitude of any emitted radiation. Other meters measure the change in an electromagnetic field over time."

Oh. My. God!

I grab my head. "Celia! Yo! You're freakin' killing me!"

"Sorry," she says with a giggle. "I tend to get carried away."

"You think?" I ask with a laugh.

"Basically, an EMF can alert you to a spirit's presence." She pauses for a minute and then taps the meter. "I'm just excited to have someone to talk to about all of this. I've been doing a lot of research on it."

As strange as this talk is, I'm enjoying Celia's company. It's nice to hang with someone since Marjorie is more than a thousand miles away, probably socializing with Andrew Arnott, who she's had a crush on since, like, forever. Man, she'll laugh her ass off at me when I tell her about all of this ghost talk, if I can ever get her on the phone.

"I'm glad you came over," I finally say to Celia. "I was starting to think I was going through a mental breakdown." Who says I'm not, though? Maybe I can tell Celia about my lack of sleep, the strange tingling in my arms, the headaches, and the overall sense of weirdness that flitters through me. Or even how I felt Courtney's and Okra's pain. Nah—that can wait until we've known each other more than a day.

I take her mini-recorder in my hand. "So, what am I supposed to do with this?"

She smiles brightly. "It's got super night vision on it and will record for up to five hours."

"Impressive. Record what?"

Her messy hair blows into her eyes and she peers at me through the strands. "You're going to set it up in your room and get some video of that ghost you've got living in there."

I think my mouth falls open. "Whuuu-huh?"

Oh yeah. I've definitely stepped off into the deep end.

CHAPTER FOUR

HIS EYES ARE HYPNOTIC. *Piercing blue and crystal clear, like pictures of the Caribbean Sea that travel agents have on their websites.*

Those mesmerizing eyes are looking right at me. Through me, almost.

"Kendall . . ." he whispers in a voice that gives me (good) chills.

I wipe at the image in the air with my hands, trying desperately to see more of him. He's not too tall and he has broad shoulders. His hair is a golden blond, cut in a short crop, but long enough for a girl to run her fingers through it and really enjoy it.

I'm falling . . .

Not in love—although I won't rule it out—but literally falling.

My arms flail about, searching for anything to stop my plunge down . . . down . . . down what? Oh . . . stairs. I'm falling down stairs. Oh God! This is going to hurt like hell.

Suddenly, I'm in his arms and I'm eyeball to eyeball with those amazing Dasani-bottle-blue orbs. I'm swimming in them, trying to find my breath that seems to have been knocked away. His strength cradles and protects me.

"I've got you, Kendall."

But who are you?

I pull back and finally see his face. Holy shit, he's gorgeous. Tan, straight nose, strong jaw. There's a small mole on his left cheek. His eyelashes are golden, just like his hair.

I can't breathe. The air is gone. And someone's shaking me. Hard.

Help me, Dasani-Blue-Eyed Boy . . . help!

The rattling is for real. "Huh? What?"

"Kendall, wake up, kiddo. Time to get up for school."

I squint in the morning sunlight to get my bearings. My dad scrutinizes my face through his wire-rimmed glasses. "Are you okay?"

"Fine, Dad." My chest hurts and my muscles ache like I've taken a spill for real. "Weird dream, that's all."

Dad ruffles my hair like he's done since I grew hair. "At least you were sleeping. I've been worried about you."

"I know," I say with a sigh. "Thanks for the white-noise machine."

He smiles proudly. "I'd read they were good for insomnia."

I don't have the heart to tell him that I think it's a lot more than mere sleeplessness, like maybe a fatal, incurable illness. Instead, I nod and sit up.

Dad's still obviously concerned. "That's all it is . . . right, Kendall?"

Since I'm not a doctor, nor do I play one on TV, I don't want to self-diagnose. I shrug. "I guess so."

He sits on the end of my bed and reaches for my hand. He rubs his thumb over mine like he has since as long as I can remember. I sense a serious conversation is about to follow.

Quirking his mouth, he says, "I know this hasn't been the timeliest move for you, kiddo, and I'm sorry about that. It's never a parent's intention to uproot their children because of a career opportunity. It must be hard for you, Kendall. You left all of your friends and your home for something completely different."

Not wanting to be a pain in his butt—Kaitlin plays that role well enough—I squeeze his hand and swallow down my homesickness. "Look, I know it was, like, an awesome thing for your career to come here."

"It's a benefit for the whole family," he adds. "My salary goes so much farther here than it ever would in Chicago. And we'll be able to save more for your college in a couple of years."

"I totally appreciate that, Dad, I do!"

I pause a bit too dramatically.

"But?" he asks.

"But . . ."

His dark eyes peer over his glasses at me, almost as if he's looking into my soul for the truth. He knows me so well—what can I say, I'm a daddy's girl and there's nothing wrong with that. David Moorehead's a great guy who loves his wife and family and wants to take care of them—duh, us—even if he did bring us to a place that's barely on the map and apparently chock-full o' ghost chronicles. "Is everything okay at school? Are the kids treating you well?"

I laugh. "I've only been there one day. Pretty hard to assess my future at this point."

He frowns.

"Really, Dad. It's not school. I even made a friend yesterday."

"What is it then?" He tightens his grip on my hand. "You've always been able to tell me everything, kiddo."

"I'm just . . . adjusting." In the past, I have told him whatever was bothering me. But that was before all the weird feelings, sensations, emotions, and voices through the white-noise machine. How the hell do I explain that without someone slapping the latest straitjacket fashion around me and carting me off to the loony bin?

"Are you sure that's all?"

I swallow hard again, trying to get at that dry lump of unease. "Do you, like, believe in ghosts, Dad?"

He pulls his hand away and chuckles heartily. "You're not listening to *those* stories, are you?"

"Which stories?"

Tugging off his glasses, he cleans them on the end of his striped silk tie. "You know, that Radisson is 'a hotbed of paranormal activity'?" He punctuates his speech with air quotes, glasses dangling from his fingers, and then dismisses the notion. "Oh, and that city hall—particularly my office—is haunted and dangerous."

My eyes widen. "It *is?*"

He plops his glasses back on the bridge of his nose. "So my executive assistant tells me. I don't believe rumors like that, though. They're only meant to attract tourists, or weirdos, to the area. I don't put much credence in stories of odd footsteps, strange voices, and 'a feeling.'" He tacks on a laugh for good measure.

"Why do they say your office isn't safe?"

"Seems the city planner they brought in before me quit three days into the job because he was allegedly attacked by what he described as 'an unseen entity.'"

I almost rip the covers trying to get out from under them. This is some serious shit, especially if what Celia told me about our house and this town is true. Now there's a potential threat at Dad's office? This is too much to take in. "Dad, you have to be careful!"

"There's no need to worry about me, kiddo. I'm not afraid of something that's not there. And don't you be either."

I drop my gaze to my comforter and fiddle with the corner of it. Do I tell him what I've experienced? What I've been feeling? Hearing? About the alleged psychic cats? "I'm not afraid, Dad." I change the subject. "I just want to find my place here and fit in."

"You will. If anyone can do it, it's my Kendall."

Rrrrrrrrr-aaaarrrrr . . .

A big black fur ball jumps up on my bed between us. It's huge and must weigh about fifteen pounds. It's not a cat, it's a mountain lion.

"I didn't know we had a kitty," Dad says, looking at the tag. "Well, hey there, Natalie."

OMG! It's Natalie, one of the cats Mrs. Elliott abandoned. The furry girl rubs Dad's knee, leaving black hair on his tan suit pants. Then she comes over to me, starts purring, and flops over with her fat belly exposed. I reach out tentatively and rub her stomach. The purring only intensifies.

I do notice that Natalie thumps her tail like crazy as I continue to love on her. I think nothing of it, though, despite Celia's warning about the cat knowing when danger was around the corner and communicating that by thumping her tail. *This* is the cat I'm supposed to be afraid of? Yeah, right.

"Can we keep her?" I ask.

"She's got a tag, Kendall. Which means she belongs to someone."

"Yeah, the crazy old woman you bought the house from left her when she moved."

Dad looks at Natalie and then smiles. "Seems like we have a pet then."

"Thanks, Dad!" I lean forward and kiss him hard on the cheek.

That's when everything spins out of control. Like I'm sucked into some sort of vortex and I'm falling through cold, shivery darkness toward nowhere. Suddenly, my mind flashes like a wicked lightning storm. A vivid, brilliant image of my dad appears front and center in my transcendental state. He's very upset. Hurt even. There's a patch of red blood trickling down his forehead between his eggplant-colored bruised eyes.

I jerk back and shriek something fierce, breaking the trance.

Dad laughs at me, though. "What's wrong, Kendall? Did I miss some whiskers when I shaved?"

My chest pounds like a nail gun on a two-by-four and my pulse does the Riverdance underneath my skin. "No, umm . . . I . . . I . . ."

"Kendall?"

Holy crap! Natalie was thumping her tail. Is this cat really predicting something horrific on the horizon? Should I panic and take heed? I glance down at her. She closes her kitty eyes and curls up peacefully. No. Natalie had nothing to do with this. How could she? The image came from somewhere else, like my own demented mind, obviously. How do I explain this vision to Dad when I can't even explain it to myself?

"Sorry, Dad. It was just some static electricity."

"Ah, well." He stands. "Hurry up and get ready. Your mom's making a frittata for you girls this morning. Extra cheese, like you like it."

When my stomach growls out, begging to break the overnight fast, my breathing acquiesces. *Mmm . . . frittata . . .* that's what I'll think about instead of images of my dad bloodied and injured. Maybe attacked by that alleged ghost at his office, like his predecessor claimed to be. No. Not possible. This is just some sort of ridiculous thought drummed up by my lack of sleep, the move, and starting a new school. Anyone would react oddly to all these life changes.

Dad leaves my room, and I crawl out of bed to grab my towel. Natalie makes herself at home in the middle of my comforter. On my way to the bathroom, I sense a razor-sharp pain in the front of my skull that mirrors the location of Dad's apparent forthcoming injury. I stop in my tracks and press the terry-cloth material against my face. Tears threaten, and I stave them off. However, no amount of deep breathing will erase the image of my dad that's now stored forever in my memory bank. It can't be real. Not now. Not ever.

But something far down—something I have no explanation for—tells me, without a doubt, that I've seen my father's future.

I'll be damned if I'll let that hallucination come true. Nobody messes with my dad and gets away with it, whether I believe they exist or not.

I truly am going insane.

I need a shower.

The hot water blasts full steam to help knock me back to reality. I breathe in the orangey scent of my Victoria's Secret body wash and try to escape from my own brain. Thoughts of Dad subside and I concentrate instead on replaying my fantasy about Dasani-Blue-Eyed Boy. That dream was *so real*. As I lather the soap across my arms, I can still feel the indentations of his fingers on my biceps. Like his hands were just there. The sensation washes away with the bubbles as the water sluices over me. It was just a dream. A. Dream.

But what a dream.

Dasani–Blue-Eyed Boy . . . oh, man, was he drop-dead gorgeous. Too bad they don't make cute guys like that outside of the Hollywood city limits. I certainly won't find anyone who looks like *that* here in Radisson.

When the final school bell rings, I gather up my physiology notes and rush down the hall to the chemistry lab, where I know I'll find Celia, who texted me. I want her to come over and look at the video from my room last night. Not that I'm buying into her whole ghost theory *juuuuuuuuust* yet. (Although . . . my MP3 charger cord did mysteriously reappear last night. Someone is definitely trying to make me think I'm losing my mind by hiding things on me.)

I get to the chem lab and see Celia standing at a counter, wearing goggles and gloves. Her tongue wiggles out of her mouth as she concentrates on not spilling whatever she's working on.

"Hey," I say, tentatively. "What are you doing?"

She adjusts her goggles. "I'm running an experiment that tests the amount of lead in hair products."

I frown. "Why would you want to do that?"

"See, the lead acetate darkens the hair by reacting with the sulfur in the hair color and in the amino acids cysteine and methionine. These amino acids are integrated into the protein structure of hair. The product of this reaction is black lead sulfide—"

"Celia, you're doing it again," I say with a giggle.

Unfazed, she says, "Oh, well, I'm calculating the amount of lead acetate present by measuring the amount of an insoluble lead compound formed when a sample of the hair color product is reacted with potassium chromate."

I reach to stop her with my hand. "Really. I got it. All set."

"You asked," she says.

Trying to show more interest, I cross my arms in front of me. "What hair product are you using?"

Celia holds up a box with a picture of an older man on it. "Grecian Formula."

I let loose a belly laugh. "You're awfully serious and dedicated for only the second day of school."

Celia doesn't blink behind her goggles; a lock of hair has fallen in her face. "I asked for extra-credit work already to beef up my scientific credentials so I can get into a college of my choice."

I've wanted to go to the University of Michigan since, like, birth. They've got a great school of architecture and urban planning where I can become a second-generation planner and be just like dear ol' Dad. Besides, loves me some Wolverines football! Go, Blue! I think I'll major in football my freshman year. I'm curious to know where a smart Southern gal like Celia Nichols would want to go to college. Georgia Tech? Emory? Vandy? "Where's that?" I ask.

She stops what she's doing and says, "There are dozens of fine institutes of science technology throughout the country. My focus will be on microbiology, chemistry, and physics, to enhance my major. Over the summer, I narrowed my choices to three places. First, Princeton University; second, Duke University; and third, a long shot, is the University of Edinburgh."

I wasn't expecting *that!* "As in Scotland? Are you serious?"

Celia curtsies as if she's doing it for Queen Elizabeth. "Sure thing! I mean, an Ivy like Princeton is a long shot coming from a school as small as RHS; that is, unless you're a legacy, which I'm not 'cause my dad went to Georgia Tech and my mother didn't even go to college—"

Uh-oh, here she goes again. "Celia . . ."

"But Princeton has their PEAR—Princeton Engineering Anomalies Research—program that studies consciousness-related physical phenomena. Of course, Duke has the Rhine Research Center and lots of seminars and workshops in my field."

I can't keep up with her and what this has to do with an experiment about lead content in Grecian Formula.

Celia takes a deep breath and pushes her hair out of her face with the back of her hand. "The granddaddy of all programs, though, is the University of Edinburgh. One of the most highly respected programs, and believe me, I've done my research."

My eyebrow twitches. "What programs? What exactly *is* your chosen major?"

"Parapsychology," she says, not missing a beat.

Shaking my head, I say, "Are you still on that?"

"Of course."

"That stuff's not for real, Celia. You can't spend your life chasing something that doesn't exist."

She gives me her own headshake. "There are more things in heaven and earth, Kendall, than are dreamt of in your philosophy."

"*Hamlet*. Act one, scene five," I say. "Although it's *Horatio,* not *Kendall*."

"Whatever," Celia says. "The point is, if we're arrogant enough to think we're alone in this world without the presence of spirits, ghosts, angels, demons, entities, energies, what have you, then we're as ignorant as the bureaucrats who refuse to fund this kind of scientific research for the betterment of—"

"Okay, Madame Curie! You win!"

Celia laughs and sticks her tongue out.

"You wanna walk home together?" I ask.

"Sorry. Can't. I have my Segway." She examines the setup in front of her. "Besides, I need to finish this. I'll be home in an hour or so, though. Tell you what. Bring the video recorder over then." She lowers her voice and looks around. "You know . . . we'll *look* at it."

"Oh, okay. Sure." I am curious to see if there's anything on there. "I'll see you then."

As I'm headed out of the classroom, Celia calls out to me. "Yo, Kendall. Go take a walk around town. Get to know Radisson. It's not a bad place. You'll see."

Celia Nichols knows what she wants to do with the rest of her life. I don't even know what to do this afternoon. I suppose a nature walk will do me some good.

I smile and wave back at her.

Sure, why not? I have an hour to kill.

All right, I'll admit it. Radisson, Georgia, is a quaint little town.

I say *little* because, well, it is. The welcome sign at the city limits boasts a population of 14,877. Obviously, that's not counting the four-person Moorehead family who just joined the ranks. Talk about a downgrade from Chicago's nearly three million people.

I'll stop comparing, though. This sojourn around town is supposed to be about getting to know Radisson. I'm stuck here until I graduate, so I might as well kick back and get comfy.

From RHS, I walk east on Main Street four "city blocks" until I reach the Square, in the middle of town. The Square is Radisson's main drag and shopping area. My dad's office in city hall is across the way, in the building with the large clock tower on top of it. Lining the perimeter of the Square are charming yet kitschy stores, such as Delver's Drugs (with an old-fashioned soda counter) and Karol's Kountry Kitchen restaurant, featuring "down-home mac 'n' cheese" and some kind of concoction I've never heard of—what in the world are rutabagas? There's a fabric store, a hearing-aid place (love the name: Stick It in Your Ear), an arts and craps place (because, honestly, it all *is* crap), and a coffee shop named Central Perk, obviously a nod to *Friends*. A men's clothing store is on the corner of Main and Pace, with a shoe store across the street full of Crocs of every size and color and a sign that reads "Warning: we're temporarily out of Webkinz."

I head over to the middle of the Square where there's a well-kept park, complete with shade trees and flowers in planters. In the center of the park is a tall granite Civil War memorial with a Confederate soldier facing south. It says he's a soldier at parade rest. Hmmm, doesn't look too restful to me, clutching that musket to his side. There is a fishpond to the right of the monument that has a small fountain gurgling away. I can see how someone might like sitting on the nearby bench and enjoying the afternoon. Not me, but someone.

Suddenly, the wind shifts and seems to dance around me. My skin grows cold and clammy, and my footing falters. Oh, man, I'm terribly lightheaded. Whew. Where did that come from? Okay, maybe I *will* be someone who sits in this park. I drop to the bench, and my heartbeat accelerates, pounding ferociously against my lungs. My head is woozy and I sense all the blood rushing straight down to my feet. On top of that, my stomach hurts. It's like I've eaten bad pizza. You know, when you think the leftovers still look good after three days in the fridge, then you have to make that quick dash to the bathroom. Yeah. Just like that.

I wonder if I can run into Central Perk and use their washroom.

Since there are no crosswalks, I look both ways, wait for the pickup truck decorated with Georgia Bulldog stickers to pass, and then scoot across the street. I grasp a nearby lamppost with a death grip to keep from falling to my knees. Something serious is happening to me. Words tangle in the back of my throat. I cry out for help in my head. *Someone call 911. Or my mom.* Man, it's like there's a firecracker show going off in my head. I hear pops and music and voices and talking and . . . whoa . . . what's going on? I spin around to see if a store is piping Muzak out onto the sidewalk. Nope.

A mosaic of colors dances around me in a fuzzy rainbow effect. Is this for real or am I hallucinating? Were those mushrooms that were in my lunch salad of the magical type? No, that's absurd. Maybe I breathed in too much of those acetate fumes Celia was cooking up in the chem lab.

A woman walks past, checking me out from head to toe. "You must be Roy and Elva's granddaughter," she says.

More random rockets explode inside my head. Or at least,

that's what it seems to be from the noise in my brain. Can anyone else hear what's going on? Is there a volume knob somewhere? I wish I could shut this off. But how?

"Ummm, no, ma'am. I'm not," I say politely when all I want to do is scream bloody murder.

The woman flattens her lips. "You look just like Elva. Are you sure?"

The mental sparklers and colors have now morphed to a full-throttle headache. I so don't want to talk to this woman right now. "Yes, ma'am. I'm sure of who I am."

"Of course you are," she says with a dainty laugh. "It's just that Elva's granddaughter is about your age and I thought . . ."

Her words become a mangled mishmash lost in the cacophonic orchestra of my mind as a slow realization penetrates the brain traffic and noise, forming one painfully clear notion: *I know her name.*

I see the letters in my mind: H-e-l-e-n P-e-a-r-l-m-a-n.

Helen Pearlman was born here in Radisson and . . . I rub my temple. She leaves town only once a year to go stay at her beach house in . . . I wince, searching for the details on the edge of my gray matter. There's sun, water, and sand painted across my memory like I've been there myself. Of course, I haven't—I've got it! Grayton Beach, Florida . . . in the Panhandle.

My hand flies to my mouth.

How the hell do I know that?

"Are you all right, dear?"

I nod, afraid to speak.

"Y'all sure now?"

"Stomachache," I mutter, thinking it's the easiest answer.

"My Lawrence has the same problem. He eats at least two packs of Tums a day and—"

More flash cards of information skitter across my mind's eye. Lawrence isn't her son. He's her husband. For some reason, I know this as sure as I know my own name. And, umm . . . Lawrence had a goiter—*What on God's green earth is a goiter?*— removed from his neck last May. Eww . . .

I shift my gaze back to Helen Pearlman, wife of goiterless Lawrence, hoping I don't appear as horrified as I feel.

Ribbons of color surround her, and I blink to focus. Yellows and pinks seem to dance about her head in a spotlight of sorts. Is the sun playing some sort of trick on my eyes? People don't just walk around with, like, halos of rainbow hues all over them. Seriously. And the intense, sudden outcropping of anger within me is nearly frightening. I want to lash out at this poor woman, although she really hasn't done anything to me. WTF?

"You'll have to excuse me, please," I say. "Nice to have, umm, met you."

She waves after me as I stumble away. I'm completely discombobulated and I'm freaking out here! The pavement under my feet feels like quicksand, but my legs are leaden as I try to walk. My hands are tingling, and the pain in my head is massively forceful. It's like part of my head is missing. At this point, I wish it were—anything to take away this pain!

I don't think I can make it to Central Perk. It's too far down the street. Light-years away, it seems. I need air-conditioning, water, and a seat. Probably an emergency room, as well. I must be having an aneurysm or something none of the doctors on *ER* can correctly diagnose.

There's some random store directly behind me. I push on the glass door and hear the jingle of several bells when I burst inside. The cool air conditioner surrounds me, tickling my neck and causing the hairs on my arms to stand at attention with chill bumps. To my right, a woman in jeans and a T-shirt that reads "I know I'm psychic 'cause my underwear says 'medium'" stands and smiles at me.

"Hi there!" She's young. Maybe in her early thirties.

I somehow find my voice. "May I use your ladies' room, please?"

The woman stares at me with great scrutiny, like she recognizes me. Oh God. She doesn't think I'm Elva's granddaughter too, does she? Stupid small town.

Her hands spread wide and she waves around my head with a look of fascination. "Oh my goodness! You're literally bursting with energy!"

I'm bursting with something, that's for sure.

The pupils in her hazel eyes are widely dilated. From the pungent odor of incense in the room, I assume she must have been smoking some marijuana before I came in. Marjorie's older brother used to smoke the chronic in his room, so I recognize the transcendental look this lady's got.

"The bathroom," I say, trying to nudge her out of her daze.

"Oh!" She snaps out of it with a knowing expression across her lips. "Sure, hon. Up the stairs and to the right."

I smile. "Thanks."

"And when you're done," she calls out, "I'd love to have a long chat with you, Kendall."

CHAPTER FIVE

I FREEZE IN PLACE on the third step up.

My bottom lip quivers when I start to speak. "H-h-how do you know my name?"

Instead of answering me, the woman stretches out her hand. "I'm Loreen Woods." She emphasizes the words, like they're supposed to mean something to me.

"Nice to meet you," I say, still puzzled and even more wigged out than I'm letting on. Not wanting to be rude, I sheepishly reach to shake. When our hands touch, Loreen's eyes close and she breathes in deeply, clasping my palm securely to hers. A near vibration passes through me, like we're sharing a pulse. I want to pull away, but she seems entranced again. I pump our hands up and down twice and then release. Her lids remain shut, so I take a moment to check this place out.

Jeezy-chreezy. What have I walked into?

Candles and incense line one wall. Another is covered in books and CDs. I also see pyramids, crystal balls, tarot cards, and I Ching sticks, whatever those are. There's a jewelry counter that sports racks of crystals and stones hanging from chains. Not really necklaces, but something pretty. A sign over an old-fashioned cash register reads "Divining Woman." Uh-oh. Have I wandered into some sort of fortunetellery psychic-babble store? My mother would shit a gold brick and throw holy water on me if her devoutly religious self knew I was even within ten feet of this place. I feel the need to get out of here *fast*.

Loreen's eyes open. "Kendall. It's so wonderful that you stopped in."

Okay, I need to get hold of this situation. My pulse seems to have calmed down, and I no longer feel like my insides are going to explode. "Again—how do you know my name?"

"There's a connection to you that I've been feeling for several days, but I didn't know what it was until you just walked in here," she explains.

"What kind of connection?" Do I really want the answer?

Loreen lets out a pent-up sigh. "A connection between our souls. Perhaps we knew each other in a previous life? I'm not sure. All I know is that I am supposed to guide you."

Hello, Shirley MacLaine, get Larry King on the phone! Someone's stealing your act.

This is a farce. Some sort of new reality TV show that Bravo's filming here in the sticks of Georgia. Will Heidi Klum pop out from behind the rack of tarot cards? This woman's not for real.

"I think you have me confused with someone else." I move toward the door, thinking that now that my dizziness has passed, I can make it home without a visit to the necessary (as my grandma used to call it). Home, where I'm going to lock myself in a closet until all this weird shit stops happening to me. Or until it's time to go off to college. "I don't need your bathroom after all. Thanks anyway."

"Wait, Kendall. We must talk."

"Why?"

"You see, I'm a psychic healer and sensitive," she says. I suppose her T-shirt isn't a joke then. "I have to say, there is a tremendous amount of energy surrounding you."

"Thank you?" I ask more than say.

"Something brought you in here to me today, Kendall," Loreen says. "I've seen you in my dreams and had advance knowledge of you in my card readings. You've been experiencing some, shall we say, strange things?"

It's like I've been doused in the face with a glass of (sweet) iced tea. (No such thing as unsweet tea here.) I gulp down the unease lodged in my throat and say, "Yeah, how did you know?"

Loreen takes a seat on an old Victorian couch with burgundy cushions. She pats next to her. "You're what, sixteen?"

"I'll be seventeen in December." I sit down next to her.

"Capricorn?"

I smile. "December twenty-second."

"Ahh . . . on the cusp. You were born on the winter solstice." She reaches for my hand. "You're a very special girl, Kendall. And you're only discovering your powers."

Powers? Like a superhero or something? I mean, who wouldn't want Wonder Woman's curves and bosiasms—*I sure would!*—but I don't think I possess any special powers. "I don't understand—"

"I shouldn't refer to it that way," Loreen scolds herself. "What I meant is, you're just discovering your *abilities*. The gift that you were born with. Your sixth sense. You're a sensitive, Kendall. I can feel it. Your aura is strong and your energies are pulsating out of control."

Could this be what's causing my headaches? That is, if I were to believe her mumbo jumbo.

Loreen bites her bottom lip and scowls at me, as if she knows what I'm thinking. "Your mother is a sensitive?"

I try not to snicker. "No, she's an Episcopalian."

Loreen ignores my attempt at humor and studies me. "Hmm. I could be reading that wrong, but I swear, it feels like you've inherited your sensitivity."

"Not unless Mom's holding out on me." I doubt it, though. My mom's as religiously conservative as they come. She wouldn't even let me read *Harry Potter* because she said it was a "training manual" for witchcraft. Whatever! Hello, it's fiction. While I can see Mom clutching the Book of Common Prayer, I can hardly visualize her hunched over a crystal ball hosting a séance to communicate with the dead. "So you really think *I'm* sensitive?"

A nod from Loreen. "You've only started to open yourself up, and you don't know how to control your gift. The least little thing can set you off with an emotional outburst—anger, nerves, trepidation, fear—anything, especially when you're surrounded by paranormal activity."

I stand up. "What is it with everyone in Radisson being obsessed with ghosts and spirits and shit? Don't you people have a movie theater or HBO?"

"Paranormal elements are very in vogue right now," she says, laughing.

Hand on hip, I retort, "What? Ghosts are the new black?"

"You could say that. We're in an age of awareness and awakening like no other time in our society. A lot of paranormal experts"—she uses finger quotes around the word *experts*—"think there's a thinning of the dimensions surrounding us. It's almost like we're in a new age of enlightenment! I mean, who doesn't have a ghost or angel tale?"

I didn't, until recently.

Loreen adds, "Well, it's not considered taboo anymore."

Needing some distance, I walk over to the bookshelf to review titles: *Awakening Your Psychic Powers; You Are Psychic: The Art of Clairvoyant Reading and Healing;* and *Psychic Development for Beginners.* Are you kidding me? They might as well be titled *Psychics for Dummies.* That would be me, if I were to buy into this.

I'm too confused by all of this information and the physical things that are happening to me. But I'll admit to having a curiosity about this sensitivity Loreen seems to think that I have. "Maybe I should get one of these books. Which one do you recommend?"

Loreen waves her hand, shooing me away. "You don't need anything like that."

Wow, she totally sucks as a saleswoman. How does she pay her rent each month if she doesn't move the merchandise? I bet she's just reeling me in to try and get me to buy something more expensive. Like a chi machine. Marjorie's mom has one, but then, she's a little imbalanced to begin with. She's originally from Los Angeles.

"Come sit back down," Loreen instructs with the warmest smile.

I obey, because I *am* interested. Like, why is this occurring now?

"This awakening is occurring because you're in an incredible hotbed of paranormal activities here in Radisson," Loreen pipes up, answering my unspoken questions and echoing my father's words from earlier. Do they print that phrase in the brochures that the tourism bureau hands out and then make the citizens regurgitate the words ad nauseam? For Christ's sake! "How . . . what . . . ?" Man, I've got to be careful with what I think!

"This is an old town, Kendall, full of history and death and battle and scars from the Civil War. There are a lot of energies around that see your shining light of understanding and they're standing up and shouting, 'I'm here!' at you. Your awakening is coinciding with your move and being surrounded by such rich history."

Okay. Hold the phone. Now I ask my questions out loud. "Why wasn't I having all this weird stuff happening to me when I was in Chicago? We *are* the home of Al Capone and his mass-murdering gang of goons, not to mention the infamous Resurrection Mary and all the other ghosts of Archer Avenue."

Marjorie and I got ditched in Resurrection Cemetery on Archer Avenue this one time back in junior high when we were riding around with kids our parents wouldn't have liked for us to associate with. Marjorie swore then a million times over that she actually saw Resurrection Mary, the vanishing hitchhiker, when we were standing outside trying to flag down a ride out of there. She said she saw a woman with blond hair and a white dress not far from us, and then she was gone. I never really believed in things like that—and Marjorie soon got over her fear and denied the alleged sighting later, saying she was having some sort of anxiety attack and had too much adrenaline flooding her system—but now I'm starting to wonder.

"Well sure, Chicago is full of its own ghosts and spirits," Loreen says as she nods. Ha! I've gotten her! "What I'm talking about is more focused on you, Kendall. There, your mind was quiet, and here, it is alive and awake."

"Are you kidding me? It's crazy-quiet now. So much so that I can't sleep at night."

Loreen shakes her strawberry blond hair. "I'm not talking

about your surroundings. We're talking about your mind, which is anything but quiet. I bet it's like the Fourth of July in there at times. Are you experiencing loss of sleep, strange appetite, and/or odd pains throughout your body? Vivid dreams, perhaps?"

Oh, right . . . Dasani-Blue-Eyed Boy. I gulp hard and nod. "I thought it was the heat."

She adjusts on the couch. "Puberty is usually the time when sensitives have an awakening, so to speak."

"Seriously? Can't I just get a few pimples and have to start using Proactiv like all those famous Hollywood people?"

Loreen chortles, then gets serious again. "I know. I felt the same way when I was your age. Only I was scared out of my wits, hearing and seeing spirits. I fought it for the longest time because I didn't have any place to go for reference, or someone to give me advice and guidance. My parents put me on so many medications, it's a wonder I made it through my teen years with my sensitivity still intact."

I frown in confusion. "I'm not exactly at the beginning of puberty, you know? Could there be another reason?"

Thinking for a moment, Loreen asks, "You came from Chicago, you said?"

"Yep. Gold Coast." That sounds so pretentious, but I'm proud of my former address.

"Hmm . . . downtown?"

I confirm with a nod.

"It's pretty simple, Kendall. When you lived in the city, you were surrounded by cars and trucks and noise and people. You didn't allow yourself to slow down enough to know that you have these abilities and gifts. Once you moved to a more tranquil and less frenetic environment, your energies took over and you've become more open. Especially since this town has so much to offer."

"I guess that kind of makes sense." In a warped sort of way.

I begin pacing across the braided rug that feels like it was made from hemp. My fingers find my temples and I rub in slow circles as this info is absorbed. Skepticism washes over me like a summer rain shower. It's hard to believe the words of a stranger who wears a comical T-shirt, runs a New Age shop, and sniffs too much incense eight hours a day. I bet Loreen pulls this crap on every loser who wanders into her store. She's just saying I'm like her to draw me into her clientele web.

Still, she smiles so calmly at me. "Don't you believe you're coming into a psychic awakening?"

I pace more instead of answering. Sure, it was freaky-weird how I knew about Helen Pearlman, her beach house in Florida, and her husband's goiter. *Note to self: Google* goiter *when I get home.*

Loreen clears her throat. "It's a swelling in the neck, just below the Adam's apple or larynx, due to an enlarged thyroid gland."

"It's . . . I mean . . . how did you—?" Holy shit! She's a mind reader. Well, duh! She told me she's psychic.

This is ridiculous. My world is spinning off its axis. There has to be an explanation other than Loreen's crackpot theory. (Stressing the *crackpot* part.) I should stop by my mom's office and have her new doctor-boss check me out. X-ray me. Draw vials of blood to examine and test. Maybe I'm suffering from scarlet fever. Or I've become lactose intolerant? Developed asthma? Become allergic to nuts? Anything!

I'm. Not. Psychic!

If I were psychic, I wouldn't have had such a problem memorizing formulas last year in geometry class. And I would have always known what my Christmas presents were before I unwrapped them.

"I need to go," I say firmly. There's just too much to digest.

Loreen is at my heels. "Wait, Kendall. I'd like to give you something."

She goes over to the front jewelry counter and pulls out a rack of chains with dangling pendants of various shapes, sizes, and designs. "These are dowsing pendulums. Let's see if any of them are reacting to you."

"What do you mean, reacting to me?"

"Here, try this one," she says, handing me a chain with a crystal on it. My question is answered when the pendulum begins to move on its own as it dangles from my grasp. Whoa. What's doing that? I pass the crystal back to Loreen and reach for a shiny silver one on the end of the display.

"I'd stay away from the metal ones," Loreen notes. "Metal conducts electricity, and let's just say it wouldn't be good for a young girl just coming into her gifts."

"Umm . . . okay." I don't even know why I'm standing here. What do I need a pendulum for? Isn't that, like, how farmers find where to dig wells and stuff? Since I don't have any live-stock in the backyard, nor do I plan on majoring in animal husbandry when I get to college, this seems like an exercise in futility.

Loreen takes another one from the display. "Ah, just as I thought. The pink quartz with the beads of rhodonite and black tourmaline on top is perfect for you."

"Are you making these words up?" I ask. Guess I should take a geology class someday.

She just laughs and passes the pendulum over to me. "Pink quartz is good to start with because it's the stone of love for oneself, family, friends, community, the Earth, et cetera. This will help to heal your heart of any wounds and reawaken your trust with its soothing vibrations."

"But—"

Loreen continues. "The rhodonite promotes the energy of love. What girl doesn't want to enhance depth, clarity, and the meaning of one's inner experiences? Especially when it comes to boys." She elbows me knowingly. "These beads are also good for understanding the messages behind your dreams."

"Oh, that's kind of cool," I say, sort of coming around. Hmm . . . maybe this thing will share Dasani-Blue-Eyed Boy's e-mail addy or cell phone number with me.

"Finally, Kendall—and this is important—the black tour-maline is ideal for psychic protection. These crystals act like etheric vacuum cleaners, clearing your surroundings of negativity and disharmony. It's very important as you're discovering and exploring your gifts that you use protection at *all* times."

I feel myself blush horrendously in a blaze of embarrassment from my forehead to my feet. My sex life—or lack thereof—is so totally not any of this woman's business! "Excuse me, but I don't even have a boyfriend! And whenever I get one and the time is right, *of course* I'll use protection. This is the twenty-first century, after all!"

Loreen doubles over laughing, to the point where she has to wipe away tears.

What's so damn funny?

"Oh, Kendall, I'm so sorry," she says when she catches her breath. "I don't mean protection like *that,* I mean protecting yourself from evil spirits or entities and such if you try to explore your abilities."

"Oh." I should be wearing a braying donkey head right about now. What an ass I am.

"There's a lot of evil in this world," she says. "I just want to make sure you're prepared for what you might face."

I gaze at the beautiful pendulum lying in the lifeline crease of my palm and suddenly I'm shocked to see the price tag. "Holy crap! I can't afford this."

I try to return the pendulum to Loreen, but she's not having any of it. She curls the chain into my hand and closes my fist around it. "It's from me to you. You need this."

An early childhood lesson is never to take gifts from strangers. However, I feel compelled to tuck the pendulum into the front pocket of my jeans, along with an instructional sheet Loreen gives me. I mumble my thanks, unsure of what to make of this whole visit. At the door, Loreen hands me one of her business cards.

"Call me if you need *anything*."

In my haste to leave, I bump into a table displaying both tarot and regular playing cards. The boxes spill open, tossing cards about on the floor. I almost scream when I see the queen of hearts staring up at me from the patterned Berber carpet. Just like what's been happening in my room. "*You* again."

Puzzled, Loreen asks, "Have you and the queen of hearts been crossing paths lately?"

"You could say that. Every time I come near a deck of cards, *she* comes flying out to scowl at me and judge me."

Loreen bends down to pick up the card. "She's speaking to you, Kendall."

"She's creeping me out."

"Not at all," Loreen says. "See, hearts are the suit for emotions. They show pain and suffering. You're struggling with what's awakening within you. But the queen of hearts assures you that you're not alone. She's telling you of a trusted woman. Someone knowledgeable and faithful who will help you."

Loreen means herself, doesn't she?

My eyes connect with hers. She smiles and gazes deeply into my soul.

Whoa. That's intense.

"Okay, then," I say, backing out. "Well, thanks. I'll be seeing you."

Outside her store, I shake my head and try desperately to dismiss everything that just happened. Psychic? Me? Yeah, right!

I look at Loreen's business card and, after some hesitation, chuck it into the nearest city trash can. Keep Radisson Beautiful. Not only is Loreen a lousy saleswoman—giving me a twenty-dollar chain!—she's nuts, crazy, *muy loco en sombrero* . . . absolutely *pazzo!*

CHAPTER SIX

WELL, THAT WAS COMPLETELY messed up.

After my encounter with Loreen, the crazy woman, I decide to veer off Main Street and take the road less traveled, hoping it makes a difference for me, just as it did for Robert Frost. I cross back to Butler Avenue, which runs parallel to Main, behind our house. As I walk along, I notice the trees are starting to lose their leaves as the first sign of fall touches the landscape. If I were back home, Marjorie and I would be lining up at the United Arena for preseason Blackhawks hockey games. Instead, I'm in a strange land, running away from someone who says I'm awakening to my psychic abilities; oh, and I'm slinking home to check a videotape taken in my bedroom last night of a possible ghost.

How is this my life?

I tuck my hands into the pockets of my Roots Canada zip-up hoodie and keep walking. My head begins to ache slightly when I step into the next block. The aroma of honeysuckle tints the air, and I smile. Grandma Ethel used to have honeysuckle potpourri in her kitchen to cover up the smell of cooked food. That was before she died, three years ago. Honestly, if I could communicate with the dead—as per these "abilities" Loreen says I have—wouldn't I be chatting with Grandma Ethel, given how close we were?

Continuing along, I drag my fingers along the rigid top of the bush-covered wrought-iron fence. The railing is worn smooth underneath my hand, indicating that it's been here for a lot longer than I have. The tapping within my skull contin- ues, as does a newfound pressure in my chest that reminds me of when I had walking pneumonia in seventh grade and it hurt like all get out to take a deep breath.

The fence ends and I see a wide-open gate leading into ... *oh, hell no*. It's a cemetery!

I start backing away, even as something seems to call out to me. Not exactly in a "yoo-hoo, Kendall" sort of way. More like I just *know* I need to go inside. I peer in at the green grass and expertly trimmed shrubs. The honeysuckle scent is even stronger, wafting toward me and inviting me to come in. Graveyards usually skeeve me out; however, there's some- thing almost peaceful and serene about this place. I can't ex- plain it ... it's beckoning me to step in and take a look around. Why not?

There's a small dirt road from the gate that turns into a pebbled drive. From the looks of the graves and markers, this place is pretty old—probably dating back to the early 1800s, just like the town. To the right, ornate obelisks etched with family names reach to the blue sky. Massive mausoleums are scattered among plots that have been lined off with aged marble. These must be the more affluent town families from over the years.

Beyond the nicer markers are paths leading to much simpler graves. Some are marked with stacks of red bricks around them. Others are merely noted with a single rock or a wooden cross. From the few inscriptions I can make out, these appear to be the graves of slaves, Indians, and unknown soldiers.

The dull pain in my chest intensifies and I feel my breathing begin to labor. It's like I'm having an asthma attack, although I don't suffer from it, like Marjorie does. Mental illness, possibly, but not asthma. Could it be that I'm experiencing something akin to what happened at school yesterday with Courtney's throwing up and Okra's broken leg? Am I feeling something that these dead people were afflicted with?

I don't panic this time. As an alternative to freaking out, I take a moment to focus on my breathing, like Mom talks about. In doing so, I note that the tension in my chest eases somewhat. An image—an awareness, almost—appears in my mind of a Confederate soldier with the same kind of chest pains. He . . . he . . . died from . . . wait . . . it's coming to me . . . died from . . . complications from . . . pneumonia . . . made worse by his . . . "Oh my God! He had asthma."

Urged on by who knows what, I fall to my knees and begin clawing away at the marker in front of me. Red Georgia clay embeds under my fingernails, but I don't care. I move the rusty-colored dirt off the placard on the ground and pluck two long weeds that have crawled over the stone. Written on the grave is:

LT. CHARLES S. FAHRQUARSON
23RD ATHENS RIFLE BATTALION
1844–1864
DIED OF ASTHMA

I pump my fist in the air and jump to my feet, beaming with pride over this revelation. Of course, there's no one here to celebrate with me, if this truly is a celebration. Who says it's not just a lucky guess? Soldiers died of weird stuff all the time —dysentery, measles, diarrhea (*gross!*)—you name it! See, I listened in class when we studied the Civil War. Who knew I'd ever have to call upon that knowledge?

Then it hits me. "Poor schmuck. He was only four years older than me."

Here I am having a pity party for all the change in my life—which in the big picture isn't anything horrendous like marching off to war—when this guy died so young!

A sigh escapes my lungs. The pain is gone. The confusion remains.

I trek farther into the cemetery and see a babbling brook that cuts through the middle, dividing the land into two sections. There's a charming wooden footbridge that crosses over to the other side, where the landscape is lower, flatter, and the hill rolls downward, making it hard to see the additional grave markers. A marble bench is situated on the bank of the brook, next to the bridge, so I take a seat. Clear water trips and trickles over rocks and then disappears underneath the bridge. The air is silent, save for a few chirping birds and—

Marching?

I hear marching. Seriously. Like boots on pavement.

I blink once. Then twice.

Son of a biscuit eater—one of Grandma Ethel's sayings—there's a unit of what appears to be Union soldiers hiking up the hill, crossing the bridge. WTF? They're in full dress uniforms; some are tattered, torn, and stained with blood. Several of the men sport wounds or are wearing slings and bandages. For some reason, the blood makes me remember that icky image I had of Dad this morning. Maybe he's going to join a reenactment group?

As the soldiers pass by me, I shout out, "Hey there." None of them even turns his head in my direction. "Hello!" Nothing. "I said, hell-lo!" Great; not only am I possibly imagining these soldiers, I'm imagining rude ones.

I do a quick head count and get to fifty by the time they completely pass me. My mouth drops open as I watch them march together up the pebbled drive and out the front gate. Jumping to my feet, I scoot back up the path also to catch a glimpse of the unit soldiering down the road. Too bad I don't have my camera with me. It's not exactly every day you see something like that. They must be doing some sort of Civil War reenactment.

At the gate, I glance to the left. Nothing. Then to the right. Nothing.

My hair hits me in the face from the way I'm jerking my head back and forth. "What? Where did they go? They were just—"

At that precise moment, my heart feels as if it's going to burst out of my chest. I'm scared shitless. The pressure in my lungs is different from the earlier pain and asthma sensation. This way-beyond-a-flutter freak-out is courtesy of my absolute, complete, and total terror. Because at this exact moment, I truly believe that I've seen with my own eyes not one ghost, but fifty.

There's absolutely *no* sign of the soldiers anywhere.

They're gone.

"Thank you, ma'am." Celia hangs up the phone after speaking to the Radisson tourism office. "Nope. No Civil War reenactment groups in town."

"Crap!" I feel like I'm still trying to catch my breath after running the remaining half mile from the cemetery to Celia's house. I stop rubbing the ears of Celia's old English bulldog, Seamus, who's sitting on the bed next to me, panting, drooling, and enjoying the attention I've been giving him. I'm a nervous wreck, and petting an animal calms me down. Or at least it should. "That was the only explanation I had." It beat the more likely alternative, which, if confirmed, would open up the notorious whole other can of worms.

"Are you sure they were Union soldiers?" my friend pries.

I flop on her bed and press a pillow over my face while Seamus licks me on the arm. I want to scream. Plain and simple. Sitting back up, I say, "They were dressed in blue uniforms and looked just like the pictures in all of the history books. Their coats were so detailed, with gun straps and buttons and everything. Celia, it was sooooo real. *They* were real."

"You know, I've heard of things like this."

"Things like what?"

"Seeing ghosts like that."

She said the *g* word out loud. "Now, Celia, wait—"

Her eyes grow wide. "No, seriously!"

Borrrrrwwwwwhhhh! Seamus pipes up.

"Oh, you too?"

I run my hands through my hair that's messier than anything. "There's got to be a more logical explanation." As soon as I voice the words, I know I don't even believe them myself.

"Look, Mr. Spock. Logic aside . . ." Celia rubs her chin with her hand, obviously in deep thought. "It's simple. They had to be ghosts, Kendall. And you saw them clear as day! That is the coolest thing ever. I've lived in Radisson my entire life and I've never had a sighting like that, not for lack of trying or staring out the window with night-vision goggles on hoping to pick up a spectral or a—"

"Celia. Focus." I'm going to need some serious psychotropic medication now.

"I *am* focusing," she snaps at me. She pulls up Wikipedia on her desktop computer—her room looks like Circuit City, with a wide-screen plasma TV, two computers, a laptop, a stereo, a Wii, and a DVD player—and continues with her ghost theory. "I think you experienced a residual haunting."

"A what?"

"Here."

Intrigued, I move off the bed and cross to her desk. I read the Web page over her shoulder. "'A residual haunting is thought by some to be a replayed haunting in which no intelligent ghost, spirit, or other entity is directly involved. Much like a videotape, residual hauntings are playbacks of auditory, visual, olfactory, and other sensory phenomena that are attributed to a traumatic, life-altering, or common event of a person or place, like an echo of past events.'" Whoa. That's heavy. "So let me get this straight," I say, standing tall. "I'm not seeing real ghosts, just the memory of something that may have happened, like, a hundred and fifty years ago?"

"Something like that," she says. "Think of it as an eternal video replay."

Great, the headache's back. Only this time, it's clearly caused by my tension.

Celia reaches for a large atlas from the shelf above her computer. She pulls it down and flips through the pages to one particular map.

She stabs her finger on the book. "See. Look." She's

previously marked a path on the map of Georgia, making a yellow-highlighter line from Atlanta all the way to the Atlantic Ocean. "This," she says, "is Sherman's March to the Sea."

"Oh my God, Celia. You're such a dork."

She waggles her finger at me. "*History buff* is the politically correct term."

I elbow her and laugh, trying to make light of the situation. "Whatever, dudette."

She points to the small dot on the map that indicates my new place of residence. "Look. Right here is Radisson." Grabbing a magnifying glass from her top drawer, Celia zooms in on the town and the specific path of the Union soldiers all those years ago. "This is where the Union soldiers are known to have marched through Georgia. Here is the Spry River. It gets really narrow outside the Radisson city limits and turns into nothing more than a stream that's shallow and flows through here—where the cemetery is."

"That's literally right where I saw them!"

Celia claps her hands together. "Hot damn!"

"What?"

She grabs my shoulders and squeezes. "Kendall, don't you get it? You saw *actual* spectral evidence. I would *kill* to see that."

I don't exactly fear for my life here in Celia Nichols's room. However, the reality of all of this hits me like a right hook in the face from Rocky Balboa. "It's all true," I say, my throat tightening around the words. "Everything she said about me is true."

"She *who* said? What's true?" Celia asks. Exuberance is written all over her face. She's into all of this stuff, so she'll understand if I tell her, won't she?

Can I trust Celia with this info? I have to or else I *will* go mad. So I start dishing the 411 from Loreen Woods.

"Oooo, you talked to *her*?"

"Yeah, why not?"

"She's pretty cool. I've been in her store a couple of times. The tourists adore her. My dad sort of thinks Loreen's a weirdo and a fraud just sucking in the out-of-towners for their money."

"Yeah, well, I thought the same thing. But listen to this." I tell Celia everything that transpired at Divining Woman. "So, she was right. I'm a . . ." I pause, wondering if this is how gay kids feel when they come out of the closet to their friends and loved ones. If I admit this out loud, then it becomes true. There's no turning back. I swallow down my apprehension and say slowly and clearly, "Celia, I think I'm, like, psychic or something."

Celia's mouth drops open and her eyes dilate. "You're what?"

"Psychic. You know, a sensitive."

She stares at me blankly. Like *she's* seeing a ghost. Seamus, obviously bored now that (1) he's not the center of attention, and (2) the conversation has shifted to the weird, hops off the bed and struts his stout and sturdy bulldog self out of the room. I expect Celia to do the same.

It was fun having a new friend for two days . . . oh well.

"Okay then, I guess I'll get going. Sorry about—"

"No effing way! That is phenomenal!"

"Really? You think so?"

"Yes! Don't you?"

Oh *phew!* "I suppose so," I say. I'm more relieved that she hasn't thrown a crucifix at me or arranged to have me boiled in oil.

"That's why you're hearing voices, Kendall. I've read all about this. Ghosts and spirits reach out to sensitives because you have, like, this flashing sign above your head that's telling them you can see and hear them, so they're constantly crowding around you, wanting your attention."

"I know, Loreen told me the same—" Celia isn't listening. She's off to the bed to get the video recorder I returned. She grabs a USB cord, plugs one end into her laptop and the other into the recorder, cues up some software, and clicks Play, all in a matter of moments. This chick knows her electronics. Her bedroom is the best boom-boom room I've ever seen. I sort of expect her to have a secret switch or knob that opens a wall panel and reveals the passageway to a secret underground lair. "Celia, are you paying any attention to what I'm saying?"

"Yeah, sure," she says, acknowledging me with a hand wave. Then, "You know, this means we can really do some serious ghost hunting. With your abilities and my technology— and unlimited bank account—we can get anything we need, from thermal cameras, EMF meters, and temperature gauges to walkie-talkies so we can go back and forth."

"Your unlimited bank account?" Geesh, must be nice.

She waves me off with another flick of a wrist. "Yeah, you know. Plastic allowance. Mom and Dad never look at my AmEx bill. Our accountant just pays everything monthly. Where do you think I got all of this stuff?"

I screw up my mouth. "I thought maybe you were a drug dealer or something."

"Sort of. My dad is the founder of Mega-Mart, which includes one of the biggest pharmacies in the nation."

"No shit!" I clarify. "The part about him founding Mega-Mart, that is."

"No shit about it."

Well, that explains everything. Celia Nichols is an heiress. To the Mega-Mart franchise fortune, no less. Who'da thunk it? She certainly doesn't act like the girls in my class back home in Chicago who lived at the more prestigious city addresses and wouldn't give fellow classmates the time of day if their parents made under a million a year.

Before I can say anything else, Celia turns and asks, "Can you channel?"

"Can I what?" I'm good at channel surfing.

Her eyes grow wide. "You know, channel a spirit."

"I hadn't thought about it." It sounds invasive. "Loreen didn't mention—"

Celia shakes her head. "Never mind, it's something you can learn later."

"I've apparently got a lot to learn." I spread my hands out before me, gazing at the lines and creases in my palms as if they're a road map that's going to show me the way in my new world. I definitely can't take this journey on my own.

Celia jars me out of my reverie. "Friggin' A, Kendall! Check this out."

My head is reeling from her excitement, but I lean closer and stare at the computer monitor where last night's video is running. Lovely: there I am in my T-shirt and shorts, thrashing around in the bed. Must have been when I was dreaming about Dasani-Blue-Eyed Boy.

Celia points to the screen with her index finger, indicating something white and smoky on the videotape. "Were you smoking a cigarette?" she asks.

Sneering, I say, "Yeah, right. At two a.m. I don't smoke, thanks. It's something else."

"Let me zoom in."

Sure enough, we see that there's a mist moving around.

"What the—?" I ask with a gasp.

"It's some sort of, umm . . ." Celia turns her head sideways and I follow along.

"Is it a vapor?"

She nods. "It's taking a form, almost."

"There's a hand," I say, pointing.

"Oh my God. There's hair, too! Look!"

I almost choke as the recorded apparition appears before me. A white, womanly form, peering down at me as I'm sleeping. Then the woman shifts and disappears out of the frame, as if she's headed down the hall to my parents' room. Chill bumps break out up and down my arms and legs, as if I'm caught outside in a lake-effect snowstorm. Talk about major heebie-jeebies! My alarm shifts a gear into something resembling being pissed off. Who is this? And why is she messing with me and my family? An overwhelming sense of dread fills me, like I know this specter aims to hurt us because we're outsiders and are living in its house. I can't explain it other than I just *feel* it in the fabric of my being.

I put my hands on my hips, remembering the image of my father battered and bruised. Does this entity have something to do with that? Can I keep him safe from her, if it even is a her? "The hell with this. I want her out of my house, out of my room!"

"Awesome! We've got a lot of work to do if we're going to officially ghost hunt."

I never thought I'd say it, but—"I'm in. We need to read all we can on ghost hunting, what to do, what equipment we need, how to organize." Suddenly, in my mind's eye, I have a vision of football players working together. The letters *t-e-a-m* scroll through my brain. "We need a team to do this correctly, right?"

"Damn straight we do!" Celia mock salutes me. "I'm on it. And whatever we require in terms of electronics, supplies, anything, it's on me. I get a ridiculous discount at Mega-Mart like you wouldn't even believe."

I certainly won't argue with that proclamation because I know I can't bankroll this operation. Celia high-fives me, and my life has officially changed.

Something deep inside me, perhaps that awakening sixth sense, tells me this is the right thing to do. And maybe, just maybe, I'll be able to keep the vision of my injured dad from ever coming true.

Chapter Seven

THERE'S A GHOST in my house.

A real, live—well, technically *not* alive—freakin' ghost in my house.

I can't get over this.

Not while I slept last night—and dreamed about Dasani-Blue-Eyed Boy again—or when I was having b'fast with the fam while Mom read a daily devotional. Not even her blueberry smiley-face pancakes could distract me from the floaty ghost lady in my room. Nor could Dad's talking about how his coffee mug kept disappearing at work yesterday. Okay, I sort of heard that part. Maybe after Celia and I solve the mystery of the floaty lady in my room, we'll tackle city hall and investigate all the ghost stories there, starting with Dad's office.

Yep. I've accepted my fate. If you can't beat 'em, join 'em.

Celia and I are now officially ghost hunters, or, rather, ghost huntresses. Huh, I like that better. It sounds so fifteenth-century primeval of us. Not like I'm Van Helsing (Hugh Jackman was waaaaay hot in that movie) out to rid Transylvania of the vampires with a rapid-fire crossbow. Instead, I'll be like all those people on the TV programs Celia's had me speed-watching on her TiVo over the last three days. I'll use my abilities to help lost or confused spirits on their way—if that's what they're seeking. I promise to use my gift only for positive purposes. Besides, I want that apparition *out* of my house and away from my family. I thought I heard that ghostly voice last night when I passed by Kaitlin's room. Even though she's a pest, she's my little sister and I'll fight to the death for her, ghost or no ghost. If my newfound psychic abilities can help that earthbound spirit move to the beyond or wherever it's supposed to be, then I'm all over it.

Here at school now, I look across the aisle at Celia, who's furiously sketching something in her notebook instead of listening to our calculus teacher, Mr. Kline, drone on about the specific arc length of a parametrically defined curve. Celia's tongue sticks out of the corner of her mouth as she concentrates on whatever it is she's drawing. I don't blame her for being bored. How in the world are parametrically defined curves going to help me in my future at the University of Michigan? Or in Celia's quest for a parapsychology degree in Scotland—which I still think is a bit nutty.

Only six more minutes until the bell rings and we can eat lunch. I'm not sure if it's my awakening psychicness or what, but I'm so hungry I'd eat my calculus book if it was battered and deep-fried.

Mr. Kline drops the chalk to the tray and steps over to the

lectern. "Read through chapter three and do the problems on page forty-four. We'll discuss tomorrow."

Bleck. Homework. On a Thursday too. Doesn't Mr. Kline know I've got to watch *Ugly Betty* tonight? Oh . . . and surf the Web some more—finally got the Internet connection at home and have been looking at all the links and bookmarks Celia's forwarded me—on how to ghost hunt. It all still feels massively weird, but it's something to do and something to keep my mind off that vapor in my room that talks through machines. And I need to see if Marjorie has gotten my e-mail filling her in on everything that's going on in my new life here in Radisson. I also need the deets on what she's been up to. I can't believe she hasn't tried to call me. Maybe she's just crazy-busy like I am. Man . . . there's so much to do and so little time.

When the bell blares, I swoop my things off the desk and into my backpack with little care. "Let's eat!" I announce at Celia's desk. "I heard the American chop suey is actually edible."

Celia quickly snaps her notebook shut, but not before I get a good glimpse at what she was drawing. It looks like a guy.

"Who's that?" I ask.

"No one."

I furrow my brows at her.

"Seriously, Kendall. It's nothing. Mr. Kline was about to put me to sleep."

"Me too." I glance at the spiral notebook she crams into her bag. "That was really good, whatever you were drawing."

She won't look at me. "I was just doodling. No big." She slings her bag over her shoulder. "This class blows. I wish I'd opted for something else this period."

I decide to let questions about her sketch go. For now. Some people are sensitive about their art, so I won't push. "I know. I wish I could be like that dude over there." I point to a thin guy who'd been sitting in the front row and is now deep in a convo with Mr. Kline. He must be bucking for this semester's teacher's pet. "He seems riveted by calculus."

Celia glances over and shrugs. The guy catches her looking at him and a wide grin spreads across his face. Then he waves. "Oh. That's just Clay. He's a whiz at all things math-related."

He's also majorly crushed on Celia. I don't necessarily have to have psychic abilities to understand that. Look at him light up! "Are you guys going together?"

Her mouth drops. "Me and Clay? No way!"

"Why not? He's tall and cute and I can totally tell he likes you."

Was she drawing a picture of Clay in her notebook and is just too shy to tell me? Or him? I think it's kind of precious, in a geeky Celia sort of way.

Shaking her head, she bolts out of the classroom and into the hall toward her locker. "Clay Price and I have known each other since we were little. Our dads golf together."

"So?"

"So," she starts, "I'm not interested in him like that."

"How are you interested in him?"

"I'm not. In any way. All he does is tease me. He used to pop my bra in sixth grade."

I roll my eyes. "Don't you know that when a guy likes you, he's mean or teases you?" I remember Jack Dumfries pushed me off the seesaw in second grade because he allegedly liked me—or so Marjorie told me when I was lying in the dirt trying not to cry because I'd ripped my brand-new tights. Not the smartest way to my heart, but Jack and I did "go steady" for two whole weeks. This is great, though. I finally feel like a normal high school teenager having a normal high school teenager conversation. "Who are you interested in?"

"No one!"

"Don't get all defensive."

"I'm not."

I see her cheeks stain red and know I've touched a nerve. There's definitely something she's not telling me and I can't seem to break through her mind to find out what it is. I can't exactly read minds, I don't think. Rather, there's just information out there that I know, without a shadow of a doubt, is true.

"Sorry, Celia."

"No, it's not you," she says, hiding her eyes behind her hair. "It's just that I have too much to think about academically, extracurricularly—and now with our ghost hunting—that I don't have time for boys. Especially someone as annoying as Clay."

"Clay's a cutie. Was he who you were drawing?"

"Jesus, Kendall. Drop it, would you?"

I laugh heartily to break the tension. "The lady doth protest too much, methinks."

Celia rolls her eyes back at me. "Don't go get all *Hamlet* on my ass, okay?"

I can't help but hip-check her as she's stashing her books in her locker. "Whatever you say, Nichols."

"I say we quit worrying about my love life—or lack thereof —and concentrate on setting up our ghost-hunting team."

"All right, already," I state with a knowing smile. I really like Celia and I don't want to do anything that would put me on her bad side. She's fun and smart and crazy. And she's the only person who's given me the time of day (other than that one visit with Loreen) since I moved to Radisson. Everything happens for a reason, right?

Which is all good 'cause I've left two voice-mail messages on Marjorie's cell and she still hasn't returned my e-mail. See, I typed out this long message to her about what's been going on here since I moved. Like, everything. I'm trying to reason that she's just busy with school and life in Chicago, and she's not ignoring me and my e-mail confession about being psychic. Since Marjorie's mom's a big flake, Marjorie might think I'm headed down the same path.

Good thing I've got Celia now to be a friend and accept me for who I am.

In the caf, she and I buzz through the serving line, snagging salad, American chop suey—which isn't Chinese at all, just elbow macaroni, ground beef, and tomato sauce—and ice-cold Diet Cokes. Celia leads us to a table over near the window where we can begin strategizing our ghost huntressing. Where to start?

I dive into my plate of food like I've never eaten before while Celia decorates the table with printouts from websites galore on how to assemble an investigative team and all the equipment we'll need. "Most of these websites," she begins, "say you should have about eight people for a proper ghost-hunting team."

"Why eight?" I ask with my mouth full. My mom would be so ashamed of me. We won't even *go there* about what she would think of me becoming a ghost huntress.

Celia makes a note and then says, "Because you need people collecting the different kinds of scientific data and evidence."

I wipe my mouth with the paper napkin. "I thought *I* was doing the psychic stuff."

"You are," Celia says. "All good ghost-hunting teams need a 'sensitive' to speak to the spirits."

I look up and glare at her. "What's with the air quotes around the word *sensitive*? Don't do that to me."

"Do what?"

I mock her air quotes. "That. It makes me feel like a freak."

"I'm sorry, you're right. We'll call you the team's psychic investigator, how's that?"

I put the napkin back in my lap. "That's more like it." Before scooping up another mouthful, I ask, "Who else do we need?" How in the world will we—the outcast and the newbie—find people to help us out? Maybe I can get Loreen to suggest someone who might be interested.

Celia motions to one of the printouts that has a picture of a folding table with a lot of monitors, computer equipment, and other items. "See this? It's called base camp. Wherever we investigate, we'll need to set up one of these to keep up with what's going on at all times."

I crane my neck to get a good look. "Oh, okay, I get it. It's a place where you can monitor the cameras and stuff."

"Right." Celia sips her soda. "I think it's only natural that I head up all of the electronics and computer equipment—"

"—since it's all yours anyway," I say with a laugh.

"—and that we find someone with a real talent for photography." Celia pulls out last year's Radisson High School yearbook, *The Reveler,* and starts flipping through the pages. She points to a large picture of the football team in a gargantuan pile at the goal line. "Check out the cutline."

Spinning the book around, I read, "'Picture by Taylor Tillson.'" I push the annual back to Celia. "What's a Taylor Tillson?"

Celia peers over her shoulder and nods her head toward a

girl with long dishwater-blond hair sitting with one other girl in the back of the caf. Oh wow, it's the Pretty Girl from my homeroom class who waved at me.

However, I scrunch up my nose. "She looks like she's popular."

"She used to be. She's sort of pulled back socially from her regular clique for some reason since we've been back," Celia explains. "But the point is she's a photographer for the yearbook."

"That is a plus. You think she'd be interested?" I watch as Taylor laughs really hard at something the other girl says. I notice that Taylor's tan and thin and wears a little too much eye makeup. She'd probably rather hang out with the cheerleaders and football players than go creeping around God knows where late at night with Celia and me.

"Check this out." Celia spins the yearbook back to me. Sure enough, there's Taylor front and center of the French club, then in the pep club picture. She's also a member of 4-H and the honor society and the science club. Cool; in that picture, she's standing right in front of Celia. "She's totally a serial joiner around here. Any time a teacher needs a volunteer for anything, Taylor Tillson always has her hand in the air first. She's been, like, a social chair all the way back to kindergarten."

"What are her parents like?"

Celia eyeballs me. "What does that matter?"

"Trust me. It matters." I think of my own mother and how she'd be on her knees on the prayer bench at our new

Episcopal church, praying for my soul, if she knew I was dancing with the dead . . . or planning on it.

"Her mom is a housewife and her father used to be the
president of First National Bank," Celia rattles off.

"Used to be?"

"Yeah, he moved away. Taylor hasn't really talked about it.
Maybe that's why she's sort of pulled away from the RHS social scene."

Something clicks inside me and my inner thoughts focus
on Taylor Tillson. I don't exactly know how I'm doing this, but
it's happening. My interpretation of her is hazy, foggy even, like
there's some sort of defense system in her brain that no one
can bust through. Then again, I probably can't even really do
this and that's why I'm getting no reading. Abruptly, my inner
thoughts shift to a vivid image of . . . Dasani-Blue-Eyed Boy.
In this vision, he's sitting in a Jeep beeping the horn. Who is
this guy? And why am I constantly dreaming—day- or otherwise—of him?

"Kendall! Earth to Kendall."

"Sorry," I say, snapping out of it. "I was trying to get a read
on Taylor."

"Can you do that?"

"I don't know!" I say.

Celia moves her hair behind her ears. "Best way to get a
read on her is to actually talk to her."

She's got a point. "So, do you know her well enough to ask
if she wants to join our team?"

Celia shrugs. "Sure. Why not?"

"Let's go, then."

I bus our table and return the half-eaten food to the kitchen area. Celia sucks down her Diet Coke and tosses the can into the blue recycle bin. As we walk toward Taylor's table, Celia says, "So, if she signs on as our photographer, all we need to do is get someone to do the sound recordings and then we can get started."

"EVPs," I add. "Electronic voice phenomena, or the capturing of disembodied or spirit voices on magnetic tape as audio recordings."

"Ah, someone's been doing her homework."

"I've been watching *Ghost Hunters* marathons," I say proudly. "I thought you said we needed eight people, though?"

"I just said that a lot of the groups out there have eight people," she corrects. "Semantics, you know? It's whatever works for us."

"Well, don't forget, we'll need a skeptic," I add. "All those websites say you need someone a little cynical to keep us honest about our findings."

With a snort, Celia says, "Around here, that won't be too hard to find." She straightens. "Here goes nothing."

I take a deep breath and focus my mental energies on Taylor Tillson. I silently ask that she be open-minded and not start throwing her chop suey at us. It would take a lot of Tide with bleach alternative to get the tomato sauce out of my good Eddie Bauer button-down.

"Hey, Taylor!" Celia says in a high-pitched voice I don't recognize as hers.

"Hey there, Celia. How ya doing?" Taylor smiles genuinely at Celia and then cocks her head a little to check me out. "Oh, I know you! You're in my homeroom. How rude of me not to come introduce myself to the new girl in town! Sit, sit, sit."

The other girl at the table looks me up one side and down the other. Then she mumbles something about getting dessert and scoots off. I concentrate hard, hoping not to pick up on any of her thoughts, but the airwaves are relatively silent. I've got to quit being so paranoid.

I extend my hand across the table in a very grown-up way. "I'm Kendall Moorehead."

Taylor shakes my hand fervently and welcomes me to RHS. Oh God, I hope she doesn't break into song or something, à la *High School Musical*. "It's so great to have a new girl in school. Most all of us grew up together and we're sick to death of each other's company. Right, Celia?"

Celia chuckles slightly as Taylor runs through a quick twenty-question session on the who, what, where, when, and why of Kendall Moorehead.

"I looooooove Chicago," she says with an almost shimmer in her blue eyes. I'd been told that sometimes Southerners can be fake nice to you, but the vibes I'm getting from Taylor seem to be a hundred percent genuine. Maybe I misjudged the Pretty Girl.

"My mom is a part-time buyer for Nordstrom's at Perimeter Mall outside of Atlanta, and she took me with her one time on a trip to Chicago. So many amazing stores to lose yourself in for days on end. You must really miss it there."

"I do. It's the only home I've ever known," I say, a bit sadder than I anticipated. "It'll always be my hometown. Now I'm just trying to adjust to living here."

Taylor reaches over and pats my arm with her French-manicured hand. "We'll do everything to make you feel welcome here, right, Celia?"

"I already am," she snaps. I get the impression that Celia either doesn't like Taylor Tillson or envies her. Can't tell which yet, but there's something under the surface.

"So, Taylor," I start. No use pussyfooting around. Might as well dive into the deep end. "There's something Celia and I wanted to talk to you about. Well, ask you, more like."

She tosses her blond mane over her shoulder and licks her lips, already shiny with gloss. "Sure! Shoot!"

"This is serious, Taylor," Celia says softly. "Like, top secret."

Taylor leans in, eyes afire with curiosity. "Oh, goody! I love secrets."

I swallow down my trepidation and strike out. "See, Taylor, Celia and I are starting uh, uh, a club, so to speak, and we need a photographer for it."

Taylor's finely sculpted brow lifts up and she smiles amazingly white teeth at us. "Ooo, I'm the yearbook photographer. I also work on the school's website and have this amazing Facebook page you'll have to check out. Lots of emo-type pics of myself that I took in the mirror at home. And two of my football pictures from last year were used in the *Atlanta Journal-Constitution*."

Wow, she's as exuberant as Celia when you get her going. Will I be able to handle both of their strong energies?

"What kind of club is this?" Taylor asks. Her wide smile literally glistens, and the shade of pink on her lips makes her teeth appear even whiter. "I'm totally into adding another club to my curriculum vitae."

With a deep breath, I try again to see into Taylor's thoughts. She seems not to have any prejudices hidden under the surface, from what I can tell, other than she hates her grandmother's cooking, misses her dad, and thinks Courtney Langdon needs to eat a tray of brownies and not throw them up. I try not to giggle as I continue. I get the sense of a genuinely warm and friendly person. Taylor's a bit of a daredevil, even though she may not know it yet.

Celia taps me on the shoulder. "Tell her, Kendall."

Okay. Here goes.

"Celia and I've decided to start ghost hunting."

I watch as Taylor sits there for a moment, staring ahead as if she's been frozen in time. Then she blinks hard with her overly mascaraed, long black lashes. "Oh, wow. Fascinating. You've just got to tell me exactly what this would entail? Would there be papers or extra-credit work here at school involved?"

Celia and I look at each other. I say, "No, this is totally an after-school type of thing. You know, like at night and on the weekends."

"It'll all be very scientific," Celia explains. "We'll have equipment for sound and for measuring energies."

Celia and I give her more details about the ghost in my house, how people in my father's office think city hall is haunted, and how Radisson's storied history makes it the perfect place to hold investigations. Celia gives some detail about how Taylor would take pictures and videos and be an integral part of the team so that I can try to communicate with the spirits.

She zeros in on something I said. "What do you mean, 'try to communicate with the spirits'?"

Do I really want to lay all of my cards on the table? Do I want to be that girl who blurts out to everyone she meets that she's a psychic? Psycho, more like. Yet Taylor's eyes appear to be kind and understanding with an outline of pain that I can't put my finger on just yet.

I fight my apprehension and lower my voice. "I'm sort of going through this, umm, well, don't tell anyone, but it's like a psychic awakening."

Taylor's eyes widen. "Meaning?"

"Meaning I can see and talk to spirits."

I wait for Taylor to call the principal and have me thrown out of school. Fine. I guess I can finish up by being home-schooled. These days colleges accept all kinds of students.

But Taylor surprises both of us.

Her mouth flies open and she claps her hands in front of her. "Oh. My. God! That is phenomenal! You're really psychic?" She stops herself with a hand to her mouth and quiets down. "Tell me what I'm thinking *right* now. No, don't! Let me try to block my thoughts from you." She shuts her eyes and smiles real hard, bursting into a giggle. "Oh, this is going to be so much fun. Just think of all the places we can explore and investigate right here in Radisson. We'll have to have a schedule and organize everything. Wow, I'm sure there aren't many other applicants to Duke University who'll have ghost hunting as an extracurricular activity." Then Taylor raises her fist and cheers, *"Scientia vincere tenebras!"*

"Excuse me?" I ask, unaware they taught Latin at RHS.

Beaming, Taylor says, "'Through science to conquer darkness.' It's the motto of Université Libre de Bruxelles, Belgium."

"And you know that how?" Celia puts in.

Taylor waves a hand in the air. "Just one of those things you pick up."

"Oh. Okay." Damn, these kids here in Radisson are smarter than I gave them credit for originally. I guess it's not just some backwater 'burb outside of Atlanta. I sit up tall, barely believing that she's interested. She should, like, go on *Jeopardy!*

Taylor nods at me. "The motto fits here, don't you think?"

"It sure does," Celia says.

I place my hand on the table and lean in toward Taylor. "So, you're in? You'll ghost hunt with us?"

"Absolutely!" she says loudly, and claps her hands.

"Like hell you will, Taylor. Are you insane?"

I whip my head around to confront the deep-voiced intruder. Of course, the first thing I see is his blue-jeaned crotch. *Yikes! Sorry!* Wasn't expecting that. So I crane my neck up to see who has rained on our very private parade.

I take in the full details of the bellowing guy. Trim waist, athletic build, last season's Old Navy rugby shirt that's been washed too many times and has seen better days, tan arms, thick lips, straight nose. Short-cropped blond hair frames his gorgeous face, and his jaw is firm and clenched . . .

But as soon as I make eye contact with him, my ears start ringing. A wave of heat passes over me while I stare at his beautiful blue eyes. Breathing becomes difficult, and the pounding in my head returns. Bells, whistles, and lights punctuate my thoughts. It's like I'm in net for the Blackhawks and someone just scored the Stanley Cup–winning goal on me, top shelf, glove side, and I'm sprawled out on the ice like roadkill while the other team celebrates. The blood tiptoes away from my face and I hear Celia say something about "she's gone pale."

"Hey, are you all right?" the guy asks. I see his lips moving, yet his words blend into the noise of my brain that's telling me *This can't be real.* My balance on the lunch-table bench is precarious, and air to my lungs has suddenly become a precious commodity. I sense myself slipping away into oblivion.

Holy shit . . . I'm going to pass out, and Dasani-Blue-Eyed Boy—*he's for real!*—is moving in to catch me as I fall.

CHAPTER EIGHT

"KENDALL! KENDALL! Are you all right?"

I think that's Taylor screaming at me, but I can't be sure as I emerge from my hazy funk.

"Somebody get the school nurse," Taylor instructs.

"No. She's fine," Celia says, knowing I don't want to be poked or prodded. "It's just hot in here." She's waving an empty cafeteria tray over my head in an attempt to give me air.

"I could pour some water on her," Taylor says. "They do that all the time in the movies."

"You'll get me wet too," a male voice says from behind me.

Even though I'm drenched in sweat, I'm chilled to the bone. Crap on a crutch! Why did I faint? I haven't passed out like that since Easter Sunday when I was ten years old. I was singing the "Hallelujah Chorus" in the children's choir and it was scorching hot, so hot that I crumpled to the floor among the lilies of the valley. When I came to then, my dad's strong arms were holding me, just like—now? Wait! That's not Dad cradling me. It's—

Dasani-Blue-Eyed Boy!

That's why I zonked out. Because he exists! Here in Radisson. In my school.

"You okay?" he asks as he peers at me. Even from my up-side-down point of view, he's quite breathtaking. I realize I'm slumped on the floor, half lying in his lap with his arms around me. Mmm . . . it feels nice, too. Just like my dream. Whoa. My dream had been some sort of weird foreshadowing of right now. I fell. Dasani-Blue-Eyed Boy caught me. He's eyeing me with major concern on his tanned face. Wow. I'm serious. He's freakin' gorgeous. I guess there *are* guys like him in Radisson. Color me lucky. The brown mole I've seen in my dreams is right there next to his nose on the left side of his face. I resist the urge to reach out and feel it just to make sure it's real. Yeah, I need some oxygen.

"Uhh, I think I'm—ugh," I blurt out. My head is pounding with the now-familiar psychic headache. There are flashes and lights and images, but nothing's concise or coherent. I press the palms of my hands into my eyes and rub—but not so hard that I smear my mascara. Dasani-Blue-Eyed Boy is no longer a figment of my imagination.

Taylor squats down next to me. "Oh, poor Kendall." Then she turns to the mystery man who saved me from cracking open my skull on the cafeteria's linoleum. "This is all your fault, Jason!"

Jason? His name is Jason. That's a noble name. Like Jason

and the Argonauts, bringing Pelias the Golden Fleece. (So I know some Greek mythology on top of all the Shakespeare.)

"How on earth is this my fault?" he asks. "I caught her, didn't I?"

"You scared her senseless with your bullishness," Taylor accuses.

"I'm just looking out for you."

"I don't need you to look out for me, Jason."

"You certainly do," he growls. "Especially when you're talking about shit like ghost hunting. Are you insane, Taylor?"

I zone out for a moment, away from the hubbub swirling around me. My headache intensifies and I start seeing full-color images flickering through my mind, like a PowerPoint presentation. They're of the two of us—Jason and me—together. Like, doing couple things. Walking together. Talking on the phone. And me falling again. He's catching me, but it's different from just now. I sense anger and resentment in the air around me, trying to hurt him . . . or me. Then we're kissing. Whoa! What an amazing vision this is. *Come back.*

Taylor is still going at Jason full steam. "You can't tell me what to do."

"Someone should so you don't act like a jackass."

"You're the jackass, Jason."

"Y'all—" Celia tries with no success.

"Nice mouth, Taylor. Do you kiss your mother with it?"

"You should know."

From the tone of this argument, I gather that golden blond

Jason is Taylor's boyfriend. Of course, the beautiful people pair off together. Such is the way of the world. It's been occurring since the dawn of time. That leaves outsiders and geeks like Celia and me to watch in envy and wonder what their children will look like someday.

I try to sit up and find myself nestled between this Jason's muscular blue-jeaned thighs. His warmth radiates against my back, and I feel quite natural up against him like this. Rather a precarious position, I must say. I'm sure Taylor doesn't appreciate me being snuggled up to her honey like this.

She flattens her lips and death-glares at Jason over my shoulder. "I'm sick of you constantly telling me what to do! You're my brother, not my father, Jason. When are you going to get that straight?"

Brother? *Ohhhhhhhh . . . iiiiiiiiiiiinteresting.*

Celia steps forward and extends her hand to me. "Here, Kendall. Get up."

I clasp on and let her pull me to my feet. Oh my God! While she's tugging, Jason gives me a shove on the ass for good measure. My entire being tingles, from the roots of my hairs to my in-need-of-a-pedicure toes. And it has nothing to do with my psychic abilities. It's like I've been Tasered by his gorgeous looks and the crooked smile that he gave me when I was supine in his lap. I scramble away from him and mutter my thanks under my breath.

"What happened?" Celia asks in a whisper.

I don't want to tell her about my dreams of Dasa—urr,

Jason yet. She's been a good egg accepting my psychic awakening and the quest to ghost hunt, but I don't want to freak
her out too much. "I think it's all part of coming to grips with
my abilities."

She places a hand on my back and says, "Next time you
want to play fainting goat, give me a heads-up."

I chuckle. "I'll do my best."

Jason stands as well and brushes off his large hands on his
jeans. "I know you just got sick or whatever, but are you seriously talking about ghost hunting and dragging my sister into
it?"

Pushing him away, Taylor says, "No one's dragging me into
anything. I *want* to do this, Jason. And like I said before, you're
my brother, not my guardian."

A long sigh escapes my chest as my initial crush-rush wears
off and I take another good, long look at Jason Tillson. He's a
little bit taller than Taylor—his *sister*—and has impressively
broad shoulders. Just like the ones in my dream. His eyes are
the most amazing crisp blue I've ever seen. Taylor's aren't much
different, only hidden behind a thick layer of eye shadow, eyeliner, and mascara. Upon closer inspection, I swear they look
just alike.

"You're twins," I say more than ask.

Jason quirks his mouth at me. "What, are you psychic too?"

Taylor smacks him. "You're such a jerk. Yes, Kendall, we are
twins. But because Mr. Wonderful here is three minutes—"

"Three and a half," he says emphatically.

"Whatever. Since he came out first, he thinks he can tell me what to do."

"I didn't mean to cause a family squabble," I say.

"This is my life," Taylor says. "As I was saying before the Incredible Hulk moved in and nearly sent you up to Jesus, I have two digital cameras and a video recorder that registers night vision. That should come in handy, shouldn't it?"

"Absolutely. Celia says our best hunting will be at night, so any equipment that lends itself to that is perfect. Right?"

I nudge Celia with my elbow, but she doesn't look up. "Sure." She seems to be fascinated by a bend of elbow macaroni on the floor at her feet. What's wrong with her? She's totally clammed up all of a sudden. Is she afraid of Jason Tillson? Honestly, he's just an overprotective brother. I think it's kind of cute, in a sweet, distorted way. Celia sits back at the table and begins shuffling the papers we'd been showing Taylor. I guess she's focusing on the task at hand, which is getting our team set.

Turning my attention back to Taylor, I say, "I'm so glad you're in. With you aboard, Celia can concentrate on the computer equipment and I can really start honing my intuitive skills so we can connect with the spirits around here."

A harrumph escapes Jason's chest. "Intuitive skills? What's that supposed to mean?"

"It means that I actually *am* psychic." I poke my index finger against his steel-belted shoulder. "So watch your thoughts around me."

Okay, so it's a pretty hollow threat, but what Jason Tillson doesn't know won't kill him.

"Fine," he says and then turns to his sister. "Do whatever you want, Taylor. But don't come crying to me when the shit hits the fan or you screw up in some way."

"Thanks for the vote of confidence, JT."

As Taylor and Celia begin making notes and comparing calendars, I watch Jason stride off through the cafeteria. People around us seem to lose interest and go back to their American chop suey and ponderings of the fainting new girl. With one more sidelong glance, Jason's electric blue eyes connect with mine, and he half smiles like he knows a secret. It's the same exact look I've seen in my dreams. The one he gives me right before I fall into his arms.

Damn it! Didn't that just happen?

I know one thing: if I'm going to keep my sanity, I need to steer clear of Jason Tillson.

When I walk into Divining Woman after school, Loreen hands me a Vitamin Water and invites me to sit on the couch with her. "I bet you could use something cold to drink after the day you've had."

"How do you . . ." Right, she's psychic. "You sense that from my energies?"

She runs her fingers through her curly hair and nods. "Your energy is almost of a static-electricity nature. I get the sense something happened at school?"

I tell her about the run-in with Jason.

"So, this is the boy you've been dreaming of?"

I bob my head while I gulp the orangey drink. "Exactly. Down to the details of the mole on his left cheek."

Loreen shuts her eyes and breathes in deeply. I almost have to snort at today's T-shirt, which reads "I know what you did, and there will be consequences." She shifts her eyes to mine. "I sense a cosmic connection between you and Jason, but it's not very clear right now what your future holds. As you develop your gift more, you'll be able to decipher the meanings of things like dreams, images, and visions. Right now, you just have to take it one day at a time and not get too discouraged or frustrated with yourself."

I laugh. "The fact that I'm even in your store again shows that I'm trying to come to terms with what might be going on with me."

She reaches over and takes my hand. "It really is a gift from God, Kendall. There's so much good you can do with it. Take it from me, I know."

"Thanks, Loreen. I'm trying to look at it that way." Although, maybe I should start playing the lottery or betting the ponies or gambling on baseball games. I could make a fortune! I sit back and smile, thinking *that* could be the life.

"That would be an abuse of your abilities, Kendall, and you know it."

"Get out of my head, Loreen," I say with a bit of frustration.

"Sorry, I can't help myself." Loreen smiles at me. I'm so glad to have her here to guide me through this awakening and to help me not make an ass out of myself. Stupid queen of hearts was right. I did need another woman to show me the way. "You should use your psychic intuition to do something good," she says. "I use my Reiki healing all the time at the nursing home where I volunteer. So many of those elderly people have family that's moved away or no one to take care of them and most of the time, they just want companionship."

"That's awesome, and I'm sure they really appreciate it." I had no clue she spent time doing that and helping people. Here I thought she was just this kind of squirrelly lady with the New Age shop. There's a lot more to her, obviously. That was really ignorant of me to make such a snap judgment about her when I came in here before. "What's Reiki?"

"It's a Japanese technique for stress reduction that also encourages healing."

"Oh, okay." Sounds cool. Wonder if I can do that too? "So, the way I'm going to do something good is Celia and I've decided to hunt ghosts. Hopefully, I can help spirits out who are stuck here for one reason or another," I announce.

Loreen couldn't be happier. "You certainly picked the right town for it. The right county, even. The right part of the country. With all the Civil War history here, you'll have plenty to keep you busy."

I nibble at my bottom lip. "And you'll help me learn everything I need to know, won't you? 'Cause I can't do this alone,

Loreen. I'm winging it as it is. I mean, I don't know why I'm hearing certain things or seeing visions or knowing who people are without being introduced or—"

She reaches over and pats my hand. "It's okay, Kendall. I'm here for you."

I let out the breath I've been holding and feel a bit of relief. Loreen understands everything and she's going to guide me through this awakening.

"Why don't you get a notebook and I'll answer some of your questions."

"Perfect," I say, diving for my book bag. Armed with pen and paper, I sit cross-legged on her couch, nearly salivating for information. "So, what *am* I exactly? I mean, I hear all these terms like *psychic, clairvoyant, sensitive, fortuneteller* . . . What's the right thing to call myself?"

Loreen nods and thinks for a moment. "It all depends on what abilities you hone. Myself, I'm an empathic psychic healer. I'm sensitive, can feel the pain of others, can see into other people's minds almost, and I use Reiki to heal. Those are the things I've worked on in my years. But, Kendall, you have to discover your powers and grow and develop your skills. Really, it's pretty much like multitasking."

"Well, I can do that."

"Tell me what you're experiencing, exactly."

I run through the list of Things That Have Happened to Kendall Since Awakening, and then sit quietly while Loreen lets the information churn.

"You display several psychic traits," Loreen says. I settle into the couch, pen poised over my notepad. This is so much better and more interesting than Mr. Kline's calculus class. "First there is claircognizant," she says. "It's where you become perceptive to things. You don't know who's telling you the information or where it's coming from, you just *know* certain things."

"Like how I knew all of that about Helen Pearlman and her husband's goiter."

"Exactly. Then there's clairvoyant, where it's almost like 'clear seeing.' It encompasses future events, past events, even connects in a way so you can use your mind and view remote locations. Everything is visual and you're literally seeing what's going on."

I lower my brows and ponder what she's said. "I don't think I've actually had that happen yet. Unless you count the Union soldiers I saw . . . and that weird thing that happened when I saw my dad injured, like, in the future or something."

Loreen shifts in her seat. "Maybe. That leads to clairaudience, where a spirit speaks to you or you hear something. Sometimes the voice is in your head or maybe it's a whisper in your ear. That's very common with me and my spirit guides."

I think of the floaty lady in my room and how she spoke to me through the white-noise machine. I guess I've got clairaudient ability as well.

Continuing, Loreen goes on to explain about clairsentience, the ability to feel the vibrations of other people through touch or feeling. There's also clairalience, where someone gets their psychic knowledge from certain smells. It all makes sense to me. I mean, how many times have I heard a certain song on the radio or sniffed a familiar odor and then I'm taken back to a particular moment in time. Popcorn cooking makes me remember all the movies Marjorie and I saw together growing up. The aroma of sausage dogs puts me right outside the walls of Wrigley Field. Mandarin oranges make me remember when Maree Harris barfed on me in second grade and a whole slice came out of her nose (needless to say, I don't eat mandarin oranges to this day); Chanel perfume makes me think of Father Ludwig's wife, who directed the Episcopal Christmas pageant last year at church; and, of course, honeysuckle in any form takes me right back into the loving arms of my Grandma Ethel.

"It's starting to make more sense to me—no pun intended," I say.

"You'll learn as you go, Kendall," Loreen says with encouragement.

I let out a contented sigh, the first in a long time. "Celia asked me if I could channel. I Googled the term, and it was saying that channeling is letting a spirit into your body? I don't know about that, Loreen. Do you do that?"

"I have," she admitted. "Trance mediumship is interpreting and relaying energies that are around you. You let them go through you, inside you, and let them talk using your body."

"Is that safe?"

She laughs. "What in life is foolproof? As I've told you

before, you just have to protect yourself and pray before allowing the spirit to enter you. *You* set the ground rules,
Kendall, not the spirits."

I stop making notes as my hand shakes. The thought of
something inside of me, making me do and say things, kind of
skeeves me out. Maybe I won't be developing that skill too
soon.

Loreen's eyes shine in what almost seems a sense of pride.
"So you see, Kendall, you just have to be patient with yourself
and see what skills develop for you."

Pen down, I say, "I definitely have a lot of that going so far.
It's just, sometimes I hear something or I know it and I don't
know whether to speak up or not. Like when Okra Carmickle
came into class and I felt the pain in his broken leg like it was
mine. Man! If I had said something, the school nurse would
have taken me to a padded cell or something." My fingers slip
into my hair and I rub at my skull. "It's like, these thoughts are
driving me crazy sometimes. Just knowing stuff. I want someone to knock the information out of my head and let it be
out there for others to interpret."

I can feel Loreen's warm and comforting smile emanating
toward me. I know from our talk that she's sending her own
positive energy to me for courage. We spend the next half
hour chatting about my and Celia's plans and how we've got
Taylor on board to be our photographer for ghost hunting.

Loreen snaps her fingers as if she's had a revelation. "Ooo, one of the things you'll want to use in your investigations is the dowsing pendulum I gave you."

"Really?" I haven't had the opportunity to play around with it or study up on it with all that's been going on.

"Absolutely. Do you have it with you?" Loreen asks.

I pull the tiny black velvet bag that I put the pendulum in from the front pocket of my jeans. The small pink quartz pendant tumbles out into the palm of my hand. Ironically, the stone feels cold, even though it's been in my pocket, so I warm it in my fist.

"That's good," Loreen instructs, "you really have to bond with your pendulum."

"Bond?"

"Yes. It will react to your energies differently than it will to anyone else's."

"That's pretty cool," I say as I play with the chain. "So, I don't understand how this is going to help me ghost hunt. Don't you use this to find water?"

Loreen pulls a book off one of the shelves and turns to a page that has the history of dowsing. I don't feel like reading all of it, so I hope she'll just summarize. I have enough schoolwork to read when I get home.

"Okay, Miss Smarty-Pants," she says with a grin. "Historically, dowsing is known for locating water, gold, oil, and minerals, but you can use it in relation to issues of life and death."

I feel my brow raise in question. "How's that?"

"Oh, doctors in Europe have used pendulums to find cancer and detect allergies. In the Caribbean, women use them to determine the sex of an unborn baby. I even read a story once where Marines in Vietnam used pendulums to locate buried mines."

"Whoa! That's amazing. So it's not some satanic conjuring tool?"

Loreen laughs so hard she has to dab her eyes. "Dear Lord, no. There's nothing satanic about it at all. In fact, I pray before, during, and after I use my pendulum. It's a very spiritual experience. God is always with me, watching over me and protecting me with his angels."

Yeah, tell my mom that. She would freak if she knew what I was doing. Best she not know then, eh?

I wiggle around on the couch, ready to try this out. "How do I do it?"

"Hold the pendulum by the bob at the end with your thumb and index finger, and let the chain dangle over the finger. Don't move it; it'll move itself."

I follow her instruction and sit perfectly still with my elbow pressed against my side. The pink quartz hangs there, pointing down, but vibrating slightly.

Loreen takes out her own crystal dowsing pendulum and copies what I'm doing. "Now, Kendall, you have to figure out what constitutes a *yes, no,* and *maybe* for you. Ask, either in your head or out loud, 'When I ask a question, what is a *yes* answer?'"

"Oh, okay." I concentrate on the lovely pink stone hanging at the end of the silver chain. "Hi there," I say, trying to respect my pendulum. "Could you please show me what a *yes* answer is when I ask a question?"

Sure enough, the pendulum starts moving. For a moment, I think it's just my jittery nerves. However, I'm not moving a muscle. The pendulum swings clockwise, spinning around and around.

"This is the coolest thing ever! How does it do it?"

Loreen takes her eyes from her pendulum and looks at mine. "Well, you know how radios pick up information from invisible radio waves?" I nod, still trying not to move. "The pendulum acts like an antenna and reacts to the vibrations and energy waves emitted by people, places, thoughts, and things. It also connects the logical and intuitive parts of the brain."

"That's freaky amazing! Look at it spin."

"Ask it what a *no* answer is."

I follow her instructions and watch the pendulum stop spinning and then swing from right to left. When I ask what my *maybe* answer is, the pendulum points straight to the ground and begins quivering.

"Too bad I can't use this for my calculus exam," I say. Hmm, could it tell me what it means about a certain polynomial when the fifteen derivative is a nonzero constant? Probably not. Mr. Kline barely allows graphing calculators; I'm sure a pendulum would be out of the question.

I keep concentrating as I'm dowsing and practicing, but

after a while, the pendulum sort of loses its turgor pressure and stops spinning. "Did I break it?"

"Not at all," Loreen explains, "you just have to get used to each other. Let me give you a jump start."

"A what?" I'm not interested in jumper cables being attached anywhere to my extremities.

"It's sort of a psychic-energy jump start," Loreen clarifies. She stands and rubs her hands together and then places them on my shoulders. "I'm helping you tap into your sixth sense to connect you to your pendulum."

"Oh, I get it." My pendulum starts moving as I ask, "Are there spirits in Radisson?"

Suddenly, the chain starts spinning so fast I can barely make out the shape. Behind me, Loreen gasps. She hastily pulls her hands from my shoulders and steps away. I see her rub her hands as if they've been stung. "What's wrong?"

Her hands fly to her face, and her cheeks turn a fiery red.

"Loreen? Are you okay? Are you having some sort of psychic hot flash?"

Without a word, she takes my hand and smiles so warmly at me. "Oh, Kendall. Now I know why you were meant to be here with me. We're kindred spirits."

"Right. We're both psychic, intuitive, and all those *clair*-words."

"There's more to it than that. We were meant to meet each other. Of course, I saw visions of you in my dreams, but I had no idea what a connection we truly have. We're both only children who lost their mothers in childbirth." A tear trickles from her eye at that moment.

But it's soooooo not accurate in the least.

"Ummm, Loreen. I think you need to get your psychic batteries checked."

"No, Kendall. I saw it. So clearly. I'm sure of it. I'm meant to mentor you because you're without a mother . . . without a family."

I return my pendulum to the velvet bag and restash it in my jeans pocket. "No, Loreen. Not only do I have a little sister named Kaitlin, but my mom is very much a part of my life."

"You must be adopted," she says quickly, so sure of herself.

Like you can fake the pictures of Mom and me in the hospital together? "No!" Honestly, the nerve! "You're just wrong, okay?"

Loreen's horrified and turns white as a sheet. "I'm so sorry, Kendall. I-I-I swear it's what I saw. I felt the energy so clearly. I totally sensed a mother figure passing."

"Maybe it was my grandma you saw?"

Although Loreen shakes her head in a negative way, she says, "Perhaps that was it."

I give her a halfhearted smile, feeling like she's hiding something from me. "Psychics aren't always right."

Hanging her head, she says, "Sure, sure, of course we're not."

She seems genuinely upset. Aside from the fact that she just attempted to disenfranchise me from my family, I kind of feel bad for her. She's pacing around, fanning herself. Poor Loreen. She needs a boyfriend.

Geez. Just when I start to think she's kind of cool and can help me, she goes all crazy on my ass.

"It must have been crossed energies," Loreen says finally. "Crossed energies. You'll see. It'll happen to you one day and you'll understand."

"Okay. Sure."

Tamping down my agitation about the odd reading of my parentage, I gather my things because I need to get home. One day I'll understand, she says, huh? All I understand is that if Loreen really is a Froot Loop, then I'm going to need some *serious* psychotherapy.

CHAPTER NINE

I NEED TO TALK TO MARJORIE. It's been too long since we hugged goodbye in front of my building while the movers hauled away all of my earthly belongings. On the drive to Georgia, Marjorie texted me a couple of times—telling me she was hanging with Gretchen Lind, a tall blonde in our class who never did like me for some reason—but that she missed me. And since I haven't heard back from Marjorie from that long e-mail I sent, I don't know if the distance is too much for our lifelong friendship.

I pull my legs up underneath me on the bed and stack the pillows in front of me for a makeshift desk for my laptop. Powering it up, I see that Yahoo Instant Messenger shows Marjorie as offline. However, I know she sometimes switches to invisible so Brian Coey, this guy a grade behind us in school, won't stalk her online.

Clicking on **marjorie_w00t**, I type:

Kendall-doll: Hey, chica-ma-lika!

When I hit Return, the message appears in a chat box that shows she is indeed online, merely hiding out.

A wave of sadness overcomes me as I await her reply. Usually, Marjorie pounces on me before I can even fully boot up the computer. What's taking her so long now? Maybe she's not sitting at her computer at the moment.

Kendall-doll: Marj? You there?

My eyes close and I breathe deeply, projecting my thoughts all the way up across the flyover states to land in Marjorie's house. Loreen told me this afternoon about something called remote viewing, where I can actually see into places even though I'm not physically there. I picture Marjorie's townhouse. Her room is on the second floor, and her computer sits in a nook of her desk and bookshelf area. I see her. She's sitting there in her sweats, a pair of fuzzy socks, and a scowl on her face as she looks at the words on her screen.

Kendall-doll: I know you're online! It's been an eon since we've talked!!!!!!!!

Melancholy nearly dances in the air around me, swirling to encompass me as I stare at the blinking screen. My friend is just sitting there. Ignoring me. Hoping I'll go away. I bite back the palpable heartache that has nothing to do with my newly discovered gifts. This pain isn't empathic. It's mine. Because at that moment, I know, beyond a shadow of a doubt, that my e-mail wigged her out. Down-to-earth, sensible, AP honors student Marjorie with the pothead brother and alfalfa-sprouts mom—she doesn't know how to talk to me.

Bravely, I type out:

Kendall-doll: It's my e-mail, isn't it?

Kendall-doll: Don't wig on me, Marj.

In the bottom left-hand corner, the icon shows me she's typing something. My hopes soar that my best friend is still just that. Deep down in my intuition though, that claircognizant part of me that Loreen and I discussed, I know things will never be the same with Marjorie.

marjorie_w00t: hey

Kendall-doll: Hey. What's up?

marjorie_w00t: nothing.

Great. She's writing in lowercase, which blares out "annoyance."

Kendall-doll: Why haven't u e-mailed me?

marjorie_w00t: been busy.

Kendall-doll: Doing what?

marjorie_w00t: school. homework. stuff.

Kendall-doll: u hate me.

marjorie_w00t: I don't hate u kendall. I just don't no what 2 say 2 u.

Kendall-doll: Never had that problem b4

marjorie_w00t: u never claimed 2 b psychic b4

marjorie_w00t: how's GA?

Kendall-doll: I'm getting used 2 it. It's diff.

marjorie_w00t: apparently.

Kendall-doll: Y does this have 2 b so hard?

marjorie_w00t: u tell me

Kendall-doll: ur hanging out w/Gretchen Lind rn't u

marjorie_w00t: yeah. she's cool. her dad just got her a bmw convertible.

Kendall-doll: Nice.

It's anything but nice. This conversation is work. Not just for my typing abilities, but for my brain. My best friend since first grade and I aren't compatible anymore. I'm planning ghost hunts with my new friends here in the South, and she's riding around in a designer car with one of the school's most popular girls.

Kendall-doll: U've moved on.

marjorie_w00t: what did u expect me 2 do, kendall? Not find new friends? Cry 'bout how u moved away?

marjorie_w00t: u left. plain and simple.

Kendall-doll: I didn't have a choice!!!!

marjorie_w00t: Doesn't matter. U're gone. And I mean WAAAAAAAY GONE!!!

Bitch. She's referring to my gut-spill e-mail about being psychic. I thought if anyone would understand, Marjorie would. We had that experience together on Archer Avenue with Resurrection Mary. Why can't she just be a good enough friend to accept me for what I am? I mean, even if she doesn't believe what's going on, she doesn't have to get so snarly about it.

Kendall-doll: So u do think I'm a nutcase.

marjorie_w00t: i don't no what else 2 think. that e-mail wuz . . . out there.

Kendall-doll: It was from the heart.

marjorie_w00t: Gretchen said u've really lost it.

Kendall-doll: YOU LET GRETCHEN READ THAT????

marjorie_w00t: She's my BF!!

Kendall-doll: I thought *I* was ur BF. A month ago I was.

marjorie_w00t: things change. u moved on. i moved on. obviously all this is affecting u and u've made up all this shit about being psychic. I just can't hang w/crazy, kendall, and u no that.

I stare at the hateful words, remembering that old childhood rhyme about "Sticks and stones may break my bones, but words will never hurt me." Yeah, well, whoever wrote that was a friggin' idiot. Words hurt more than anything. Bruises and cuts from sticks and stones are medicated and covered with Band-Aids and then they heal. But Marjorie's typing is indelibly inscribed in my mind forever.

Tears gather in a pool at my lash line, but I refuse to blink and let them loose. Loreen told me I'm going to have challenges in my life when it comes to people, especially loved ones, accepting my abilities. It still doesn't make Marjorie's cutting remarks any softer.

Instead of fight, I choose flight.

Kendall-doll: Mom's calling me 2 dinner. I hope u'll e-mail me soon and we can still talk. I miss u.

marjorie_w00t: L8tr!

As if helping not to make a liar out of me, Mom calls up the stairs, "Kendall! Kaitlin! Dinner!"

I click off the IM window and shove the computer away.

Finally realizing that everything about my life is now different, I can do one of two things:

(1) Wallow in my own self-pity, hide in my room, and be miserable until I graduate from high school and go off to college.

(2) Embrace my new surroundings with both hands, live life to the fullest, and enjoy widening my circle of friends and acquaintances.

The answer is definitely #2. It *has* to be.

"Kendall," Kaitlin screams at me from the top of the stairs. "Mom says the spaghetti is getting cold and to get your stupid butt down here!"

I'm sure those weren't Mom's exact words. "I'm coming."

Reaching over to my bedside table, I take the framed picture of me and Marjorie at a Bears game last year and gaze at it. It's a slice of time in my life. But there are new memories ahead of me to make just as special. I carefully open the table drawer and place the picture inside.

Marjorie's moved on. So will I.

After dinner, I'm working on my @#$%ing calculus homework when I hear the doorbell ring. A few moments later, Dad shouts up, "Kendall, you've got company."

I bound down the stairs to see Celia standing there in jeans and a black "The Truth Is Out There" T-shirt, talking to my dad. She may be a tad dorkish, but she's got a heart of gold and would never tell me she "can't hang with crazy."

Two cats buzz by their feet in the doorway and run up the staircase past me.

"We have two pets now?" Dad calls out.

"I think Seamus chased them in here," Celia explains. "He's outside barking like a tree."

"Don't worry, Dad. That's Eleanor with Natalie. I told them they should both feel at home here."

As does Celia. Dad's ever the host, welcoming her to our humble abode—compared to the friggin' mansion she lives in. "I know your father, Rex Nichols," he says. "I'm working on the new Mega-Mart distribution-center development project with him."

"Yes, sir," Celia says. She adjusts a large Nike gym bag on her shoulder. "Dad says the distribution center is going to bring a lot of jobs and new people here to Radisson."

Dad nods in agreement. "The city has had this land for over a hundred and fifty years. It's finally time to do something productive with it. Something that's going to put Radisson on the map." My dad pushes his glasses higher on his nose and smiles brightly. "It's an impressive project and I'm glad I was brought in to work on it. We've lined up some builders who are bidding for the affordable-housing community that will be adjacent to the property."

I slide in and tug Celia by the arm, hoping to rescue her

from Dad's work bragging. "We've got some homework to do, Dad."

"Sure thing, kiddo. Nice to meet you, Celia."

"You too, Mr. Moorehead."

As we scoot up the stairs, Celia says, "Your dad's kind of cute in a forty-plus-year-old-guy sort of way."

I stop in my tracks. "Eww . . . you did not just say that."

"What?"

"You got all over me for thinking you should make a move on Clay Price, because he's not good enough. Yet you think my *dad's* cute?"

"God, don't start that again."

Rolling my eyes, I head off to my bedroom. "Did you bring over all the stuff?" I ask, completely ignoring the gross-out factor concerning my dad.

Celia plops her bag on my bed and unzips it, startling Eleanor, who is in full bathing mode. "It's all here. Where's your computer?"

I point across the room to my desk. "Over there."

She slides a DVD into the appropriate slot and quickly installs sound software onto my hard drive. Then she hooks up three small cameras, each monitor getting a different angle on my room.

"Make sure you get a shot of the door," I note while I stroke Natalie's head. She's curled up behind Eleanor, without a care in the world. "I think the floaty lady likes wandering out to the other bedrooms."

"You got it," Celia says. Her tongue pokes out of her mouth as she concentrates on setting everything up just right. "The cameras will capture any movement and activate the recording devices I'll leave out. Just go about your evening as you normally would."

"Right. Because every teenage girl likes to be videotaped while she's sleeping," I say with an evil grin.

Celia reaches for the bag and pulls out two small digital voice recorders. "Hopefully, we can catch some EVPs tonight."

"Why two recorders?" I ask, stroking Natalie's tail (which is not thumping, thankyouverymuch).

"I read an article online by this group called the New England Ghost Project, and their EVP specialist uses two recorders. One records real things in the room, like the white-noise machine and your snoring—"

"I do *not* snore!"

"—and the other will pick up any EVPs. It's sort of a double-verification thing. If the sound is picked up on both recorders, it's probably something environmental and not paranormal at all," she says with a shrug. "It works for them, so I thought I'd try."

"Should I leave the white-noise machine on?"

"You hear the voice through that, don't you?"

"I did that one time," I say.

"I read that things like a white-noise machine or even a ham radio can create sound waves that the spirits can manipulate to communicate with us. If spirits are manipulating the white noise, just like someone is able to rewind a tape player and listen, we can potentially hear the spirit as it plays through the white-noise machine," Celia explains. Man, she's so smart. She's going to make a hell of a scientist one of these days. She'll probably win the Nobel or something for inventing a sound machine that allows us to talk to the dead like a phone call. Although, didn't Thomas Edison invent something like that already, way back when? Oh, yeah, we learned about it in junior high school: the spirit communication device.

Not wanting Celia to think I've slacked off on our pre-ghost-hunting investigatory stage, I say, "I've been reading up on EVPs. A lot of the information is kind of skeptical about what EVPs are, because it's not really a back-and-forth conversation like you and I can have. There are a ton of websites with amazing snippets of voices, maybe even from other dimensions."

"Time's not constant," Celia notes. "It's more like the ebb and flow of the ocean."

Natalie takes a playful nip at my hand. "Right. So maybe these things I sense with my abilities are simply fingerprints or imprints left in time?"

Celia runs her hand through her messy hair. "That is a good theory, Kendall. Let's put it to the test tonight and see what we get. Then tomorrow, Taylor and I will spend the night and take some pictures and analyze the data."

I tug a piece of dryer lint off of my Old Navy flannel pajama pants and flick it onto the floor. Eleanor watches the

progress and jumps off the bed to investigate. "Mom'll be relieved that I've made friends at school."

"Duh," Celia says. "Taylor's a great addition to the team, and
she likes you a lot. You're a mystery to her and that excites her."

"She's great. But her brother needs to chill out. What's his
major malfunction? Did you see the way he glared at me?" A
tingle creeps up my back, just thinking about Jason and his
magical, dreamy eyes that bore straight through me. "So, what
do you know about him?"

"Jason Tillson?" She lifts her shoulders, not looking away
from the computer. "Not much. He runs track, plays baseball,
and used to date Courtney Langdon."

My eyes widen. "Ugh! That puking girl?"

"The one and only. He broke up with her at the end of last
year. He spent the summer in Savannah working for his uncle,
doing roofing or some sort of construction."

"Sounds like you know everything about him," I note.

Celia's face is hidden in her hair as she contemplates a USB
port on the back of my laptop. Then she says, "It's a small
town, Kendall. Everybody knows everyone else's business."

"Oh, yeah. I forgot."

Good to know Jason is single. I'd hate to be having dreams
about some other girl's boyfriend every night.

Standing up, Celia wipes her hands on her worn jeans.
"There. We're all set. Everything's hooked up and ready to go.
Just click here when you go to bed and then we'll check out
the video tomorrow and see what we've got."

"Wicked!" I hold my fist out to her, and she enthusiastically bumps it back.

"All right. I'm outies." She grabs her gym bag and salutes me as she's walking out. "We are officially ghost huntresses."

"Damn skippy."

With that, I finish my dreaded calculus homework, take a quick shower, and then settle into my fluffy bed. With Natalie and Eleanor curled up together at the foot on top of the comforter, purring like boat motors, I lie there, staring at the ceiling and waiting for . . . something.

You know how when a car (like Dad's Volvo) makes that *clickety-clack* sound all the time *until* you take it to the mechanic, and then you never hear that particular sound again? Well, that's what's going on with me and the floaty lady tonight. Now that I'm wired and recording . . . where the hell is she?

I doze off from around ten until after midnight, but the continuing vivid dream of Jason and his killer eyes knocks me out of my deep REM. Man, the vision of me in his arms is so . . . *real*. Then again, so is he.

I've been tossing, turning, and flipping around so much that Eleanor and Natalie both gave me an "eat shit" look—as much as cats can—and left to prowl the house. When I first heard the voice in the white-noise machine the other night, it freaked me out. Now, I'm dying to hear it again! And it won't come to me.

Finally, around two a.m., I get up and go to the bathroom.

When I return to my room, I grab one of Celia's recorders and sit by the white-noise machine. It's *tzujzh*ing along—yes, I know that's a very dated Carson Kressley *Queer Eye* reference, but it's the onomatopoeia that works here—like a washing machine on the spin cycle.

I lean close and whisper, "Is anyone here?"

Tzujzh. Tzujzh. Tzujzh.

"Are there any spirits here?"

Tzujzh. Tzujzh. Tzujzh.

"Are there any spirits here with anything to say?"

Tzujzh. Tzujzh. Tzujzh.

"Oh, come on!" Why am I not hearing anything now like I did before? This ghost is totally mucking with me and it's starting to annoy me. Consistency, please!

My fingers start getting tingly. Loreen told me this is connected to my psychic senses, so this time, I pay attention to the sensation instead of thinking that I'm having a myocardial infarction. (Celia's not the only smart one!) A buzz hums in my ears and I try to breathe through it, hoping to hear something in the midst of the mental junk.

Tzujzh. Tzujzh. Tzujzh.

The noise machine continues steadily next to me as the tingling awareness recedes. I wiggle my fingers and shake out my hand. Whatever the moment was seems to have passed.

I press Rewind on the recorder. Then I hit Play and listen closely.

I hear the white-noise machine and my feet padding out

of the room and then back again. There's some banging around as I not so delicately picked up the recorder.

My voice whispers out, "Is anyone here?"

Silence. And then I hear a hissed *"Yesssssssssssssss . . ."*

Awesome! I stop, rewind, and play it back.

I hear myself again. "Are there any spirits here?"

Three or four seconds pass. *"Yesssssssssssss . . ."*

Holy freaking cow! Just like the other night. Only this time, I've got proof!

Okay. I've got to be calm. I can't lose my cool every time I encounter a spirit—or a suspected spirit. I am Kendall Moorehead. Psychic. Intuitive. Sensitive. Ghost huntress. No more wigging out.

Next is my "Are there any spirits here with anything to say" question.

I press the recorder close to my ear because I damn sure want to hear this.

Four or five seconds pass with nothing. I'm about to give up when I hear *"Reeeruuuun taaahh meeeeeeeee."*

I don't know exactly what it's saying, but it *is* saying something. Huh? I rewind and play again. And again, until it finally hits me what the voice is truly saying: *"Return to meeeeee . . ."*

What?

You're kidding.

Stop. Rewind. Play.

"Return to meeeeeeeee."

"Unbelievable!" I pretty much shout out and then clamp

my hand over my mouth. People are sleeping. But how über-amazing is this? *Return. To. Me.* To *who* me? What does it mean? Ignoring the reference to the forgettable Minnie Driver/David Duchovny movie of the same title, I decide I need to take a stab at really connecting with this spirit.

I crawl over to my discarded jeans and dig out the velvet bag that holds my dowsing pendulum. I climb back up onto the bed and get in a comfy sitting position. I grip the silver chain just like Loreen showed me—clutching it with my thumb and index finger, and letting the pink quartz dangle. Not moving my arm or hand at all, I say, "When I ask a question, what is a *yes*?"

In the moonlight that's spilling into my room between the crack in the curtains, I watch as the pendulum begins to move slightly in a clockwise direction.

"Thanks. Now, please show me what the movement is for *no.*"

Immediately, the pendulum stops spinning around and begins swaying back and forth from right to left. Just like it had done at Divining Woman this afternoon. Loreen said after a few sessions like this, the pendulum and I will be used to each other and I won't have to always ask the direction or motion of an answer.

"Good. Thanks again. Now, please show me what the answer is for *maybe.*"

At that, the pendulum stops moving altogether and points down, quivering again.

"Well, what do you know about that?"

A cold breeze dances up my left arm and gives me immediate chills. On all the paranormal TV shows I've been watching, the experts say that a cold spot represents the presence of a possible spirit. Does that mean the floaty woman is here with me? I close my eyes and open my mind to accept whatever I hear or see. I also say a quick prayer, asking God to protect me from anything evil, like Loreen advised. You never know what you're up against.

In my mind, I see a vision of a pretty woman with soft brown hair flowing around her shoulders. She's dressed in white, but I can't make out the details of her features or her body. This is definitely my floaty woman, though. I just *know* it.

I concentrate on my pendulum and try to tamp down the overanxious pulse-thump under my skin. "Is there a spirit present?" I ask. I almost feel like there should be a pendulum motion for *duh*.

The quartz begins to spin clockwise, indicating that I'm not alone.

"Are you a female?"

Yes again.

"Did you die in this house?"

The pendulum changes direction and bobbles back and forth. "Hmm . . . no." Weird. If she didn't die in this house, then what's she doing here?

"Did you die in the Civil War?"

Another no.

"Were you killed by a soldier from the Civil War?"

No.

Out of the blue, my chest tightens on me. Not so much out of fear or trepidation. It's more like she's trying to tell me something. Tightness in the chest. I felt that in the cemetery, but it was a different type of pain. That was a sense that I couldn't breathe properly, which led me to believe the spirit I was feeling had died of asthma. This sensation is more of an ache, like someone's got a fist around my heart. Is this really happening to me? Or is it that empathic stuff Loreen was telling me about and I'm just feeling what the floaty lady experienced? How can I even tell? What if this is serious and I need to go to the emergency room? (Can I possibly ask myself *more* questions?) I don't think I need medical attention, though. This isn't about me. It's about *her*, whoever she is. The awareness of her suffering permeates my whole body, and I double over a bit. I'm definitely feeling the ghost's pain. I take some deep breaths and expel them slowly.

"Your torment is awful," I say, hoping she can hear me. "What did this to you?"

I shake off the numbness and continue dowsing.

"Did you have a heart condition?"

The answer is in a clockwise spin.

"Oh, man . . . that's horrible. You poor thing. Was it back in the days when they didn't have the good medical treatment we have today?"

Back and forth the pendulum goes. No, huh?

"So, you're not like a hundred and fifty years old?"

I get a very active *no* response, the quartz swaying vigorously.

"Okay, okay! Sorry. I wasn't trying to offend you," I say with a laugh. "I'm trying to find out how I can help you. I've got this gift, you know, and I need to see if there's anything you need from me." I pause for a moment as the pendulum slows down. "Do you know that you are not alive?"

A *"Yesssssssss . . ."* murmurs from the white-noise machine instead of the recorder this time. "Whoa!" Again, this ghost is playing with me, but I'm stoked! I've got another audio confirmation. We're totally getting somewhere. "Oh, wow. Thanks. That's you, huh?"

The pendulum indicates a *yes*.

Man, I'm champing at the bit here. I wish the floaty lady would just appear and talk to me, like how Patrick Swayze blabbers with Whoopi Goldberg in *Ghost*. I know this isn't a movie, but I wish it were.

Excitement skitters through my bloodstream, powering me. I wonder if I should call Celia and tell her. Nah, drunk dialing is one thing, but spook dialing is another. I'll wait until I see her at school and then tell her everything. Hopefully, we can repeat all of this tomorrow when she and Taylor are here.

"Are you happy?" I ask.

The pendulum begins to almost vibrate as it moves, not

giving a clear response. Loreen said that some things out there in the universe just aren't any of my business, so I wonder if I've offended the ghostly spirit.

"I'm sorry," I say. "That may have been inappropriate. Is it okay for me to ask you about your happiness?"

As I'm watching to see what the pendulum will do next, the door to my bedroom opens up with a squeak and a groan.

"Kendall, what are you doing up this late?" Mom snaps on the light and squints at me.

I curl the pendulum into the palm of my hand. "Umm . . . nothing."

She scowls and walks toward me, gripping the neck of her bathrobe. "It's after two in the morning and you're in here making enough racket to rouse the neighborhood."

"I'm sorry, Mom. I didn't mean to wake you up. I couldn't sleep."

"I understand that. Isn't the noise machine helping?"

I smirk at her. "In more ways than you could know."

"What do you mean?"

"Nothing. Sorry." I crawl across the bed and tuck myself back under the covers. "I'm going to sleep right now."

I can tell she's not buying any of this. She's got that concerned-mother glower going—the one that gives her that vertical wrinkle right between her eyebrows.

"Kendall, your father and I are *very* concerned about you. You can't go on not sleeping like this. It's not normal."

"I know, Mom—"

"I'm going to make an appointment with the doctor and we're going to get you a prescription for Rozerem. You know, it's been proven to help people with sleeping ailments."

Oh my God. "You sound like one of those TV commercials, Mom."

She quotes the marketing campaign. "'Your dreams miss you.'"

Not the ones starring Jason Tillson. "You had pharm reps in your office today, didn't you?" From what she tells us at the dinner table after a long day, there's nothing more aggressive in a doctor's office than the pharm reps coming in with their pamphlets, samples, and gimmicks. Thing is, Mom always falls for them.

"Now, Kendall. Don't get sarcastic."

She's always like this—trying to cure any ailment Kaitlin and I could possibly have after she gets the hard sell from the reps who make the rounds of medical offices offering free packets of trial pills. I swear, if there's a pen in this house that doesn't have the brand name of a drug on it, I'll eat it for breakfast.

"I don't need medication, Mom." Honestly! I'm not getting hooked on something that's going to screw with my memory and my newfound psychic abilities. Besides, I'm sure the side effects are things like drowsiness, fatigue, dizziness, paralysis, bloody stools, diverticulitis, smoking ears, constant burping and farting, shakes, tremors, severed nerves, loss of eyelashes, teeth falling out, tongue swelling to twice its size, toenails turning black, goiters—you name it. I don't think so. "It's not something that needs medicating."

"What isn't?" she asks, her irritation now turning to parental worry.

I burrow into the covers and pull the sheet up close to my chin. "Nothing," I mutter. My heart slams against my rib cage and I wonder if I've said too much. It's not that I don't want to talk to Mom; it's that I honestly don't think she'll take it well. I don't think any of the sample pills in her medicine cabinet are capable of "fixing me" this time.

But Mom can't take my evasive maneuver. "Kendall! I'm your mother and I'm worried sick about you." She stops and plunges her hands into her hair. "Talk to me! It's bad enough we uprooted you from the only home you've known, but we did it in your high school years." She pauses and then sits down on the bed and reaches out to me. "My father was in the army and we moved around my whole life—Texas, Colorado, Georgia, Alabama, back to Texas, Germany, and finally Illinois. I never had any kind of settled life and friends, but I also never had sleep disruptions like you're experiencing. I know what you must be going through. But you've got to give Radisson a chance. Your father's an integral part of this community now, and you'll make new friends. Trust me, sweetie."

I cover my head for a second and groan. Then I peek at Mom. She's really concerned about me. "Mom, I've made friends. In fact, they're coming over and spending the night tomorrow, or rather, later today."

There's that Mom smile I love. "Oh, well, that's nice. Certainly. Just promise to tell me what's going on with you." She pats the bed and then gets up to leave. "I'm your mother, but I'm also your friend. You can trust me with anything."

My heartbeat accelerates even more and this time I know it's nothing to do with the paranormal. I need to come clean. Mom says she'll understand. My psychic intuition clearly tells me "trust your mother" and "tell the truth." I've always been forthright with her in the past, but I've never had to tell my very religious mother that I'm talking with spirits from beyond. Can she really handle it? The sheen of love radiating from her troubled eyes tells me that she can.

I sit up. "Mom?"

"Yes, sweetie?"

I bite my bottom lip and glance down at the pendulum in my fist. "I can really tell you anything?"

"Always, Kendall."

"And you won't, like, fly off the handle and freak out?"

She takes a deep breath. "I'm going to freak out if you *don't* tell me what's going on."

Okay . . . here we go.

"You're not going to believe this, but . . . but . . ."

"But *what,* Kendall?"

"It's just that this whole sleep problem is because I'm having this, er, awakening of sorts."

"I don't understand, sweetie."

I sigh big-time. I don't want to do this. I don't want to do this. I don't want to do this. Can't I keep this secret just a little bit longer until I fully understand what's happening to me? Mom's concern is at an all-time peak, and I have to believe that she'll listen and let me work this out.

"I think I'm . . . psychic."

She stares at me as if I've just committed the most heinous crime ever. The look of love is replaced with disbelief. "It's extremely late to play games, Kendall."

"I'm serious, Mom. I think I'm psychic."

"You're *what?*"

My trepidation and anxiety is replaced with nervous chatter. Everything spills out of me like water overflowing the edge of the bath. I can't stop myself.

"I know it's hard to believe," I explain. "I didn't understand it myself at first. I'm apparently going through this psychic awakening and that's why I can't sleep. I'm on pins and needles with every sound and light that I hear and see. I'm feeling all these things and I know what people are thinking and I get these physical pains that match theirs. Oh, and I met this woman who's also an intuitive and she's been helping me through this and teaching me how to concentrate and breathe and how to use this pendulum to talk to spirits." I hold up the pink quartz pendulum for good measure.

Mom blinks hard. Then does it again. "You t-t-talk to spirits?" she asks in a hoarse voice.

"Yeah, Mom. You're not going to believe this, but I see dead people."

After what feels like two decades of silence, Mom lurches forward and snatches the charm out of my hand. Incredulity crosses her features while sheer horror and shock reverb off her like invisible microwaves. I absorb it straight into my psychic energies and sense a blackness coating me. Uh-oh. This confession was not such a good idea.

So much for that motherly understanding.

As Grandma Ethel used to say when she was playing hearts and losing badly to her gang of geriatric girlfriends: I am totally up shit's creek without a paddle.

CHAPTER TEN

OKAY, I SHOULD HAVE KEPT *The Sixth Sense* reference to myself.

"Yes, Father Ludwig," Mom says into the cordless. "I'll tell her. Bless you for your time so early this morning. Goodbye."

Mom places the phone back into its base as Dad walks into the living room, finishing up the Windsor knot in his tie. "Sarah, you didn't call Father Ludwig in Chicago and wake him at this hour, did you?"

"Of course I did, David." Her lips are flat. Like nothing I've ever seen. The woman is *très* upset with me. All I can do is sit quietly in the middle of the couch—where I'd been directed to perch after I finished getting ready for school—and await the parental verdict. Although, since Mom brought in our Episcopal priest from back home, there may be a more theological judgment coming my way.

Mom paces. I bite my bottom lip. Dad retreats to the kitchen for coffee.

"David, we have to talk about this *now.*"

"I'm coming, I'm coming."

Kaitlin tromps down the stairs and barges in. She rubs her eyes and assesses the players in the room. "Why is everyone up so early?"

"Go eat your cereal, Kaitlin," Mom directs, shooing my sister toward the kitchen.

"But Mom! Why is Kendall—"

"Do as I say, Kaitlin, or else *you'll* be in trouble too."

"Oh, man! She's in trouble? Cool!"

"Cereal. Now!"

Kaitlin doesn't even try to hide her wide-ass smile as she heads off to the kitchen. Dad returns with a steaming cup of java—I wish he'd just hand it over to me to help jolt me out of this unfortunate reality—and sits next to me on the couch. Calmly, he crosses his left leg over his knee and takes a sip from his WGN Weather mug. I know what's coming. I mean, I don't have to be psychic to see how this is going to play out.

"Sarah, sit down and let's talk this out."

"What's to talk about?" she nearly shrieks. "Our daughter was up in her room in the middle of the night practicing voodoo."

I can't help but laugh, which is so not the right reaction. "I was not practicing voodoo."

Mom plows her hands into her sleep-disturbed hair. "Look at her, David. She thinks it's funny."

My eyes connect with my dad's, begging him to believe me. "I don't, Dad. Seriously. She's making way too much out of this."

"She's your mother and she's concerned about you."

I bite my bottom lip so I won't burst into tears. Already did that enough during what was left of the nighttime, knowing what I'd face this morning.

"You're damn right, I'm concerned," Mom says emphatically. "Kendall, you're inviting evil spirits into this house, and I will not have it."

I sit forward on the couch and plant my hands next to me. I have to make them understand. Make Mom understand. "Mom, I'm not inviting any—" I stop the additional words from leaving my mouth.

Mom holds out my dowsing pendulum to show my dad. "Father Ludwig says this is used to contact spirits. It's a form of divination. Deuteronomy 18:10 says that none among you should use divination. And yet you sit in your bedroom under my roof and do that? You tell me, Kendall."

I reach for the pink quartz and nearly teeter off the couch when Mom yanks the pendant away from me and tucks it into the pocket of her bathrobe.

"It *is* used to communicate with spirits—" I admit.

"See?" Mom interrupts.

"I can't battle Bible quotes with you because you know more than I do," I say in my defense. Why would God give me this gift if I couldn't use it? "I just know what I'm doing is not a bad thing. We have a ghost here in this house and I was just trying to talk to her and find out what she wants."

Dad sets his cup on the coffee table, which is the only

barrier between Mom and me. "Kendall, you're not actually buying into all of the ghost stories here in Radisson, are you? It's just a waste of time and energy. Don't get sucked into that vortex, kiddo."

How can I get them to believe me when I only just recently started believing myself? "I swear, Dad. We have a ghost. I've seen her and heard her. I was communicating with her last night and asking her questions about if she knew she was dead and how she died and other stuff."

Mom's hand flies to her mouth, and her eyes mist over with tears. "I don't understand. Any of this. Not at all. I've raised you to be a good Christian girl, Kendall. And you repay me by . . . by . . . by dabbling in the occult!"

Oh my God. She did *not* just go there!

I bolt up and run to her side. "Mom, it's not like that at all." Hot, gushy tears obscure my vision as I try to explain myself. I put my hesitation aside; I've got to make my parents understand. "I didn't conjure this up. I'm not in a cult or trying to worship Satan or anything. You've got to believe me. *This* is why I can't sleep. First it was too quiet, and then I started hearing a voice through the white-noise machine, and now, I'm just hearing the voice in my head."

This makes Mom cry even more. "I knew you needed medication. I'm taking you in to see Dr. Murphy today."

"Please don't! It's not anything mental at all! I'm telling you guys, I've come into an awakening. At least, that's what Loreen calls it."

"Who's Loreen? An imaginary friend?" Dad asks. His eyes shift from me to Mom and then back to me.

"No," I say emphatically. "Loreen's the lady who owns Divining Woman in the Square. What do you mean, imaginary friend? I'm almost seventeen, Dad."

He sits back and fidgets with the rim of his glasses. "When you were a little girl, you had an imaginary friend."

"David . . . don't."

"I so did not." This just doesn't seem like me. I never did anything you'd expect a little kid to do: I never sucked my thumb or wet my bed. I didn't play with Barbies or baby dolls, so I certainly wouldn't have had an imaginary friend. Would I?

"You did too," Dad continues. "Never knew her name, but you said she sang to you and taught you songs. Your Grandma Ethel always said it was just angels watching over you."

Awww . . . that's really cute. Mom even has a wistful look on her face; however, it quickly morphs back into the concerned-parent scowl.

"I don't remember that," I say in my defense.

"After Kaitlin was born, you quit talking about your friend," Dad says. "So we never thought anything of it. It's normal enough for children to do that."

Right, because children have pure souls and they can see things that adults don't recognize. They accept unexplained things in their lives and are more sensitive to their sixth sense. At least, that's what I've read on all these websites that Celia and I have been trolling. Could I have been talking to spirits or ghosts way back then? Of course, the thought of me sitting in my room thinking someone named Tony was living in my head, à la Danny from *The Shining*, kind of creeps me out. Since my *Sixth Sense* reference didn't work on my parents, I highly doubt that telling them I "shine" would do much good either. They're not very cinematic.

I need for them to believe me, even if I don't quite understand this myself. "You guys, I'm telling you. I've developed psychic abilities."

"That's just absurd, Kendall," Mom snaps.

Kaitlin chooses that moment to butt in. "You've got what?"

Dad turns. "Kaitlin, this is between your sister and us."

My sister sticks her tongue out. "You're a freak, Kendall."

Dad points at the stairs. "Kaitlin, enough! Go get ready for school."

"Well, she *is* a freak," she mutters as she runs up the stairs.

"Just wait until *your* awakening," I scream out. "It's hereditary, you know."

My parents look at me like *they've* just seen a ghost. My mother has gone completely pale, and Dad's eyes are dilated.

"You're going for Communion this afternoon," Mom announces. "We haven't been to Christ the Redeemer Holy Episcopal Church yet, but Father Ludwig said he'd call the priest and do an introduction for us."

"Mom, this has nothing to do with religion. It has to do with my awakening." I feel like I'm practically begging here.

She leans closer to me. It's like she's aged ten years overnight because of her concern for me. I hate that I'm causing her pain and confusion. How does she think *I* feel?

"Who told you about this awakening you keep referring to?" she asks.

"Loreen. Loreen Woods. The lady at the store in the Square. I told you."

Dad pauses. "What kind of store is it? Divining Woman?"

I swallow hard and bite my bottom lip again. "It's uhhh, an, ummm . . . New Age store." Then I jump to defend Loreen. "She's a psychic/sensitive/intuitive herself, so she understands what I'm going through." I try explaining everything Loreen and I talked about. Especially how my sensitivity is a gift. "It is, Mom. It's something special that God has given me." Although, at the present moment, it seems like a curse. "I'm not making this up and I don't need mind-altering medication. This is *real*."

Dad pulls Mom aside and lowers his voice. I can hear him plainly, though, thanks to my sensitivity. "Sarah, I'm sure this is how she's coping with all the change. This move can't have been easy for her or Kaitlin. They're each adjusting in their own way. They need our love and support more than anything."

"I always provide that to my children," Mom says quickly but quietly. "I will *not* have some strange woman giving my child guidance on how to cultivate psychic abilities. It goes against everything I believe in. It goes against the Word of God. You go to work, David. Trust me to handle this."

I watch as Dad gives Mom a quick kiss and then winks at me. "We'll talk when I get home tonight, okay, Kendall?"

"Okay, Dad." Not like it's going to do any good. They think I've gone off the deep end. And I haven't even gotten around to telling them about my ghost hunting with Celia and Taylor. That's something I'm going to have to keep to myself for now. Mom would blow a gasket.

She won't look at me when she speaks. "Go get ready for school, Kendall."

"Yes, Mom," I say, not wanting to push her any further.

As I pass by her, she takes my elbow to stop me. "One more thing, Kendall."

"Yes, ma'am?"

"I forbid you to see or talk to that Loreen Woods woman anymore. Is that understood? You're not to call her or go into her store or anything. You will stop all of your unusual behavior at this moment. Am I understood?"

My chest constricts, making it hard to take an adequate breath. Mom's words slice through me, bisecting my life into compartments labeled *normal* and *abnormal*. All I wanted was to fit in here in Radisson. So I have psychic abilities and I see ghosts. And I have friends that appreciate that. Aren't those good things? I guess not.

I echo my previous words. "Yes, ma'am."

"Good." She hugs me and kisses the top of my head. "I love you, Kendall. I'll protect you against anything in this world."

Yeah, but what about the *other* world? Can she protect me

from spirits? Can she shelter any of us from what I've seen and heard? Can she shield Dad from the harm that's possibly going to come to him?

The ghost huntress in me knows she can't.

"Thank you for the pizza, Mrs. Moorehead," Taylor says. She's as perky and vivacious at eight thirty at night as she is during the school day. My mom's eating it up, though. And there's been absolutely no reference to this morning's family discussion. It's like it never happened.

Mom beams at my friend. "Glad you enjoyed it, Taylor. Since I lived in Chicago so long, making deep-dish pizza is second nature for me."

"It was really awesome," Celia chimes in.

I get up off the floor and move to escort my mother out of my room. "Thanks, Mom. Really. We're all set."

"I'm baking chocolate chip cookies," she calls out. Who is she, all of a sudden? Some genetically engineered combination of June Cleaver and Betty Crocker?

"Moooooooom," I moan, like Kaitlin.

She smiles warmly. "I'm going." Then she lowers her head and whispers, "Isn't this much more fun, Kendall? Hanging with normal girls and making new friends?"

"Right, Mom." Little does she know about our shared interest.

It's like these are Mom's first friends, too, and she doesn't want to leave. I have to remember, she lost her close friends—

like I lost Marjorie—when we moved here. "What are you going to do? Watch TV, listen to music?" she asks.

"Talk about boys," I say, knowing it's the perfect teenage answer she's expecting.

"How fun! Enjoy!"

I close the door as Giggly McGiggleton—a.k.a. Sarah Moorehead—goes down the stairs to tend to her baked goods. Love the woman, but she seriously needs to give me some space.

"Your mom is *trop adorable pour des mots,*" Taylor says with a heavy French accent.

Sorry, I only know a few German and Spanish curse words. "She's what?"

Taylor's eyes shine. "Too cute for words."

Celia wipes her mouth with a napkin. "Can we get down to business, ladies?"

"Oh, come on, Celia. It's a slumber party. We *should* talk about boys first," Taylor says. She reaches into her purse and reapplies her shiny lip-gloss that had been eaten off with her pizza.

Celia opens her laptop and starts it up. "I don't want to talk about guys. We've got to start focusing on our ghost hunting and what our plan is."

I wouldn't mind talking about guys if we talk about one in particular. I'm sure Taylor could give me all the scoop on her brother. However, I don't want her to think I'm just friends with her because her brother is a mad-hot cutie any more than I want her to think we're only friends because she's the school's best photographer. And Celia's certainly not interested in the opposite sex these days, even though she was doodling some guy in her notebook. So I decide not to push the guy issue right now.

"We'll dish dirt later," I say. "First, let's get all of our equipment set up and then start thinking of places we can investigate after we rid my house of this floaty woman."

An hour later, we've got all three laptops juiced up, the sound equipment recording, and the infrared cameras strategically placed around the room. Funny, Mom was so exuberant about bringing us her homemade chocolate chip and pecan cookies, she didn't even notice that we weren't painting our nails, doing each other's hair, or gabbing about guys, but instead were all peering at the screens of our respective computers.

As Celia is demonstrating the EMF meter to Taylor, I suddenly experience a swirling of energy coming into the room like a fine mist. I don't see anything, but that familiar heavy chest pain is back.

I reach over and touch Celia's arm. "I'm feeling something."

Expeditiously, she turns the EMF toward me, and the meter starts flashing red. "This means there's a strong electromagnetic energy present," Celia explains. "Can you reel it in, Kendall?"

Taylor's mouth forms a perfect, round O. "Reel *what* in?"

The tingling sensation in my fingers sparks out all the way

to the tips. We're totally not alone here. I just know it. Taking a deep sip of breath to steady myself, I say, "We have company."

Celia moves the meter around me, concentrating on the readings it's giving off. "Direct me to where it is, if you can."

I sit still on the floor and breathe as regularly as possible so I can withstand the ache in my chest. It's as if my heart isn't right. If I had to explain it to a TV reporter or something, I'd say it's like someone has a fist around it and is squeezing the shit out of it.

"It's . . . everywhere," I say. "I just feel the energy around me and in the room."

"You should take some pictures, Taylor."

She jumps to her feet. "Oh, right! That's what I'm here for. I'm the photographer. Should I use infrared or digital?"

"Digital right now," Celia instructs. I watch a smile break out on her face. "This is pretty cool."

I nod in return, not wanting to break my concentration.

The sound of Taylor's digital camera clicks and beeps around me. She's got one of those models with all the bells and whistles, literally. Maybe she should put it on the museum setting and not scare away the floaty woman.

"I'm going to kill the lights," Celia says. "You know, to, like, encourage the spirit."

"Ooo, I've got goose pimples!" Taylor stretches out her arm to show the tiny mounds all over. I know exactly what she means, as I've also got chill bumps dancing all over my skin.

"Let's try to make contact," I say.

"Excellent," Celia exclaims, then shushes herself. We certainly don't want the Happy Homemaker busting in on us and totally wigging out. It would be the final nail in my custom-built parental coffin. Something like this would put Sarah and David over the edge and have me sent off to a convent or, worse, a mental institution.

I reach in my pocket for my pendulum and remember it's not there. "Shit!"

Taylor's eyebrow arches when she pulls the camera away from her face. "What is it? You're not possessed or anything, are you?"

"No, Mom took my pendulum."

"Double shit," Celia adds. The EMF meter is raring red for all to see. "Something big is here and it wants to make contact."

Think fast.

I look over at Taylor and take note of her silver heart pendant hanging from a chain. "Hand me your necklace, Taylor. I can use it as a pendulum."

Her hand moves to her neck and she balks. "It's Elsa Peretti."

"Will she mind?" I ask.

Taylor giggles. "*Mon dieu, au contraire.* Elsa Peretti. She designs for Tiffany and Company."

"Oh. I don't care. It'll swing, won't it?"

Celia interrupts and points to my dresser. "Do you have anything in your jewelry box?"

Yeah, Taylor's not budging on her designer necklace. I don't blame her. If I had something name brand and expensive like that, I'd tell people to piss off too.

But wait, I sort of do have something that nice. Well, sentimental, at least. Following Celia's suggestion, I rummage through my jewelry box and pull out a very personal black velvet bag.

"What's in there?" Celia asks.

Taylor snaps a few pictures, nearly blinding me with the megaflash she's got on that thing. "Sorry, I should warn y'all next time." She slants toward me. "Oh, Kendall! That's gorgeous! *Très magnifique!*"

"Shhh! I don't want my mom to hear and come in. I already told you guys I'm in big trouble."

I slowly draw the family heirloom from its protective place. It's a long silver chain with a pristine crystal teardrop on the end of it. Grandma Ethel left it to me in her will because I used to always want to look at it whenever I visited her house. She told me it was made from angels' tears.

"This'll work perfectly."

The three of us return to the middle of my room, and I take a seat on the floor. Taylor scurries around snapping pictures—and saying "Flash!" beforehand—and Celia monitors the computer. There are spikes on the sound equipment that make me think she's picking something up on the recording. I try and tune in to my subconscious to see what, if any, messages I'm getting. I'm not exactly thrilled with this, but Loreen told me that I've got to conquer my fear because the spirits will feed off it. Sort of like that thing about dogs knowing when you're afraid of them and charging you. That happened to me in sixth grade when Marjorie and I were walking home from getting frozen yogurt. A neighbor's Doberman pinscher got loose from his chain and damn near chased me up a tree because I screamed and ran when I saw him. Stupid dog was just after my chocolate-vanilla swirl, but he sensed my terror.

I can't let the floaty woman—or any other spirit—key in to that, so I stuff my emotions deep down into the pit of my stomach, to be digested along with the pizza and cookies. My job as a psychic intuitive is to make contact at all costs.

I hold the necklace like I would my pink quartz pendulum. The quivering of the chain tickles at my fingers and I'm ready.

"What does that do?" Taylor asks. I give her a quick *Dowsing for Dummies* explanation and continue with my questions.

"Are there any spirits with us?"

The crystal drop moves slowly at first, clockwise.

"That's a *yes,* isn't it?" Celia asks.

I nod. Taylor takes a picture.

Suddenly, I'm ice-cold, like I've been sitting in a deep freeze.

"Y'all, it's way cold in here," Taylor whispers.

Celia agrees. "Cold air just rushed around my feet." She takes a small black meter from her pocket and points it at the floor. "Fifty-eight degrees."

"In here?" Taylor questions.

"Right here," Celia says. Then she points the temperature gauge over by my bed. "Seventy-two."

"That's quite a change," I say with a tinge of excitement in my voice. Sure, I want this creepy ghost out of my house and away from my family. However, it doesn't mean that I can't get a thrill that it actually exists and we can track it.

"I don't understand," Taylor says. "I know I'm here for my photographic abilities, but I'd love to know what's going on."

Celia pushes her hair out of her face. "It's generally thought in the paranormal community that when you have extreme temperature drops, there's an entity around."

"Oh. My. God." Taylor's about to go whack. "Like, seriously?"

"That's why you're taking pictures," Celia explains. "Anytime we report a cold spot or if Kendall tells us where she's feeling something, snap as many pictures as you can."

Taylor executes a perfect military salute and gets back to work. I think she must be on Prozac or Ritalin to be that cheerful and at ease all the time. Even when she seems frightened, she has a rosy outlook. Too bad some of those happy genes didn't rub off on Jason.

All right. No thoughts of him tonight. I have a spirit to chat with.

I return to my dowsing. "Celia, you ask the questions and I'll give you the answers and anything else I'm feeling. Taylor, take as many pictures as you want."

Wetting her lips, Celia asks, "Are you a male?"

"No."

"Are you a female?"

I look up at her. "Like . . . duh. If it's not a male."

Celia screws up her mouth. "Just see what it says, Kendall."

"Yes."

"See?"

Taylor fusses. "Y'all!"

For a second, I thought my mother had walked in and caught us. Holy crap! But no. She's downstairs with Dad watching one of the medical dramas they love so.

After a series of questions, I ask Celia to read back the notes she's been taking.

"We know the ghost is female, she's sixteen to twenty-one years of age, she's not at rest, she's not happy, but she knows where she is." Celia taps the pen on her notepad. "After going through the first four letters of the alphabet, we know that her name starts with an *E*."

I close my eyes and think hard on the letter *E*. A *Sesame Street*–like flip-flash of the alphabet whizzes through my mind as I try to find the remaining letters of her name. *E-E-E,* concentrate on *E*. The vision in my head shifts to that of a book. An old book. Oh, wait, this book is on my shelf. Just then, it's as if a tremendous amount of energy surges from my chest, propelling me outward and upward. I feel like I'm being pulled up by the wings of an eagle that's asking me to soar with it. *Come with me* . . . But I can't. I've got work to do. Remembering how Loreen talked about grounding myself, I lift my lethargic hands to touch the floor next to me, and suddenly, I'm released. My eyes fly open and I scoot over to the corner of the room.

"What's wrong, Kendall?" Celia asks. She points her EMF meter in my wake.

"I know her name."

Taylor's flash illuminates the shelf, filled to capacity with my mom's books from our old den in Chicago. There was nowhere else to unpack them, so she put them in here since I've got this awesome bookcase built into the wall. I reach for a crimson-bound hardback and slide it out.

"Letters of Emily Dickinson," Celia reads over my shoulder. "So, our ghost is educated."

"No, don't you get it? That's her name. Emily."

"Damn, Kendall, you're good," Celia exclaims and then hugs me.

"Y'all better come over here and look at this," Taylor says, her face lit by the video display on her digital camera. "While y'all were doing that, I thought I'd scroll through the pictures I've taken to see if I got anything."

"And?" Celia prompts. I can tell she's trying hard to be professional when she really wants to do round-off back handsprings across my room.

"And, look—"

Taylor turns the camera so we can see the display. In the first shot, there's a very large, textured orb over my left shoulder. I shudder a bit, thinking something was that close to me.

I can't be afraid though. I must be strong. Nothing will hurt me. I am surrounded by a bubble of white light, and God and his angels will protect me. At least, that's what Loreen told me to chant in my head.

"Aren't orbs supposed to mean something?" Taylor asks.

Celia explains. "Most of the time they're dust or bugs. But they can be entities."

"Do you see any bugs flying around my room?"

Celia and Taylor both laugh as Taylor clicks to the next picture.

"Whoa! Is that ectoplasm?" Celia asks. Sure enough, there's this misty white blobby thing (I'm sorry, that's the best way to describe it) next to me.

I nudge her teasingly. "How would I know what ectoplasm looks like? Holy shit, look at that picture!"

"I'm very proud of this one," Taylor says, unfazed by the fact that she's just captured our spirit on film. "It's clearly a hand. See the fingers curling there?"

"Double whoa! It's reaching out to you, Kendall." Celia makes a note of this.

Taylor holds the camera close and then scrolls forward a few. "And the pièce de résistance. Voilà!"

Celia gasps. "It's phenomenal!"

I swallow the lump in my throat. Girlie emotions—akin to PMSing—bubble up within me and I sort of want to cry because the image is so amazingly beautiful. The blobby white mist that had formed a slender arm and fingers reaching out has now turned into an electrifying bolt of glowing light that seems to be exiting straight up. None of us saw this with the naked eye. It was only captured on the camera. And what a photograph! That was the moment I felt as if I were being pulled up into an invitation to fly. Emily wanted to take me— or my spirit—with her. I'm not frightened or freaked out. In fact, I'm painted with a calmness, a beauty, a peace.

I glance over at Celia, who's grinning like the clichéd cat that swallowed the canary. She winks, and I smile back. We both know we've turned a tremendously important corner.

"Oh yeah, *chicas,* we've made contact."

CHAPTER ELEVEN

AFTER A WEEKEND of stealth paranormal research with Taylor and Celia, I'm ready to get back to school and out from under the ever-watchful eye (i.e., stifling observation) of my mother. Don't get me wrong. I love her, honest to Pete, but she needs to quit looking at me like I'm about to go all *Exorcist* on her. (I woke up last night to see her praying at the foot of my bed. As Celia would say, "Bless her heart.")

Mom's at work today and should be more concerned about who's on Dr. Murphy's flu-shot list than if I'm cutting pentagrams into my arms with her Gillette Venus razor. (Okay, that was harsh, but if she can react in such a retarded way, I can poke fun at it.)

The RHS lunchroom is packed and boisterous. I grasp my tray containing tuna salad and pita bread (trying to be healthy) and weave my way through the tables to where Taylor is sitting with her laptop.

"What's up, T?" I say, really comfy with her after spending the weekend together. Sure, she's a little high maintenance and loves to throw French words at you. But she's a lot of fun too, and she's into being a ghost hunter. It's like she has this special purpose now. Celia certainly pegged that one.

"Kendall!" her singsongy voice shouts out. "Sit, sit, sit."

I slide onto the bench and pop open my Diet Coke. "What are you working on?"

She licks her lips and smiles. "A report on our activities this weekend. I figured the best way to track our progress with each case is to keep a log file we can refer back to."

"That's a great idea," I say. "Mmm, they put apples in the tuna salad."

Taylor waves it off. "It's a Southern thing."

Just then, another tray smacks down next to me and I see Celia's long, jeaned legs lace underneath the table. "Hey, y'all. Sorry, got stuck in the hallway talking to Clay Price." She sighs and blows her bangs out of her eyes.

"Oh, he's a hottie," Taylor says, her eyes wide and shiny. "You should go out with him."

"That's what *I* told her!" I say.

Celia attacks her beef and potato casserole and shovels a way-too-hot mouthful in. "Shit!" After putting out the fire with a big chug of soda, she says, "Clay and I have known each other since, like, birth. That would just be . . . ewww."

"Don't even try with her and Clay, Taylor. I've been there, done that."

Taylor tosses her long golden hair over her shoulder and doesn't miss a beat. "That's fine, because we have our hands full. Boys are nothing but a distraction for dedicated paranormal investigators like us." She tilts the computer screen toward us and I see her neatly charted notations and observations from our weekend ghost hunt.

"Awesome idea, Taylor," Celia says. "I have so many EVP files, I have to figure out a way to organize them. It's almost too much to keep up."

"Those EVPs really are phenomenal! I mean, even if you don't believe that it's an actual ghost, it's definitely something," Taylor says. "How else do you explain it?"

"But it has to be paranormal activity," Celia nearly pleads. I'm in awe of how passionate she is about this subject. "There are a lot of paranormal investigators out there who suggest that EVPs, in addition to being the voices of people who've died, might also be psychic echoes from the past, or even psychokineses unconsciously produced by us and others around us." She reaches for her notebook and thumbs through it while she spoons in another bite of her casserole. "Here, right here. There are some other pragmatic explanations, which include apophenia—finding connections between insignificant or unrelated phenomena—and pareidolia—interpreting all sorts of random sounds as words in your own language. Then there's the possibility that we just misidentify what we're listening to or—"

"You know what, Celia?" I say, stopping her from going off the deep end. Damn, she's one smart cookie. It's hard for me to keep up sometimes, and I get As! "We need someone to focus on the sound, so you can concentrate on the equipment and working with me on my abilities. If we have someone doing sound, it'll take that burden off of you."

"True. We do need more people. But who?"

Celia's not much of a school socialite—apparent by her hanging out with the new girl—and I'd venture a guess that Taylor's regular friends wouldn't think too much of what we're doing, since even she doesn't hang with them all that much anymore.

As I listen to the funky House music that plays through the caf, I think about the kind of person we can approach. "I think it should be a girl. And she should have a really good ear for sounds."

"That's not exactly a trait people put on their Facebook page," Taylor remarks.

I tap my foot to the Kaskade remix of a Seal hit, feeling the rhythm and beat spread through me. Turning to Celia, I ask, "Do you know anyone in band? You know, musicians have great ears."

Celia looks like I just poked her with my fork. "What? The dorky girl knows other dorks? Geesh, Kendall."

"That's not what I meant." Man, she's Little Miss Sensitive today. Who peed in her Rice Krispies this morning? "I just thought you'd know who was who more so than me. Chillax, hon."

"Sorry. My mom was all over my ass this morning about

not being home most of the weekend and thinks I'm slacking off on my schoolwork. As if! That's not even an option." She turns her dark eyes on me. "You know that's not true. You know how badly I want to escape Radisson and go off to college."

"It's okay, Celia. Why don't we have an outward show of studying at your house today. That way, your *mom* will chillax."

"Chillax? Is that a Chicago word?" Taylor asks.

"Chill . . . relax . . . chillax."

"*C'est bon . . . oui,* I must use that," she says with a giggle. Then she starts humming along with the overhead music.

Right then, it hits me!

I glance across the lunchroom and spot a girl with dark makeup, spiky hair, and a noticeable tattoo on her right forearm. She's wearing a headset, standing at her DJ station, and concentrating on mixing out the cafeteria beat. She clearly reeks of *Rebel Without a Cause,* and I have the perfect cause for her to take up. Why didn't I think of this before?

Trying not to be too obvious, I point her out to Taylor and Celia. "Who's she?"

"That's Rebecca Asiaf," Celia explains. "School DJ, obviously. She does all the dances and gets paid to do weddings and other parties on the side."

Taylor clasps her hands. "Oh! I see where this is going. She'd be awesome to listen to our EVP recordings and decipher what we've captured."

"She's obviously got a great ear," I note. "Do you guys know her?"

Celia fixes on Rebecca in front of the turntable. "We had physics together last year."

"I think Jason knows her," Taylor says.

Just the mention of Jason's name makes my stomach clench. I gulp deeply, hoping I don't, like, pass out again. He's not around, is he? I mentally scan the caf. Nope, he's not here. Phew! Didn't want to get another tongue-lashing from him today.

"Jason and I were invited to her sweet-sixteen party last year," Taylor adds.

"*She* had a sweet-sixteen party? I find that hard to believe," I exclaim. It's probably the nose piercing and the black nail polish that sort of wash away the "sweet" image. This girl's dark and hard-core.

"Wouldn't know. I didn't get invited," Celia says, but she doesn't seem too disappointed about it. "I do know that her transformation to the dark side, shall we say, happened not long after that."

I zero in my attention on Rebecca, seeing if I can pick up any energy from her. My psychic senses must be working because I can feel a lot of anger in her. Annoyance she hasn't really dealt with yet, thus her rebellion. I see her, though, as a girl of about ten or eleven. She's in a pretty pink dress . . . in a beauty pageant? A woman is there, cheering her on. No. She's fussing at her for not doing better in the contest. Little

Rebecca is crying. The woman is chastising her. Then the image disappears.

"Whoa."

"What happened?" Celia asks.

"Umm. Nothing. Just, you know, my Spidey senses," I say, trying to laugh it off.

"Let's go talk to her," Taylor says. "What do we have to lose?"

The three of us approach her as she transitions from a Dance song into one with more Deep House rhythms. I'm feeling a tremendous amount of energy coming from Rebecca. It's almost as if she's surrounded by bands of color radiating from her. Not that I can read auras or anything, but this chick comes alive when she's spinning her tunes.

"You're really awesome," I finally say.

Rebecca sneers at me; the diamond stud in her nose almost winks my way. She puts the large headphones up to one ear and totally ignores us.

"How's it goin', Rebecca?" Taylor asks ever so sweetly.

Celia shifts in her Timberlanded feet and tucks her hands into the back pockets of her jeans. The look in her eyes says exactly what I'm thinking: *This isn't going to work.*

Rebecca pulls the headphones from her ear, tosses them on the table, and then downs a gargantuan gulp of Mountain Dew. "What do you Barbies want?"

Barbies? The three of us? You've got to be frickin' kidding me! Taylor, maybe. But me? Certainly not Celia.

Taylor steps forward to make the introductions. Not even addressing Rebecca's slur, she says, "You know Celia Nichols, right? This is Kendall Moorehead. She just moved to Radisson from Chicago."

"Charmed, I'm sure," Rebecca tarts off.

"Hey." Deep inside, I understand that this isn't about me. It's about people who look like me who may have treated Rebecca differently because of her chosen attire. Or maybe it's something deeper. I don't exactly want to examine the psyche of my fellow classmates, so I focus on the music. "Like I said, you're wicked amazing. I heard a lot of DJs in Chicago, and you're good enough to spin in clubs."

This seems to crack the veneer a little. She nods her head, her product-filled hair not moving. "Thanks."

"Go ahead, Taylor," Celia presses. "Ask her."

Rebecca locks her dark eyes on mine. "Ask me what? I'm sort of busy here."

Taylor surges on, ever sparkly, charming, and determined. "Rebecca, we've got a *projet reserve* going on."

Celia knocks her in the back with her elbow. "English, Taylor."

"A secret project."

Rebecca clears her throat. "And this interests me how, exactly?"

"You know how Radisson has thousands of ghost stories? Well, we've decided to form a ghost-hunting group. Celia is our technology specialist, I'm the photographer, Kendall here is our sensitive. She's psychic."

"Get the hell out of here," Rebecca scoffs.

"Seriously!" Taylor says, like it's a perfectly normal thing.

"She's a lunatic if she's telling you that."

"No, I'm not. Why would anyone claim to be something they're not?"

This stops Rebecca for a moment. "Why do I care about any of this?"

I step forward. "Because you have an amazing ear, apparent by your music, and we think you'd be the ideal person to handle all of our sound needs." My pulse snare-drums away under my skin for no reason at all.

Rebecca runs her fingers through her hair, not messing it up at all. Then she hooks her thumbs into the belt loops of her jeans and starts laughing. "You're serious."

"As a heart attack," I say. "When you're ghost hunting, you pick up a lot of sound anomalies, and we need someone with a trained ear to decipher what's real and what's not real. It's a very important position on the team. We all agree you're the person for the job." I pause and make eye contact again with Rebecca through her black liner. "It was a decision we didn't make lightly, I assure you."

Rebecca doesn't blink for at least five seconds. Neither do I.

She lets out a whooping laugh that causes other students to

turn and stare. "Y'all bitches are full of shit! You don't have the guts to actually hunt ghosts. Why don't you go play with your other Barbie friends and leave rational people like me alone?" And with that, she places the headphones firmly over her ears and continues to snicker as she shuffles through CDs.

We skulk off to an appropriate distance.

"I think that went quite nicely, don't you?" Celia opines.

Rebecca tucks a thumb into the waistband of her low-slung jeans. I have the overwhelming sensation that she's either thinking of our offer or thinking of how to have me exterminated. When her head pops back up and the middle finger of her left hand points my way, I have my answer.

I nab Celia and Taylor both by the arms and pull them away. "What. A. Bitch."

"Yeah, well, I could have told you that," Celia says.

I hear a sniffle and turn to see Taylor's bright blue eyes swimming with tears. "She just flipped me off."

"No, she flipped *me* off," I correct.

"She flipped all three of us off," Celia adds.

Taylor sniffs. "A bird's a bird. I haven't been flipped off in my life . . . *ever*."

"Oh, Taylor! Don't cry," I beg. I hand her my unused napkin from lunch. "It was worth a shot."

She snivels a little more and then wipes the water away from her bottom lid, not messing up her impeccable—obviously waterproof—makeup one bit. "I just don't understand why people are like that. Why they have to resort to name-calling and finger motions like that. Rebecca and I used to be friends before she went off the deep end and got all tough and stuff."

"Taylor, it's okay. It's about her, not—"

"What have y'all done to my sister?" a voice roars out.

I don't have to be psychic to know what I'll see when I pivot.

Jason Tillson.

Gorgeous and *pissssssssssssssssed*.

Celia steps backwards and I somehow find my voice. "Jason, it's okay. We were just—"

"You were just *what?* Upsetting my sister. Which I knew you'd do with your asinine plan to form this ghost-hunting group." He's totally in my face. I can smell the slight scent of musky cologne, mixed with his own boy sweat. My heartbeat accelerates and not because of any of my sensitivities. Okay, my normal girlie sensitivities are on maximum. Does this guy even know how hot he is?

"Look," I start to say.

"No, *you* look here," he says forcefully. He holds a finger in my face, and for a moment, I swear he's going to poke me with it. "Taylor's been acting all weird since you waltzed into this school. She's got a lot of personal shit going on in her life and she doesn't need any craziness added to it. I won't have you"—he turns and looks at Celia—"or anyone else doing anything that's going to make things worse for my sister or make her cry more."

More?

Poor Taylor. I had no idea there was something bad going on in her life. I mean, Celia mentioned the isolation, but I didn't pick up on anything. Some sensitive *I* am.

Taylor pushes her way between us. "Grow up, Jason. It's not about that. Leave Kendall and Celia alone. They're my friends."

"I'm just watching out for you."

"For the six millionth time, I don't need a protector."

He laser-beams his startling blue eyes at me. "You'll need an MD and a psychologist if you keep hanging out with her."

"Hey now!" I say in my defense. But then I feel an incredible squeeze around my heart. Not like I'm having an attack or like I'm sensing a spirit's pain. Uh-oh. Here we go again. This agony is all my own. Like my heart is breaking—shattering, really—into a million tiny pieces. I steady my breath and put my hand to my chest. While the Tillsons name-call and argue, I completely foresee myself falling again in the future. Dizziness trips me, along with a fear similar to dropping three floors in an elevator. This time, I call out to Jason for his help, and he catches me swiftly in his grasp. Before I know it, we're kissing. Not just any kiss. A kiss straight out of the pages of a romance novel. Like magical-moment-in-the-movies kissing.

Celia puts her hand on my arm. "Kendall?" she whispers. "Are you all right?"

"I-I-I don't know."

It's right here and now that I know without a doubt that Jason Tillson is destined to break my heart.

Chapter Twelve

"Kendall, you shouldn't sleep over at someone's house on a school night," Mom says Thursday evening as she loads the dinner plates into the dishwasher. That's supposed to be Kaitlin's chore, but she's in front of the television playing Guitar Hero with Okra Carmickle's little sister, Penny.

"But Penny's spending the night here," I nearly whine. God, I sound just like Kaitlin.

Mom waves a towel at me. "That's different. They're young and can't get into as much trouble as you can."

Jesus, Mary, and Saint Joseph! "I'm just going to Celia's to work on a project we're doing together. I'll be in the backyard, practically. I can wave at you from her window."

Dad strolls in and looks at my backpack slung over my shoulder. "Running away from home, kiddo?" Then he winks.

"I'm trying to go over to Celia's to spend the night. Mom's giving me a hard time."

I know she's still concerned over the whole talking-to-spirits thing and probably thinks if she just keeps me in her line of sight, nothing will happen. And you know, she's right. Because I *am* going to Celia's to do some research on the people who owned our house previous to Mrs. Elliott. And I *am* ghost hunting under my own roof, right down the hall from Mom.

"Why, Sarah?" Dad asks.

She totally gives Dad the hairy eyeball and flattens her mouth. "You know exactly why, David."

Dad reaches into the fridge and refills his iced tea. "Come on, Sarah. We talked to her like she's an adult and told her our expectations on her behavior moving forward. I don't think we have to do a house arrest."

Right, considering this particular house seems to be actually haunted.

"Hello! I'm standing right here."

"I know, kiddo. Go on over to Celia's. We trust you to be an adult. Right, Sarah?"

Mom knows she can't fight both of us. Besides, how much trouble can I get into, looking at the names of the former tenants of our house?

I quickly kiss Mom's cheek and then go to do the same to Dad. Something stops me, though. Cold in my tracks, right on the tile kitchen floor. A warming sensation throbs on my left hand, between my thumb and forefinger. It's like there's a gash there. But not on *my* hand . . . *Dad's* hand.

Reaching out, I seize his left hand and spread the fingers out. Sure enough, there's a large Band-Aid covering its side. "What happened?"

"It's nothing," he says.

Mom, the nurse, steps forward too. "Oh, David. Why didn't you show me this? Kendall, go get my kit, would you?"

Dad stops me with his hands raised. "It's fine. I'm fine. It's just a little cut."

No, it's not.

"How'd you cut your hand, Dad?"

"I was working on some plans and I guess I knocked my coffee mug off my desk. I cut myself when I picked the pieces up and threw them away."

"Didn't that happen to the guy before you?" I ask.

"I suppose so. Maybe the office is too close to the train station."

"There's no train in Radisson," Mom notes, as concerned as I am.

"Oh, well. I'm just a klutz then." He holds up his hand. "I'll be fine. No harm, no foul."

The words come out of his mouth in a normal enough way. A common office mishap. However, I know—that part of me that suddenly just *knows* things—that it wasn't merely an accident. It was knocked off his desk on purpose. By someone.

Which means we've got to amp up this ghost hunting before Dad's next boo-boo is something that lands him in the hospital.

"Sorry I'm late, girls."

Taylor plops on the floor with Celia and me. We're perusing

the printouts from her Googling and backdoor researching of the previous owners of my house.

"Did you have any trouble getting away?" Celia asks Taylor.

"Jason was being a turd blossom."

I almost snort Diet Coke out of my nose. I've concocted many descriptions of him in my head, and *turd blossom* is definitely not one of them. I catch my breath of laughter and ask, "Has he ratted out our activities to your parents?"

"Not yet," she reports. Taylor hangs her head a bit and pouts, something that doesn't go unnoticed. Worry crosses Celia's face, and I do believe it's time to dig a little deeper into the psyche of Ms. Taylor Tillson.

"What's going on with you, girlfriend?" I ask, trying a playful tone. "I mean, it's great that you've joined us in our adventures, but you don't hang out with anyone at school other than us, and your brother acts like your own personal National Guard unit."

She sniffs and then rubs her nose. "I'm sorry, y'all. It's just that there's so much going on in my life right now and I'm really, really thankful to have the ghost hunting to focus my attentions on instead of thinking about how horrible things are."

"What's so horrible?" Celia asks.

"My dad moved to Alaska to be a park ranger. It was just supposed to be this finding himself thing at first. You know, instead of hiding his bald head under a Braves cap and buying a convertible, he thought he'd get in tune with the great outdoors."

"Alaska's certainly the place to do it," Celia says, and Taylor smiles.

"About a week ago, he called and I heard Mom say she's going to file for divorce. I never factored that into my life plan, you know? Divorced parents?"

"No one ever does," I say.

Taylor wipes a lone tear from under her eye. "Dad and I were close, and he was real overprotective of me. I guess that's why Jason's always Mr. Attitude about things now. He thinks *he's* my dad now. Mom started off a basket case when Dad left in June, but now, she's all into herself. Everything's moving so fast, too. She went to Buckhead three weeks ago to consult with this doctor about having a nose job and breast implants. When she was there, she met this Delta Airlines pilot named Fredrick, and they've been e-mailing each other. She's more concerned about her looks and her UDC activities than us, so Jason and I are pretty much on our own."

My parents may be a little overbearing right now, but at least they're still together. I couldn't imagine what I'd do if Dad up and moved to the frozen tundra and I couldn't see him regularly. And then, what if some other guy slipped into his place? Ewww! "What's UDC?" I ask, getting my thoughts back on track.

Taylor quirks her mouth. "Oh, it stands for United Daughters of the Confederacy. They're like a sorority dedicated to honoring those who served and died in the Civil War. Well, on the Confederate side, that is. It's all a bunch of hooey, if you ask me. Mainly, they get together and carp about their weight, their kids, their husbands—if they still have them—and drink mint juleps and play Bunco."

"Oh . . . okay," I say. Taylor's mom sounds like a woman with a new lease on life. Too bad her offspring aren't part of the equation. Maybe this is the shit that Jason was referring to earlier when he went postal on me in the caf. I can see where both Tillson kids would be stressed out from a separation, to a divorce, to parents dating again. Guess I should cut Jason some slack next time he takes a verbal pop at me.

Taylor snaps back into her positive self and says, "Seriously, y'all. I'm okay. I love what we're doing."

I'm glad she could tell us what's going on in her life. Now, for her sake, we should get back to work so she can concentrate on other things. "Okay then. Let's get down to business."

Celia slides a box out from under her desk. "I got this stuff in the mail today from GhostMart.com." She starts plundering through the plastic shipping popcorn like a kid on Christmas morning. "There are three EMF meters, some flashlights, another temperature gauge, and this cool vest."

"Abercrombie and Fitch, it's not," Taylor comments when Celia unfurls this *brown* thing.

It's a vest with a ton of pockets. "What on God's green earth is that for?" I ask.

Slipping it on her long, lean limbs, Celia says, "It's super comfortable!"

"Yeah, but what the hell is it for?" I press.

"It's specifically made for paranormal research and ghost investigations because it's got tons of pockets to hold everything," she says proudly. "Check it out. I can carry all my gear wherever we go. Everything's easy to access. Look at this small spot here. I can carry extra batteries in this one."

I pull my grandma's crystal necklace from my pocket and say, "This is the only equipment I need."

"Some of us ain't psychic, Kendall," Celia says with a laugh.

Only Celia Nichols would put on something so ridiculous and still manage to look completely at ease and adorable. I wish Clay Price could see her. I bet he'd freak, in a good way. Okay, okay, I promised not to go there anymore.

As Celia's loading up the vest with all of her Mega-Mart-sponsored purchases, I return the ad hoc dowsing pendulum to my pocket and then pore over the names she's printed off the computer.

"It's amazing what you can find on the Internet," I note.

"I know," Taylor says. "My dad found some chick on the Internet. She lives in Reykjavík."

"Like, Iceland?" Celia asks.

"Yeah. She's a flight attendant for Icelandic Air, but she really wants to get into life coaching. She and my dad met in a chat room and she flew out to Alaska to meet him. Crazy, isn't it? Thus, Mom filing said divorce papers. What's with them getting involved with airline personnel?"

Celia cocks her head to the side. "At least you'll be able to get some good discount family fares, right?"

I gaze open-mouthed at Celia and then over at Taylor. She's shaking her head. Looking back at Celia, I say, "I don't even know what to do with that one."

Not missing a beat, Taylor says, "Maybe you can learn to do tarot readings and we can find out what's in store for them."

"Maybe so."

"First, we need to focus on Emily and the Moorehead house," Celia says, bringing us back to reality.

I agree. "Right. Dad got hurt at work today and I have a bad feeling that Emily followed him there." I fill them in on his flying coffee mug and how the previous office tenant had a similar problemo.

"I think you're looking at this all wrong, Kendall," Celia says. "If this happened previously at your dad's office, then I don't see how it could be Emily. I think we're dealing with another entity."

"But I saw that image of Dad getting hurt, like, really bad."

Celia holds her hand up. "Yeah, I understand. Maybe it happens at work, though, and not at home."

"I don't want it to happen at all!" I screech.

Taylor reaches over to hug me. "We've got to get on this, ASAP!"

Getting a grip on my emotions, I deliberate over the print-outs. "I just feel like everything starts at the house with Emily. The names on this list go back to the 1840s, Celia. Awesome work."

"Told you I was good with research."

I read off the names. "Elliott, Saunders, Curtis, Hinckley, Barrington, Richards . . ." Pausing, I breathe in deeply to see if I'm picking up anything on these names. "You know, I think I saw a couple of these names in the cemetery. We should go tomorrow and see if we can find anyone named Emily with one of these last names."

A mischievous grin crawls across Celia's lips. "Why don't we go right now?"

Taylor wrings her hands. "Now? Like, in the dark? It's almost nine."

"Ghost hunting is best done at night," Celia explains. "Especially in the dark. That's when the spirits come out. Like a witching hour. You know, researchers offer a wide array of opinions on the optimal time for successful ghost hunting. Some say dusk, others will tell you nine p.m., many say midnight, and then there are those that say it's three a.m., which is the exact antithesis of the time of Jesus's crucifixion."

"Celia, now's no time to get all deep on our asses," I fuss.

"Taylor asked. I'm just saying. These are all factors we need to take into account."

Taylor reaches for her camera bag. "There's so much to remember."

Celia grabs the list and three flashlights from the new box of equipment. She tosses one to each of us and says, "Follow me."

"Won't your parents hear us?" I ask.

Shrugging, Celia says, "Dad's watching TV in his den and Mom's probably zonked out on her medication du jour. If Seamus doesn't bark and give the game away, we won't be missed. Just leave the TV on and they'll never bother me."

Taylor fluffs her hair and puts the camera bag strap over her shoulder. "I'm ready when y'all are."

"'Why, then, to-night let us assay our plot,'" I say with a wink to Celia.

"Thanks, Helena," she says with a giggle.

Taylor's confused. "Huh?"

"Shakespeare—*All's Well That Ends Well,*" Celia explains.

I let out a deep sigh. "Let's hope so."

After sneaking out of Palace Nichols through the back slider doors, the three of us creep along in the darkness toward the cemetery. So far, so good. No weird feelings, sensations, or abnormalities. Ironically, Taylor's handling this whole actual ghost hunt quite well. She's far from the Barbie that Rebecca Asiaf accused her of being. And for that matter, what I'd judged her as in my head. Barbies would be home washing their hair, giving themselves home manis and pedis, or surfing Sephora.com for the latest top beauty products. They wouldn't be slipping their sneakered feet into the wrought-iron railings of a cemetery gate.

"Careful, Taylor," Celia whispers from the other side of the fence.

"Here, hold my camera case."

Celia catches the gray bag and sets it on the ground. Then she holds her hands up above her head to spot for Taylor as she swings her leg over the top of the gate and crawls down the other side.

"Come on, Kendall. It's a breeze."

Last time I climbed something was Jenny Enos's attic ladder in eighth grade. She'd said we could see into Walker Pittman's—a real eighth grade babe and a half—room from the attic window. All it got me was an allergic reaction to the dust mites and a nosebleed from her accidental elbow in my face when we were fidgeting with the binoculars.

I grasp the railing and hoist myself over the fence with little or no incident. There is a slight ripping sound, but these are old jeans, so I won't worry about it. With my grandma's crystal fisted in my right hand, I join the other two.

Our three flashlights cross like swords on the battlefield as we weave our way through the worn stone paths. The moon shines brightly above, casting a spot on our activities and outlining each of us in a blue-gray glow. Taylor's taking pictures left and right, following behind Celia with list in hand. I'm clutching the EMF meter like it's a lifeline, watching to see if the red lights catch any electromagnetic energies.

We find a Hinckley, a Richards, and a Barrington. "No one named Emily buried here," Celia notes. She points down toward the bridge where I'd seen the Union soldiers—or, rather, what appeared to be Union soldiers. "Let's go to the lower level."

"Don't you think that's risky?" Taylor asks. "Not that I'm, like, scared or anything. *Tout à fait le contraire.*"

On the contrary, I *am* starting to feel something. My eyes slowly shift downward, and I see that the EMF is flashing like a state trooper's light bar. "Celia . . ."

"Yeah, just a sec."

"No. I think you need to come over here. Now."

Even in the moonlight, I can read the excitement on her face. "The meter is going apeshit! Awesome!"

"What does that mean?" Taylor asks while snapping some brightly flashed digital pictures.

Celia shows her the device. "It means there are high measures of electromagnetic energy present, and that usually means spirits are trying to manipulate the energy fields to make things happen, like to manifest themselves." She focuses on me, her hair pushed out of her eyes for almost the first time. "What are you feeling, Kendall?"

I swallow the dry lump in my throat. Then I close my eyes tight.

"You have to talk to me," she says in a voice as calming as my mom's. "Just tell me what's going on with you. Taylor, take pictures around Kendall."

Stretching my hands out in front of me, I can tell they're trembling something fierce. I don't have to open my eyes to know this. "You see that, right?"

"Yeah," Celia notes.

"There's a lot going on here."

I feel the camera flash on my skin. My hands are tingly. "My lips are numb." Anticipation is in the air like I've never felt, crackling all around. "There's some serious energy surrounding me. By my knees," I instruct.

I sense Celia move the EMF meter near me and know that her readings are continuing to spike off the chart. "Something's definitely causing this," she says.

The numbness increases and it's like I've gone to get my teeth pulled. I know my face is there, I'm touching it with my fingers, but I don't feel a damn thing. A ringing sounds in my head, reverberating from ear to ear. I can't answer it and it won't go away.

"Talk to me, Kendall." Celia's voice remains calm.

"Strong, strong energy. Like wintertime, when you get out of the car too fast and your coat rubs up against the upholstery and then you touch the door and it shocks you into the middle of next week."

"Good description," Taylor says. "Should I switch to the infrared camera, Celia?"

"Good call." Turning her attention back to me, Celia asks, "Are there any spirits here?"

I nod.

"Should you dowse?"

"Not yet." I swallow again, and my throat tenses up. My chest hurts with the same empty hollowness it had when

Smokey, our black and white cat, slipped out of our house and got run over by the FedEx truck. Sadness cascades over me like an ocean wave. My breathing becomes shallow and uncontrollable.

"There's . . . there's . . . so much . . . so much *sadness,*" I manage to get out.

Click. Click. Click.

I block out Taylor's photographing and just concentrate on my surroundings. It's so dismal and . . . full of lives cut short, of heartache and heartbreak and physical suffering. Of course, it *is* a cemetery, so one would assume these things are in the atmosphere. But the sensations literally encompass me, garroting me with their persistent fingers.

Opening my eyes slowly, I see them. All around me. Scattered about the cemetery.

"Holy freakin' crap," I can only whisper.

"What?" Celia asks.

Click. Click. Click.

I hold my fist to my chest. "There are so many of them."

Taylor's hair flips over her shoulder as she whips her head around. "So many what?"

"Ghosts."

Her hand flies to her mouth, and I beg her with my eyes not to completely freak out.

Then there's shouting and screaming. Not from Celia, Taylor, or me. From *them.* Calls for attention and pleas for help.

It's like being on the floor of the Chicago Mercantile Exchange at the height of trading. The school took us to the Merc on a field trip one time, and I remember the vibrations from the voices and noise echoing clear into my bones, almost. How people can do that all day, I'll never know. But it's like that for me now, and the voices are only getting more boisterous. I slap my hands over my ears, as if that's going to do any good.

"Kendall! Talk to me!" Celia screams.

"They're everywhere, Celia!" I twist to the left. To the right. I swat. I cover my face. "They're all over me!" Faces, eyes, hands. Grasping and reaching, pulling me to them. Jesus! I can't believe no one else can hear or see this.

Celia's face joins theirs, breaking through the furor. "Kendall! What are you seeing?"

"I can't hear you all at the same time. Shut up, would you? Stop talking. One at a time. Get in line or something! Take a friggin' number!" A deli I'm not, so my pleas go unheeded. The face of an older woman. The war cry of an Indian in full headdress. The musty smell of a wrinkly old man. The rebel yells of a Confederate soldier. The bloodcurdling cries of a cholera-stricken baby. "It's too much. Please stop!"

"What's too much, Kendall?" Celia is begging. "Let me help you."

I close my eyes again, but I can feel them in front of me, next to me, behind me, above me. A jarring dissonance of voices, buzzing together in an unharmonious opus with no conductor. "You can't help, Celia. You can't see them." Tears sting my eyes, and every fiber of my being is on the highest of high alerts.

Celia's so composed. "Tell me about the ghosts."

Click. Click. Click.

"I can't. Can't think. Can't anything." I shake my head, eyes still squoze—*yes, I know that's not a real word*—shut. "Loreen told me this happens." I struggle to exhale as I explain. "That when spirits recognize someone that can see them, it's like a neon light over your head and they become like puppies, suddenly yapping at your feet for attention. It's seriously too much. They're coming at me too fast. Sooooooo many. Make it stop, Celia."

She grabs my upper arms and holds firmly. My knees wobble underneath me and I don't think I can sustain my body's weight. My heart quickens to the point where I can hear the blood whooshing in my ears, and then nothing. A steady beep of a monitor sounds, and I hear a doctor pronounce, "His heart has failed. We've lost him." My eyes fly open to see, on my right, the grave of Edmund Kline Stanley. "He's here," I say as I point. "He had a heart attack in the eighties. In 1985, to be exact." My temple is flaming with searing heat and throbbing like nobody's business. "Over there, someone died of a gunshot wound to the head." Aches and nausea from my stomach cause me to double over. I bend to my waist, praying for the pain to go away. "S-s-stomach. Stomach cancer behind me."

Celia helps me up; the red light on her EMF meter is solidly in the high zone.

Click. Click. Click.

Taylor pulls the camera away from her face. "What are they saying to you, Kendall?"

"Everything. It's all jumbled together. So many of them." It's like being the most popular girl at the school dance—not that I'd know—and everyone's pulling you in a different direction, singing various songs to you. They're shouting, "Dance! Dance!"

A whispered scream rips from my windpipe as an aggressive spirit shoulders all the others aside and is seriously in my face. I mean: In. My. Face. "Back off, buddy!" I scream.

"What? Kendall! Damn it!" I hear Celia's frustration and I know she needs more info, but I can't concentrate on that right now.

"He's on me. Literally. What do you want?"

He laughs at me. Not anything sinister or evil. Playful. Jovial. Like he wants to entertain me. I just want to go home. Why is this happening?

Son of a bitch! It hits me! Loreen told me I need to protect myself whenever I go into a situation like this. Not like I have holy water in the kitchen cabinet at home, but I could have strapped on my cross or said a prayer or surrounded myself in God's love and light—anything. I did nothing. And now they're everywhere. Completely invading my personal space.

Mr. Aggressive, though, truly takes the cake. He wants in.

"In? He wants in?" I ask out loud. "What does that mean?"

Celia's mouth drops. "He wants you to channel him, Kendall."

"Channel? Like, let him speak through me?"

"Exactly."

"Don't you even think about it, Kendall Moorehead!" Taylor shouts, her voice trembling. "Oh my God. What are we doing here? This isn't right!"

I try to explain. "His pain is intense."

With that, I collapse to my knees. My entire body hurts, like there's poison filling my veins. I break out in a massive sweat, unable to control the slightest motion of my limbs.

Let me in . . .

"No! Not just no, *hell* no!"

"Fight him, Kendall. We don't know who he is or what he wants," Celia instructs with such force that I think for a minute she's an exorcist.

Gritting my teeth, I seethe. "I'm trying. He's . . . so . . . sooooo strong."

Taylor drops her camera to the ground and reaches for her cell phone. "This has gone too far! I'm calling nine-one-one!"

"And telling them what?" Celia says sarcastically. "'Hello, my friend is being taken over by some crazed spirit in the graveyard. Can you send an ambulance?' No, we have to help her." Celia kneels next to me and grabs my arms again. "Kick him out, Kendall. Tell him to piss off."

I'm not exactly sure how to fight him off. *Oh, Loreeeeee-*

eeeeeen! Why didn't I listen to you? Loooooooooooooooreeeeeeeeeen!
Can you hear me? Can you feel me? Help me!

He laughs at me inside my head.

Beeps. More beeps. Oh, it's Taylor dialing the phone.

I reach out to her. "No . . . we'll . . . I'll . . . get in trouble."

Celia shakes me. "Kendall, stay with me!"

"He's trying to get in. I can feeeel it." In my head, I scream bloody murder to get him away from me. He backs off a step. Oh, good. It's working. I screech again until all the breath is out of my lungs.

"Hey, it's Taylor. Something horrible is happening and we need help!" I hear.

Crappity-crap-crap-crap. Please tell me she isn't calling my mother.

"I'm dizzy, Celia."

She holds me close. "It's okay, Kendall."

"No, it's not okay." Nausea rushes in like a tsunami, encircling me in blackness until I have no idea what's happening.

One last mental push to Mr. Aggressive and then I feel myself passing out.

Warm hands settle firmly on my shoulders and I hear a familiar voice in my ear, soothing me. "Hang on, Kendall. I'm here. I've got you."

CHAPTER THIRTEEN

I PEEL MY EYELIDS BACK, somehow expecting to find myself in Jason Tillson's arms again. Instead, I see soft strawberry blond curls and a novelty T-shirt that reads "A Happy Medium."

"Loreen?" I barely manage to get out.

Taylor falls to her knees next to me. "Oh my God, Kendall. I was screaming so loudly. You didn't even hear me. You're not possessed or anything, are you? Do I need to go get a priest or something? Although I don't exactly know one, since I'm Baptist."

I sit upright as Loreen calms my friend. "Everything's going to be okay. I'm here to help."

"You're Loreen Woods, right?" Celia asks, her eyes alight. "How did you know to come?"

Shifting her eyes to me, Loreen says, "Kendall and I are connected. I was driving around looking for you when you called out to me." Then her tone changes. "It's a good thing you did. What were you girls thinking? Coming out here into the cemetery without protecting yourself. Haven't you listened to anything I've taught you?"

I rub my head—now free of feelings of gunshot wounds, tumors, and everything else—and let out a sigh of relief. "I know, Loreen. I'm sorry."

She grits her teeth, and I don't have to be a mind reader to know what she's thinking. She's royally pissed at me, and I guess I can't blame her. We did come out here tonight sort of half-cocked, not planning or taking care of ourselves.

"If you're going to be heading up this ghost-hunting group," she begins, "you've got to take responsibility not only for yourself but for your teammates. *Everyone* needs protection, Kendall. You, the equipment, everything. You don't know what you're dealing with in the spirit realm. Not everything is nice."

I nod my agreement. "Don't be mad, Loreen. Your shirt says you're a *happy* medium," I say with a small, weak chuckle.

"Yes, well. I didn't know I'd be talking with you about such foolishness. It's a good thing we're connected, Kendall. Something horrible could have happened to you."

"But it didn't."

She scowls.

"I said I'm sorry."

"Sorry indeed." She reaches into her pocket and withdraws a small spray bottle.

"What's that?" Celia asks.

"Holy water." And with that, Loreen proceeds to spray me with it up one side and down the other while reciting a prayer: "Saint Michael the Archangel, defend us in battle. Be our protection against the wickedness and snares of the devil; may God rebuke him, we humbly pray. O Prince of the heavenly host, by the power of God, thrust into hell Satan and all the evil spirits who wander through the world for ruin of souls. Amen."

"Aye-men!" Taylor echoes.

I mutter the same and wipe the water off my face. It smells like the stuffing my mom makes to go with our Thanksgiving turkey. "What else is in there?"

"Sage," Loreen says.

"What for?" Taylor asks.

"It cleans the energy fields and gives you protection." She passes the vial over to Celia. "Here, you girls spray yourselves as well."

Loreen helps me up, and together we brush dirt and grass off my jeans. "Thanks for coming," I say. She tweaks my nose and smiles at me. "Seriously, I'm grateful you're here."

Someone else is here too, though.

And as per usual, he's fit to be tied.

Jason barrels his Jeep through the side gate and slams it into Park. He jumps out and immediately starts lecturing. "Tell me something, are y'all purposely looking for trouble or are y'all just incredibly stupid dumb-asses?"

"Hey now—" I start to say in our defense. I move toward him, but my energies are as drained as a dead Duracell and I can barely stand without Loreen's help. "Look, buddy, I don't care how cute you are, you've got one hell of a bad attitude toward me and I'm sick of it."

Celia looks at me in shock and awe.

Yowlza-may! Did I just tell him he was cute?

He tries to glare at me, but I notice the corners of his mouth want to curl up into a smile. His eyes drop, and he toes his boot in the dirt.

I gulp noticeably and see Celia rolling her eyes.

Coming back to his senses, Jason shakes off whatever humor had overcome him and stomps up to me. Less adversarial, he says, "I should have known when Taylor called me for help this had something to do with you."

I look over at her and she bites her lip. "*Pardonnez-moi.* What can I say? You weren't exactly playing debutante hostess just now. I was a bit freaked out."

"And you called *him?*" I nearly spit out. Of course she called Jason. He's the only family she really trusts these days. Turning back to him, I say, "Look, things just got out of hand. We're all new to this and learning as we go along. Cut us some slack."

His face shades a dark red—even in the moonlight—and I think his head's going to explode like a cartoon character's. There's no mistaking the intent of the energies coming off him. "Get in the Jeep, Taylor. I'm taking you home."

"But Jason—"

"Do what I say!"

"Are you okay, Kendall?" she asks with her hand on my arm.

"Yeah, I think so."

Celia puts her arm around my waist to support me and watches the ground.

"Now, Taylor!" Jason growls.

She pouts and then tromps off to the Jeep with apologetic eyes. "Bye, y'all."

Jason lasers his eyes on Celia and me. "You better get home too before I call your parents and tell them what you were up to."

Pushing away from Celia, I spin on Jason. "Who do you think you are?"

"Kendall, it's okay . . . Don't," Celia says softly.

"It's not okay!"

Blue eyes cut through the night and connect with mine. "Cemeteries are no place for young girls. Especially late at night."

"Who died and left you in charge?" I say with my hands on my hips, feeling a surge of strength return.

"I'm responsible for my sister since my father walked out the door and my mother's too caught up with her new life. I'm too old to be putting up with teenage crap like this!"

Now I'm in *his* face, like the spirit was in mine earlier. "What are you? Ninety? No! You're a teenager yourself on paper. But you know what you really are? You're a bitter old man, Jason Tillson. You need to get over yourself ASAP!"

I seem to have hit a nerve with him because the anger in his eyes immediately morphs into embarrassment. I bite my tongue at what a bitch I've become. It's not like me at all to scream at someone like this. Especially a cute guy who's basically a stranger to me.

"I'm sorry for all of my inadequacies," he says and then backs away.

Great. Now I'm racked with guilt for yelling at him when all he was doing was looking out for his sister.

"Jason, wait—"

Celia stops me. "Let them go, Kendall. We're in enough trouble as it is."

At the Jeep, Jason shouts back with a concern that warms me. "Will y'all be okay getting home?"

"I'll take care of them," Loreen assures him.

"Thanks." And with that, he cranks up the Jeep and backs away into the darkness.

Celia and I sigh at the same time. She can easily sneak back into her house unnoticed, but I have a feeling that Loreen wants me to go home and that she won't let me enter Casa Moorehead without her speaking to my parents.

Loreen lifts a knowing smile my way.

I blow a raspberry. "Let's get this over with."

Sarah Moorehead is soooooooooooo not happy.

She is, at least, cordial to our guest.

I stand there fidgeting with a hole in the pocket of my

jeans, waiting for the shitteth to hitteth the fan . . . eth. (And no, Shakespeare didn't come up with that particular quote; *10 Things I Hate About You* did.) Loreen has just finished regaling Mom with the short version of what happened tonight and why she's bringing me home. Dad went out for a drink with one of the contractors, so at least I'm not getting the double-barreled-shotgun treatment . . . yet.

"I'm glad I was available to help out your daughter," Loreen says.

"Well, thank you for bringing her home," Mom says to Loreen in the foyer of our house. While I'd love to talk to Loreen about what happened, I don't exactly want her and Mom to bond over coffee and cookies in the living room.

"Anytime. Kendall has a very special gift, Mrs. Moorehead." Not waiting to see if Mom asks her to, Loreen moves deeper into the hallway and takes a seat on the piano bench that's just inside and to the right. "Because Kendall is still learning to hone her abilities, she needs to be especially careful when dealing with the spirit realm. She must protect herself at all times, and in fact, she shouldn't try to connect further with those on the other side until she's more fully trained."

Mom's lips flatten and her cheeks go ashen. "I appreciate your concern, Ms. Woods, but let me assure you, she won't require further training at all because she is forbidden to do this kind of thing anymore."

"Why's that?" Loreen asks, her hands folded in her lap. "Kendall has a gift."

"I don't believe so."

"I'm sorry to hear that. You must realize she needs to—"

Mom cuts her off. "I believe I know what's best for my daughter."

Loreen frowns. "And that is?"

"She's been told she's not allowed to dabble in these dark arts any further. And I've told her she's not to see you or to be *taught* by you."

"Oh."

"Mom, Loreen was only trying to—"

Mom's livid gaze slices over to me, and I immediately clamp my mouth shut. Kaitlin might not know when to stop talking, but I do. "I think you've had enough excitement for one day," Mom says. "Kendall. Go to bed. Now. We'll talk about this in the morning with your father."

"Yes, ma'am."

Holding the front door open, Mom says, "Thank you again for your trouble, Ms. Woods."

Talk about not letting the door hit you on the ass on your way out. Poor Loreen.

I grab her arm and then hug her tightly, whispering my thanks. She pulls back and takes my hand. Then she reaches over to my mother, joins our hands together, and lays hers on top. "Be good to each other," she says.

I see Mom suppress a faint smile. However, I also sense a change in the energies around the three of us. My first thought is that Emily is here and might try to harm either Mom or

Loreen. But then I hear Loreen take a deep, deep breath. She's almost trancelike as she stands there gripping our hands.

Mom appears taken aback. "What's she doing? Some sort of voodoo? I will *not* have that in my house."

"It's okay," I say softly.

Loreen breaks the contact and faces me. She knows something. Information of some sort was transmitted when we were all connected like that. I know she won't tell me though.

Loreen faces my mother and whispers a quick prayer. "I wish you nothing but the best, Sarah Moorehead. I know you've taken a huge responsibility on your shoulders with Kendall's life, and she will need all the support that any mother could give a daughter. Your secret is safe with me."

"That's just about enough! Leave!"

And with that, my mother, the polite Christian woman, shoves Loreen out of the house and slams the door.

"Why did you do that?"

Mom is shaking. "That woman is trouble. And she needs professional help."

"No, she's not, and no, she doesn't. She's a little odd because she's not like you and your friends back home. But Loreen understands me."

"Not anymore, she doesn't. I said it once and I mean it this time, Kendall. You are *forbidden* to ever speak to that woman again. She'll just confuse you and tell you lies. I've had enough of your back talk and disobedience for one night. I didn't raise you to act like this."

I thrust my hands into my hair. "How am I acting?" This is all so confusing to me. All of it that I've been experiencing and trying to deal with.

"Telling me you're psychic and then—what were you doing?—ghost hunting."

"Ghost hunting is a natural way to use my abilities to help people, Mom."

"You don't have any abilities, Kendall. You're making it all up just to get attention. Well, you've got my attention. Are you happy?"

Tears well up in my eyes. Why won't my own mother believe me? Celia and Taylor believe me. Loreen does too. Jason probably thinks there's some truth to my claims. Mom won't accept it, though.

"I'm not trying to cause trouble, I swear. I'm just trying to understand everything that's happening to me. And on top of that, I'm trying to make new friends and fit in."

Mom's voice is shaky too. "You're certainly going about it in an odd way."

I'm so physically and mentally exhausted, it's not even funny. I slump down onto the piano bench and let a wayward tear trickle down my face.

"When your father gets home, I'll discuss things with him. Until then, consider yourself grounded, Kendall. Until you're at least in your thirties." Mom leaves me sitting there as she heads off into the kitchen. I hear her banging pots, pans, and plates—her only real way of dealing with anger is to clean.

Fine.

I'm too tired to fight anymore.

I slink up the stairs and collapse on my bed, fully dressed. It's only ten o'clock, but I don't care. The bed shakes and I hear the *rrrrrarrrr* of a cat. Two, actually. Eleanor and Natalie pad their way up the mattress to me and then both nestle down in the small of my back. They begin purring and bathing each other, which sends the emotional ball right over the fence for me. The tears of overtiredness brim over the edge, and I bury my head in my pillow for a good cry. It's times like this that I want nothing more than for my mom to hug me and tell me everything's going to be all right. Only, I'm the last person she wants to hug right now, and I don't blame her. Who'd want a screwed-up kid with psychic abilities who almost gets taken over by crazed spirits in a cemetery? Yeah, that's what she signed up for in her Parenting 101 classes.

As my tears begin to retreat, I reach over and turn on my white-noise machine. Natalie finishes up licking her back leg and then moves to my hand. The sandpapery scrape of her tongue against my fingers is oddly soothing.

Several moments later, I hear a whisper. So soft. So sweet. So caring.

"I'm heeeeeeeeeeeeere . . ."

"Emily? Is that you?"

"Yessssssssssssssssss . . ."

Lovely. Just what I need. Another ghost mucking around with me tonight.

Then I hear her distinct words through the white-noise maker.

"I'm heeeeeeeeeeeeeeeeeeeere . . . for yoooooooooooooou."

Yeah, whatever, ghost. "Not tonight, Emily. I've had a shitty day."

I roll over and pull my knees up to my chest. Eleanor meows and walks around to plop herself down around my head like some sort of live mouton. As her motorboat of a purr begins to lull me into a stupor, the tears begin to trickle again, warm and sticky on my pillow and leaving a wet spot. I don't care though.

I close my eyes tight, willing the fears, trepidation, and anxiety into a small corner pocket in the bottom of my stomach. There will surely be a nice ulcery hole there soon, in that place where all the pain goes.

I sigh.

I don't know what Emily the ghost wants from me. How can I help her when I can't even help myself?

Chapter Fourteen

You know how in all those teen movies, there's a point when the hero or heroine walks down the hall at school and all eyes seem to be on him or her? I always thought it was a device to have the audience focus on the character's accomplishment or achievement in the overall journey.

But shit like that really *does* happen in real life.

I'm not even kidding.

Celia and I are walking together to our lockers Monday on the way to lunch period, and I swear, it's like every pair of eyes at RHS is looking at *us*. Not in an outcast "oh my God what were you thinking wearing those jeans with that top" sort of way. They're checking us out in a kind of amazed awe.

"What's going on?" I whisper to Celia.

"Everyone knows," she says, barely moving her lips.

"Knows what?"

Sean "Okra" Carmickle limps down the hallway in front of us and stops. "Y'all got balls," he says.

Is this a good thing? "We do?"

"Yeah, I heard all about y'all going to the cemetery last night and ghost hunting like they do on those TV shows. Wow," he continues. "Never thought a bunch of girls would do something like that. Y'all a'ight."

Okra fist-bumps Celia, then me, and hobbles off to his next class.

"How did he know? How does everyone know?" I ask, looking about.

"Welcome to small-town living," Celia says. "You think in a city where people chase the fire truck that folks wouldn't find out about a bunch of teenagers sneaking into the cemetery to ghost hunt?"

"Hmmm, I never thought about it," I say.

Girls I don't even know nod as we pass. Guys I've never seen check us out and smile.

I hear the padding of sneakers on the floor approaching us and have a feeling who it is.

"Hey, Celia!"

"Hey, Clay," she mutters without looking up.

"You're Kendall, right? I'm Clay Price," he says, extending his hand to me in a polite way.

"Yeah, Kendall Moorehead. Nice to meet you."

"I know all about you," he says with a wide, perfect smile. "I heard y'all scaled the fence at the cemetery last night and had a séance right there in the middle until the police showed up."

"Not exactly!" Celia snaps. "We were just ghost hunting and Kendall made contact with a spirit."

"Several," I correct.

"That's awesome," he says. "Can I go next time?"

Celia's cheeks stain and she starts getting flustered. "Things aren't really set in stone for our team yet, you know, and we're still trying to get all of the aspects of a proper ghost-hunting unit together. Right now, it's an all-female team and we may not have anything for you to do and—"

Clay laughs. "A simple *no* would suffice, Celia." He winks and then heads off. "Catch ya later."

My mouth falls open. "Why'd you do that?"

"We don't need him tagging along."

"Celia! It's obvious he's crazy about you."

"Which is exactly *why* I don't want him ghost hunting with us. Guys will just distract us from our investigations."

I chuckle deep in my throat. "Whatever you say, Cap'n."

Taylor rushes up, nearly out of breath. Her high ponytail swings vigorously as she weaves through the throng of students.

"Watch it!" a guy shouts out. "You'll put someone's eye out with that thing!"

"Sorry!" she sings. "Celia! Kendall! I'm so glad I found you. We're all anyone can talk about today. Isn't it the most exciting thing ever?"

"It's something, all right," I say.

"Look," she says. "I got this text message last period."

We gather around Taylor's pink Razr phone: Cum c me @ lunch.

"Who's it from?" I ask.

Taylor snaps her phone shut. "Rebecca. Asiaf."

"No way!"

"Way!"

"What does she want?" Celia grimaces. "Didn't we get enough from Bulldozer Becca already?"

I pop my head back and belly laugh. "Bulldozer Becca? Oh, yeah, I see that."

Nearly sparkling, Taylor says, "She may be coming around."

So we stash our books in our respective lockers and head toward the caf. My stomach is growling something fierce from missing breakfast this morning. I was too hung over from crying myself to sleep. And I didn't want to face my parents. I was grounded. What else was there to say or do? Barely in my new town for a full month and I am forbidden to do anything. My whole life in Chicago, I never had any problems. Then I move here, and all hell busts loose. It's not like I can hone my skills if I can't talk to Loreen. I bet if I try Googling *ghost hunting* or *psychics,* a red light and alarm will go off somewhere in the house, alerting my mother to my further "dabbling." This is no way to live. I'm damned if I do and damned if I don't.

At the lunch counter, I pile fried chicken, green beans, mac 'n' cheese, and something called pear salad—a pear half with a dollop of mayonnaise and shredded cheddar on top of it—on my tray and follow Taylor and Celia to our table over by the window. The lunchtime music mix is playing out, so I know Rebecca Asiaf is around.

I'm halfway through my finger-licking chicken breast (and totally through with the ridiculously yummy pear salad) when I sense someone approaching our table. Instead of turning around, I return the forkful of chicken to my plate and wait for Rebecca to speak.

"Yo, Tillson. I told you to come see me when you got here."

"Oh, hey, Rebecca," Taylor says, all nice and friendly. "We were just eating first. Music sounds great today, as per usual."

Rebecca swings a booted foot over the bench and sits next to Taylor. She peers out at me through her dark, black-lined eyes and purses her blood-red lips. Most people going for the Goth look seem a little silly to me, like they're playing dress-up. Not Rebecca. The fashion suits her and makes it hard for me to believe that she used to do beauty pageants only a couple of years ago.

"Thanks," she says. "It's a Dirty South mix."

Celia pipes up bravely, and I want to give her props for being so assertive. "What did you want to see us about, Rebecca?"

I focus on the hoop in Rebecca's lower lip and how the silver shimmers in the afternoon sunlight that's streaming in the window. She lifts her eyes and leans back a bit.

"Well, I felt compelled to tell you that I'm impressed."

Celia's brow shoots up. "You are? With us?"

"Us Barbies?" Taylor says a bit sarcastically.

I take another bite of my chicken to have something to do. (And to keep from saying something I shouldn't to this girl. Like, I know her home life is total crap.)

"What can I say? I was wrong, okay? When I'm wrong, I say it." Rebecca nods her head. "I'm completely blown away that you did what you did last night. Barbies don't put themselves out there for what they believe in like you did."

Wow.

I swallow the dry chicken. "Geez, thanks, Rebecca."

"Becca," she says. "To my friends, that is." She extends her hand, nails painted black and a skull-and-crossbones ring on her middle finger. *The better to flip you off, my dear.* "I'd like to be friends. 'Kay?"

I put out my own hand and shake. "I'd like that."

"And I'd like to join your group. You know, in your ghost hunting. It sounds pretty intense."

"All *right!*" Celia shouts out. She and Taylor high-five and then Taylor leans over and awkwardly squeezes Becca to her.

"This will be so awesome!" Taylor says.

I get the feeling Becca hasn't really belonged to anything in a while, so this may be a good thing for her. At least, my instincts tell me so. "Thanks, Becca. You won't regret this."

Celia pulls out her notebook and starts explaining. "See, Kendall has a ghost in her house that we think might be a threat to her family. There's also something going on at Mr. Moorehead's office and we don't know if it's the same entity following him to work or if there's something else there. We've taken a lot of pictures and have gotten some ectoplasm mist to show up in the digitals, but what we really want to concentrate on is the EVP work because the voice is not only coming through the white-noise machine in Kendall's bedroom, it's also in some digital recordings."

I can see Becca's dark green eyes begin to enlarge with the information overload. Celia must pick up on it too, because she says, "Don't worry, I'll teach you what all the acronyms stand for. Basically, what you'll be doing is heading up our EVP—electronic voice phenomenon—branch of the group. For that we really need someone who specializes in recording equipment and someone who can manipulate the sound data using the software I've got on my—"

A realization rushes in hard to my brain and I slam my fist to the table. "Damn it!"

Jumping at the sound, Celia says, "What? Did I tell too much?"

"No, I'm sorry, Celia. It's not you." I let out a long sigh and feel my psychic headache starting to come on. Or maybe it's just the residual pounding from last night's cry-fest. "It's just that now that everything's falling into place, I can't do anything because I'm grounded."

"You're grounded? For what? Last night?" Celia asks.

"Yeah. Busted."

"That's jank," Celia says with a strong sigh.

Becca frowns. "So you're not ghost hunting anymore?"

I bite my bottom lip. "I'm not allowed out of the house other than for school activities. I can't go over to Celia's or Taylor's, and I'm forbidden to see Loreen."

Taylor reaches over and pats the top of my hand. "We'll all go over and talk to your mom, sweetie. It'll be okay."

I shake my head.

Becca clicks her tongue. "I gotta get back over to the boards. Look, keep me posted. If you're hunting and need me on the team, I'm there. Just let me know."

"Thanks, Becca, you're the best," Taylor says, ever happy and jovial, no matter the challenge.

"We'll do all we can until your parents come around," Celia assures me. "Maybe we can show them some of the evidence we've collected?"

Head in hands, I say, "That'll only make things worse. Mom's kind of religious and none of this sits right with her. She's not going to let me off the hook from last night. She thinks we were careless and acting in a dangerous manner. It doesn't help that she holds Loreen responsible for what happened to me. Mom thinks she's bewitched me or something."

Celia fingers her bangs while she thinks. "Well, I'm still testing out equipment and getting our notes and stuff organized. Taylor and I can archive the photos and tag them, and then when your folks let you out again . . ." She trails off. Then she glances over my shoulder and quickly moves her eyes to her food.

"Hey, y'all," I hear next to me.

Taylor's perkiness fades and she glowers. "Jason." I watch her toy with a bite of her green beans. She pops in a mouthful and then says through clenched teeth, "What have I done wrong now? I'm eating vegetables. One of the essential food groups. I don't see how that can cause you to come over and correct me."

He drops his head down and then reaches up with his hand to scruff at his short gold hair. "Taylor, I told you last night I was sorry. We'll talk later, okay?"

"Whatever, Mr. Bossy McBosserton."

I stare at the mac 'n' cheese on my plate that's turning into something that resembles wallpaper paste. Or maybe that's just the way my tongue feels as I sit here and await the next wave of attack from Jason.

"You mind if I talk to Kendall for a mo'?"

Celia glances at me and I nod that I'm okay. She scooches her tray out of the way and into her hands. Taylor joins her, and suddenly, I'm left alone with Jason and his clear blue eyes.

I place a forkful of the cheesy noodles into my mouth and chew slowly. If I'm eating, then I'm less likely to tell him to go screw. Sad. My dreams and visions showed us being so close, not butting heads like this.

"Look," he says. He stops and puts his hands one on top of the other on the table. "I'm an asshole, okay?"

I can't help but laugh. "No argument there, skippy."

He seems flustered. "I'm trying to apologize here."

"Then stop being so judgmental—especially about me. You know nothing about me."

"I know."

"And you're always acting like an adult. Like a parent. Like *my* parent. Hell, I come to school and hang with my friends to get away from adults who are always telling me what to do. But there you are to pick up the slack."

"I know."

I flail my arms about to make my point. "You're sixteen, Jason. Just like me. Just like Taylor. Just like Celia."

He reaches out and nabs my wrists in his large hands. Lightning bolts shoot up my arms, down my torso, and go rapid-fire down my legs, like my entire circulatory system has been seared from the inside. "Kendall. I said I'm sorry. Okay?"

Slowly, reluctantly almost, he loosens his grip and lets me go. I return my hands to the table, stretching them out in front of me and mirroring his own position. I nervously wet my lips with the tip of my tongue and try to gulp down that stupid lump in my throat. "Ohhhh-kay. What's the catch?"

A sigh escapes from him. "No catch, Kendall. I'm just trying to make peace with my sister. Since you're a close friend now, I need to quit being such a jerk to you. You aren't the problem."

No, I'm not. That's too snarky. I'll take the high ground instead. "For what it's worth, I think it's sort of sweet that you look out for Taylor the way you do."

He lifts his eyes to mine and smiles. Wow, what a smile. He should definitely do that more often. "Thanks. I try."

"I mean, I'm the oldest too," I say, hoping I'm not rambling in the face of such amazing cuteness. "My little sister, Kaitlin, is a total head case, but I'd do anything for her. Especially if I thought she was doing something that would hurt her."

"Then you know why I have to watch out for Taylor. She's so innocent and has a heart of gold. She doesn't think there's anything bad in this world. I just want to prevent her from being hurt again." He lowers his eyes, but I don't think he honestly believes I want to harm his sister.

"I know that means a lot to her. Especially considering what's going on with your parents. It can't be easy, Jason." I want to touch him again, but I don't dare. Just because I've had fantasies about him doesn't mean he'd take too kindly to my acting on them.

"She told you, huh?"

"Yeah. Don't worry. Taylor's my friend and I'd never repeat anything that personal about her. Or you," I tack on.

Jason toys with the spoon Celia left behind. "I have to watch out for her. She's always been a daddy's girl, whether she'll admit it or not. She's bummed in the biggest way that he took off for Alaska. So I try to be there for her as much as I can," he admits.

"She knows that," I assure him. "But you have to realize she can take care of herself. Meanwhile, your teenage years are passing you by. Shouldn't you be hanging with the guys?

Playing sports? Dating a cheerleader or something? You don't have to be the grownup, Jason."

He's quiet for a minute, and then he bobs his head. "You're right, Kendall."

About which part, I wonder. The dating-the-cheerleader part? *No, no, no . . . focus.*

We're silent for at least a full minute as he listens to the music that Becca's mixing. Something about "taking advantage of a once-in-a-lifetime chance" is playing out. I try not to read too much into the meaning of the lyrics. It's too late, though. I believe I'm falling into a black abyss of crushdom on this guy, although I know he's just making the effort to be nice for his sister's sake.

"Speaking of acting my age," he says, startling me a little bit. "I did a lot of research on ghost hunting last night. I'll admit, it's some really fascinating stuff."

I toss my hair back and concentrate hard, trying to get a read on him to see if I can tune in to his thoughts, like Loreen can do with me—but nothing. He's a steel wall of mental resolve. Guess I'll have to get info from him the old-fashioned way. "*You* were checking out how to ghost hunt. Now why would you want to do that?"

His eyes widen. "It's not to check up on Taylor or anything. It just seems interesting. I had no idea how popular or 'in' it was. There are tons of paranormal groups out there on the Internet that are doing what you're doing."

"Planned on doing," I mutter.

"Past tense?" He scrubs his hand through his blond hair. "Shit, Kendall. I hope my tirade last night didn't have anything to do with it."

I shrug my shoulders. His performance and anger hadn't helped, but it was all my doing. "I knew my mom would be upset if she found out that I was trying to contact spirits. I probably shouldn't have gone into something like that so green, you know? I think getting nauseated to the point where I wanted to puke and then passing out was enough to put the whole ghost-hunting thing over the edge for her."

"So, give your mother some time to settle into the town, and her job, and to make new friends, and then she won't pay so much attention to your activities."

Jason just might have a point there.

Nodding in agreement, I say, "I'd really like to finish what we've started." My family's safety may depend on it. How can I tell my parents about that without them thinking I *do* talk to Satan on a regular basis?

"You'll be hunting again soon, if Taylor has anything to say about it." He snickers a little and then doesn't miss a beat. "You know, in the stuff I was reading on the Internet, I noticed one thing most all of those groups had in common."

"What's that?" I ask.

He tosses the spoon aside, obviously bored with it. I hope he's not bored with me too. "They all have a skeptic on the team to keep things honest."

"Celia's mentioned that."

"Do you have one?"

"One what? A skeptic?"

"Yeah. Someone who can debunk your findings and keep you down-to-earth and realistic."

A laugh bubbles up from my chest. "I suppose you think Taylor can be objective?"

Clearing his throat, Jason says, "No, actually, I thought *I* could do that."

I wasn't expecting that! "You? Are you pulling my leg?"

Jason ducks under the table and then pops back up with a smile. "Nope. Not me."

Oh, that dimple just about does me in. "You think you could work with a psychic?"

"As long as she doesn't go psycho."

We laugh together, and it feels good. Natural. That's when the misty dream or vision or something crosses in front of me in a soft, seductive movie sequence. It's me. And Jason. We're embracing. Not just a hug or holding each other. It's a warm, romantic gesture. My throat is parched, and swallowing right now would take an act of Congress. Sweat covers my skin and I suddenly feel sticky-hot in anticipation of when this vision might come true. Or *if* it'll come true.

"Kendall?" he prods. "Hey, you okay?"

The lunch bell rings and knocks me out of my daze.

"Uh, yeah. Fine. Sorry." I quickly gather my things and start backing away from the hunk and a half of guy who has thrown me off balance. "I'll, um, think about it, Jason. Thanks."

"You do that," he says with a dazzling smile that leaves me breathless.

Like the grounded child that I am, I head straight home from school Monday afternoon as soon as the closing bell rings. Mom said she was going to have a list of chores on the counter for me to "get straight to." Great. She'll probably have me grouting the tile or peeling off that god-awful acorn wallpaper in the downstairs bathroom. Or worse, I'll have to babysit Kaitlin and be tortured with episodes of *Hannah Montana*. No. Thank. You.

As I'm walking up our drive, though, I see not only Mom's Sienna but Dad's Volvo in the driveway. What are both of them doing home from work at three in the afternoon? I snicker at the thought of them having some "afternoon delight," and then my fingers begin to tingle. This signifies anything but good news. Gravel crunches under my feet, sounding more like falling boulders than mere pebbles. My pulse ripples away under my skin. My head aches in a throbbing way over my left eye, and I blink hard at the soreness emanating from my skull.

The pain's not mine. It's someone else's.

I open the back gate, only to be passed by both Buckley and Natalie, meowing and pawing at each other. Buckley runs under the porch in a gray and white blur, but Natalie stops on the path in front of me.

Rarrrrahhh. She rolls over at my feet, purring and rubbing her head in the dirt.

I squat down and scratch her between the ears. "You act like I never give you any attention." Natalie closes her eyes and enjoys the affection. This distracts me from my piercing headache, but only until I notice that Natalie's tail is thumping. Not just the happy thump of a contented kitty. It's rhythmic. It's got motion. It's more like it's pounding out a message I'm supposed to listen to. My instincts perk up.

Thuuuuuump, thump, thump, thump, thuuuuuump, thuuuuuump, thump, thump, thump, thuuuuuump, thump.

Can she really be trying to tell me something, or is she just in kitty ecstasy?

Then she does it again, and I sit down and pay closer attention.

Thuuuuuump, thump, thump, thump, thuuuuuump, thuuuuuump, thump, thump, thump, thuuuuuump, thump.

"What are you saying, Natalie?"

Thuuuuuump, thump, thump, thump, thuuuuuump, thuuuuuump, thump, thump, thump, thuuuuuump, thump.

I pull a pen from my bag and jot the pattern down on the palm of my hand. Looking at what I've drawn, I see a series of long and short marks that remind me of some sort of code. Long, short, short, short, long, long, short, short, short, long, short—like Morse code.

"That's not even possible, though! You're a freakin' cat."

Natalie peers at me through squinted eyes, continuing to

purr without a care in the world. She stretches her mouth in a bored yawn as if to say, *Just keep rubbing me, person.*

I am insane if I think this cat is sending Morse code to me. I've been hanging with Celia the Conspiracy Theorist too long. But Natalie *is* trying to get my attention and tell me something, I just know it. The throbbing in my head continues in a migraine-type way. I know as sure as I'm sitting here that something's not right inside my house. Especially since both of my parents are home. Suddenly, letters appear in a vision that I can't control. Poster boards, like you see cheerleaders hold at a pep rally when they're leading a chant, or in a phonics lesson on *Sesame Street.* The letters are different sizes, shapes, and spacings, but the message is clear.

"D-A-N-G-E-R." I suck in the biggest gasp of air, which nearly gags me. "Holy shit! Dad!"

I pull my hand from Natalie and she quickly scrambles away in the direction Buckley ran. Dad! Something's happened to my father! Has Emily gone and done something to him? Is Natalie warning me? I fly across the porch, through the kitchen, and skid to a stop as I enter the living room. My parents are both sitting there on the Jennifer sectional, zombie-like.

Mom's obviously been crying, but she's also got her first aid kit out, which means something's happened. Dad turns and looks at me. He's scary-pale, and has a nasty-ass deep purple bruise on his head. Mom's applying a compress to his face. When she moves it away, I see dried blood on the side of his cheek. I grab my head and breathe scorching hot air into my lungs.

Holy hell. My vision has come true.

"Did Emily do this to you?" I manage to get out.

"Who?" Mom asks.

I try to tamp down my anger, which is mixed with border-line panic. "The ghost who lives here."

Mom's brows knit together. "Kendall, I won't have you talking like that."

"But Mom!"

Raising his hand to stop us both, Dad says, "Sarah. Please." He turns to me. "No, kiddo. This happened at work. I'd heard there was a ghost in city hall, but I didn't believe it. Didn't believe the stories about my predecessor and how he quit because of . . ." He trails off. He touches his head and winces at the contact. "There's just no other explanation. I was alone. No one was around. I didn't imagine anything. Someone . . . *something* . . . unseen attacked me."

"David, we don't need to encourage her."

"I think that's *exactly* what we need to do."

Mom sniffs back her tears and grips Dad's hand. I notice when she swallows hard, like she's trying to get past all of her beliefs and the way she's bringing me up. Pain and confusion dance in her eyes, speaking volumes to my heart and mind. This is beyond her control. Her reasoning. She doesn't want to okay this. It goes against everything she stands for. Bottom line, though, is Dad's been hurt—like I foresaw—and something has to be done.

"We can't fight it, Sarah. If our daughter can help, we need to let her," Dad says softly.

I blink hard, and I know exactly what Mom's reluctantly thinking.

The parental-imposed grounding is off . . . for now.

The ghost huntress is back in business!

CHAPTER FIFTEEN

"Okay, here's the four-one-one."

I perch on the end of my bed with the notes that I took after I talked to my dad two days ago, after the Incident. Taylor sits at my desk, Celia's sitting cross-legged on the floor, and Becca Asiaf is leaning against my wall, picking at her black nail polish.

An impromptu dowsing session with Grandma Ethel's crystal necklace and Emily the ghost told me that Emily's not at fault for Dad's injury. We're dealing with a whole other ball of paranormal wax. For now, Emily will have to wait.

We have our first official case: File #GH-0001—Radisson City Hall.

"My father's city planner office was completely ransacked on Sunday night. He discovered it when he went to work Monday morning. Aside from pens and papers all over the place, the architectural model of the new city development he's been working on had been cut into a zillion pieces; looked like lawn shears had gone at it."

"That's phenomenal," Celia says with a shine in her eye.

"That's definitely some genuine poltergeist activity. Imagine if we can get that on video."

Becca snickers a little. "So you're saying Edward Scissorhands lives and bullshitted your dad's office?"

"Not exactly." I slip from the bed and sit on the floor opposite Becca. "His office was locked after five p.m. The security guard said no one was in the building after seven. A quick scan of the security cameras didn't show anyone going in or out of the office after Dad."

Taylor taps her pen on her bottom lip and then says, "We should take a look at the security camera to see if we can see anything that others might have missed. Like orbs or anomalies."

"Or ectoplasm," Celia adds.

Becca drops her eyes. "I can listen to the tape too, to see if I can pick up any sounds, you know. Like, isn't that what you want me doing?"

"Absolutely!" I'm stoked. They're into this.

"So what, like, happened exactly to your dad?" Becca asks.

I sigh and my chest hurts from the trapped feelings of guilt and remorse at not having warned him of my visions. Would he have believed me, though? Probably not. "Dad was cleaning up the mess when he said he felt himself being dragged backwards into the hallway. Like someone had him by the collar. Then he was shoved down the stairs."

Taylor gasps in horror, her hand to her mouth, even though this is the third time she's heard this story.

"Heavy shit," Becca says.

"No kidding," I say firmly, trying to hide my fear over the entire sitch.

"Fortunately, Mr. Moorehead was able to grab the banister and didn't fall all the way down the stairs. He wasn't hurt too badly," Celia adds.

I glower. "If you consider a mild concussion and a bloody cheek as not hurt too badly."

Celia looks over at me. "Sorry. Just that it could have been worse."

"You're right, Celia. I know what you meant. He is lucky. It could have been a hell of a lot worse if he'd busted his skull on the marble."

Taylor scribbles in her notebook. "Fascinating. Just fascinating. Oh! Not the part about your father's skull busting. Just that I'd love to get a couple of cameras set up in there on timers so we can get some still images and see what we're up against."

Celia turns to Becca. "I've got the recorders for you and I'll install the sound software on your computer."

"Cool."

Then Celia says to me, "Can you get in there to dowse, Kendall?"

"I'd like to," I say.

Stretching her long legs out, Celia adjusts her seated position and says, "I did some quick research on the city hall building. It dates back to the early 1800s and was a flourishing center of the town during and after the Civil War. Apparently, there were a lot of trials following the war that centered on local landowners."

"Fighting carpetbaggers and stuff?" Taylor asks.

"Probably so. Maybe other things," Celia explains. "We'll check it out further with some more research. Main thing is for all of us to be on the same page before going to the site. Becca, you're in charge of all the sound recordings. Taylor, pictures, pictures, pictures. Video, mini-DVD, you name it. I'll set up the base camp with the computers and monitoring for the infrared cameras—"

I straighten up. "You got them?"

"Six of them," Celia says with a smile.

I tilt a brow upward.

"What can I say?" she says with a laugh. "I knew your parents would eventually come around and we could do this for real. Had them FedExed a couple of days ago."

I reach over and high-five her. "You're the best!"

Looking around at the ragtag group of girls gathered in my bedroom, I can't help but be excited. We'll bring this ghost to justice. It'll regret the day it ever messed with my dad.

"Okay, ghost huntresses. Let's go kick some major spirit ass at city hall!"

Five o'clock in city hall, and the official business is done for the day. Our work has just begun.

We've got three hours to set up and "go dark," as Celia's

heroes the *Ghost Hunters* say. Since it's Wednesday and a school night, we won't stay while our recordings are going on. We'll just set up, make sure everything's working, and then head home to let the spirits frolic as they may. Then we'll come back Friday night and get serious about having fun. That's the time we'll dig in and I'll try my hand at a psychic connection with whoever—or whatever—this entity is. It'll also give us time to do more research.

Celia and Becca have set up a card table at the base of the grand marble staircase that sits in the middle of city hall and leads to the second-floor offices where Dad works.

Taylor starts to spray some Oust to cover up the mustiness of the over-two-hundred-year-old building, but I stop her. Smells—no matter how sneeze-worthy they may be—are essential in the hunting as well. The clear windows let in the last remnants of the afternoon sun, casting an orange glow on Celia's monitors and Becca's recording equipment.

A tickle skulks up my back, making the hair at my neck stand at military attention. My heartbeat picks up and I sense someone is coming. Not a spirit, though. Human.

I spin around, hoping that Loreen has come to watch our first ghost-hunting expedition. However, I nearly pant when I see those blue eyes I'm obsessed with.

"Hey," Jason says, a bit out of breath.

"Hey," I mimic. "What are you doing here?"

"Taylor told me what was going on, so I skipped out of track practice to help out."

And apparently ran all the way from RHS.

He shifts his weight from one foot to the other, as if he's unsure what to say to me next. Honestly, am I *that* scary? No! At least, I hope not. After all, he's just doing this to keep an eye on his sister. Still, a niggling deep down in my stomach tells me he's watching me as well. He's so close. My senses are piqued, and my insides are like a bowl of mashed potatoes. Not such a good simile, but I feel squishy, warm, and comforted. I'm too attached to Jason Tillson. How will I be able to really sense what's going on here at city hall if his gorgeousness is distracting me from properly ghost hunting?

"So, use me," he says with a roguish smile.

My mouth falls open. "Huh?"

"You know. To help."

Get a grip, Kendall. "Oh. Well. I hadn't exactly decided whether we needed a skeptic or not on the team," I manage to choke out.

He smiles. "I figured I'd make up your mind for you by showing up."

"Jason, I appreciate—"

"Besides, I can lend a hand with heavy lifting or whatever you need. You know, guy stuff." His eyes nearly sparkle in the twilight of the room. "Come on, Kendall. Let me."

Becca snaps her gum. "Might as well, Kendall. If this friggin' spirit pushed your dad down the stairs—and he's a fair-sized dude—we may need some muscle around here to ward off any evil."

Jason reaches out and fist-bumps Becca.

Knowing I'm going to regret this—and hoping it doesn't hamper our investigation—I give in. "All right. Come with me."

Celia doesn't exactly look thrilled, but she remains silent.

Jason and I leave them to finish setting up base camp. Together, we climb the monstrous marble staircase. I firmly grip the railing, never knowing when the spirit—or spirits— might lash out again. Don't want to go flying ass over tits with a cute boy around.

"Where are we going?" Jason asks, keeping pace with me.

"Up to Dad's office."

"To do what?"

"Observe. Listen. Investigate. You know, 'cause we're ghost hunters?"

"Listen to what?"

I flinch. "Too many questions, Jason."

He nods and steps a pace behind me. "Right. Sorry."

At the landing, Taylor is setting up one of the infrared cameras in a corner, pointed just right to get a shot of the top of the staircase. She stands and brushes her hands together. "There! All set. Now if that mean old ghost tries to push anyone else down the steps, we'll get it on tape."

"You're really into this, aren't you?" Jason says to his sister.

Taylor beams a brilliant smile at him. "You're darn tootin'!" Then she runs off down the hallway to the room where the security tapes are kept.

"Darn tootin'?" I ask, with a quirked grin.

His eyes squeeze shut and he sighs. "She's adopted, from another planet, anything but my twin . . . I don't know," he jokes.

"I think she's adorable."

Jason stares at my mouth for what seems like an hour and I almost hear his words in my head. *You're adorable.* A blush paints me from head to toe, and I step away to break our moment. "Well. Okay, then. Let me fill you in on everything that's going on." I point down the hallway. "Taylor's setting up cameras in Dad's office, as well as the hallway and the top of the steps. She's also got two tripodded cameras on timers to take still photos throughout the night. Celia's software not only tracks but records temperature changes, so we can analyze it later. Rebecca's been bugging the joint with microphones so we can pick up any EVPs tonight. Those are—"

"Electronic voice phenomena. I know. I've been reading up on this stuff."

"Oh. Okay." Wow, he really is serious about helping us now. Maybe my "quit acting like an adult" speech had a more positive effect on him than I originally thought. I certainly don't mind watching his broad shoulders as he walks in front of me down the hallway. Or his cute butt that fits nicely into those Levi's 501s. Man, I have *got* to stop ogling him and worry about this asshole ghost who's after my dad. Or is it that the spirit is specifically targeting the city planner? Hmmm.

As I'm mulling this over, Jason knocks me out of my thoughts. "What's Celia doing?"

"She's manning all of the computer equipment at base camp. She's also responsible for all these tech toys, courtesy of Mega-Mart. Thanks to her AmEx, we've got temperature gauges, flashlights, cameras, wiring, computers, you name it."

Jason spreads his arms wide. "This is amazing. I had no idea."

I smile and wink. "You ain't seen nothin' yet."

Oh my God! Did I just flirt? I did, didn't I? I overtly flirted. *Down, girl!*

"I, umm, uhh, want to check out my dad's office. You know, to debunk whether anyone could get in at all." I hand him the small meter that I'd picked up from Celia's base-camp table. "You want to, like, take temperature readings?"

"Sure."

Our hands touch innocently enough as I pass the meter to him, sparking that tingly sensation from the tips of my fingers to the ends of my hair. This isn't like my psychic tingling awareness. This is all about him.

"Why do you take temperature readings?"

"If the temperature drops dramatically," I explain, echoing what I've learned from Celia and the Internet, "it's a sign that a spirit could be present."

"If you believe in that stuff."

I look him square in the eyes. "I have to, Jason."

"Or else what?"

"Or else I'm just a crazy lunatic who sees and talks to people who aren't really there."

He hangs his head a little. "I guess I understand where you're coming from."

This is my job now. My mission. To right the wrong done to Dad. And to get this spirit to move on . . . if I can do that.

Entering Dad's office, I take a few deep breaths and then try to center my energies. Last night, Loreen called Celia, who then three-wayed us together (so my mom wouldn't know I was talking to Loreen). Loreen told me I have to tune in to everything my body is trying to say because the slightest itch, twitch, or even indigestion could be a sign of something. One breath. Two. Third one. Hmmm . . . Jason's wearing some amazing spicy cologne.

Stop it!

Focus. Focus. Concentrate.

The noxious stench of paint fumes is up front and present in my mind. Ahhh . . . the clairalience ability Loreen was telling me about. Guess I have that, too. "The windows in this office are painted shut. They have been since the seventies," I say, very sure of myself.

Jason goes over to the sill next to Dad's desk, and there's no way in hell that even his athletic bulk could open the frame. "Yep. That's pretty stuck. How'd you know that?"

I shrug. "That's how it is. I just *know* things." I keep looking around. "So, no one could have come in that way." Eyes closed, I face the door. "The office was locked. Everyone was gone. Yet the model of the development, which was over on the table, was completely destroyed."

Quietly, Jason stands by my side while I mull this over. Then he nudges me.

"Am I supposed to tell you when the temperature drops?"

"Sure," I say.

He shows me the reading. "It just went from sixty-eight degrees to forty-two."

"What?"

He shakes the monitor. "It must be broken."

Spoken like a true skeptic. "It's brand new."

"Then how'd you do that?"

"*I* didn't."

I crouch down and fan my fingers out in front of me. Sure enough, the air feels like a gust from an air conditioner. I can almost see its path sweeping out the door. Is this the entity? Or simply some peculiar HVAC problem in this old building? Pulling Jason by the arm, I instinctively follow the trajectory of the breeze. "This way."

Twenty or so steps down the hallway and I'm back to the staircase. "Dad was standing right about here when he got manhandled."

"Don't worry, Kendall," Jason says. "I won't let anything hurt you."

Oh, there's that delicious ache in the bottom of my stomach. Just like when I would ride the Ferris wheel at Navy Pier back home. That unbelievably scary-yet-thrilling *wheeeeeeeeee!*

Of course, just as I relax and take my concentration away from the ghost hunting at hand to bask in Jason's words, something happens. Rather, something knocks into me, hard. Before I know what's happening, my feet are lifted right out from under me and I'm teetering toward the edge of the top step. I open my mouth to scream, but it's like someone's gripping my throat. I hear laughter. And I see my own demise as I begin to plummet down the marble flight.

That is, until Jason's strong arm reaches out and grabs me in the nick of time. He jerks me into his chest and we both collapse backwards onto the floor. *Bam!*

There's nothing in my lungs, and I struggle to get a mouthful of air. "I-I-I can't . . . can't . . ."

"Shhh," Jason says.

Although he's holding me steady, I realize that I've had the wind knocked out of me. It happened once at vacation Bible school when we were playing red rover and I got clotheslined in the throat when Nancy Pulkki forgot to let go of Aaron Murray's hand. Only this is nothing like that. I'm not a little kid anymore and I'm up against something much more ferocious than Nancy's and Aaron's joined hands.

"Just breathe, Kendall. I've got you."

His voice is so soothing. So calming. So reassuring.

Then it hits me painfully in the face. I'm in Jason's arms. Not like that time in the cafeteria; more like what happens in my dream. I quiver in his grip. "Holy crap!"

"What? Are you all right?"

I'm anything *but* all right. I'm half sitting in Jason's lap and I can feel his body heat radiating out at me. I sense his pulse picking up to join the rhythm of mine, and his eyes search my face. His hand moves to cup my face, and I know exactly what he's about to do.

Because it's exactly what I dreamed he would do. And what I truly want him to do.

Jason leans over and kisses me. His lips are cool at first, tentative, as he moves in. He's waiting for my reaction—or participation. Without thinking twice about it, I tilt my head slightly to the right and part my lips. He takes that as a green flag and pulls me closer. Mother of pearl . . . that's *niiiiiiiiiiiiiice*.

I'm not a pro in the art of kissing, but I've watched enough movies and read enough books that I'm able to fully kiss him back. There's lots of heavy breathing and shifting and hands in hair and stuff. We're totally making out on the stairs, like we have no care in the world.

He moans. Or I do. Who can even tell at this point? We bump noses and scrape teeth, but it doesn't stop us from continuing our snog-fest at the top of the stairs.

What does stop us is the staticky click and beep of the walkie-talkie clipped to my jeans.

"Y'all about finished up there? Over," Celia says over the airwaves.

We freeze midkiss.

My heart starts beating again when I hear Taylor say, "I'm done. Over."

I push Jason away like he's got the plague. "Taylor's coming."

He looks as wild-eyed and dumbfounded as I feel. There's no hesitation on either of our parts as we scramble to our feet and step far away from each other. Neither of us wants to get caught by Celia, Becca, or especially Taylor.

I try to get my composure—*how?*—and head down the stairs with Jason on my tail. Two steps down, I stop and turn to meet his gaze. "Thanks for catching me just then."

I don't want this thing—*whatever it is*—between Jason and me to get in the way of our ghost hunting. I think I'll keep this turn of events all to myself for now.

He winks those beautiful gold eyelashes at me and says, "Anytime."

Oh, man. This. Is. Not. Good. Not good at all.

Chapter Sixteen

I CHECK MY WATCH as I leave the house. The homeroom bell at RHS won't ring for another twenty-five minutes, so I've got time for my stealth reconnaissance side trip this Thursday morning.

I need protection and I can only think of one place to get it.

No, I'm not going to the sexual-health aisle at Mega-Mart to purchase family-planning products just because Jason and I kissed. Get real! (Although I have hit Rewind and Play like ten zillion times in my head to relive the moment.)

Currently, I'm in need of something from a higher calling.

Twice now I've been around spirits where something not good—to say the least—has happened to me. First in the cemetery, when I nearly passed out from the overwhelmed-ness (I think I just made that word up, but it works here), and then yesterday, when I was nearly killed on the stairs at city hall. Loreen told me never to go into a ghost hunt without protection: a prayer, a cross, or whatever works for me. I should've listened to her.

So, now I'm after holy water.

I turn down Pace Street and then cross over to Market to the large building with the lush green lawn. I slip up the front steps and through the brick portico. I push the sturdy red door open slowly, making it groan on its hinges. My used but thoroughly sterilized Clinique Happy perfume bottle is in my backpack and should make a good receptacle for splashing myself with the blessed liquid. I just need to get a stash of it that I can funnel into the small container.

I move through the vestibule of Christ the Redeemer Holy Episcopal Church, wondering if it's a mortal sin to swipe holy water from a baptismal font. I certainly hope not, and God forgive me if it is.

Once inside the sanctuary, I take a moment to soak up the majesty of such a breathtaking cathedral in the middle of Nowhere, Georgia. The ivory marble floor is smooth and immaculately clean against the redwood pews, which have crimson velvet kneeling benches between each set. Up front is the altar, five steps up, decorated with a large gold cross, white tapers, and mossy green ferns. Pipes and chimes from the organ fill the back wall in shimmery brass. The Gothic ceiling forms a ship's-hull-like pattern, culminating at the front of the church with a fantastic stained-glass window of Jesus and his disciples.

Not thinking of how I'm disturbing the serenity of the quiet morning, I slip over to the baptismal font that sits at the back of the sanctuary. It's an oval marble stand about three feet high, with a wood finishing around the rim that coordinates with the benches. I lift the lid of the fountain and smile when I see the clear water filling the bowl.

I pull the Ziploc bag out of my pocket and I'm just about to dunk it in the depths when I hear, "I'm afraid you're a little late for Wednesday night's Eucharist."

I spin around and squelch the words *Holy shit!* that threaten to tumble off the tip of my tongue. "Oh! I'm sorry." My eyes connect with the crisp white liturgical collar. "I mean, sorry, Father." I feel like I should curtsy or something, although no Episcopal church would ever require such action.

"No worries," he says with a kind smile. Then his eyebrow lifts. "May I help you with something this morning?"

Man, am I busted or what? And by the priest, no less! At least, I think the guy's a priest. He's tall, dark, cute, and waaaaay young. Maybe in his midtwenties. He must be straight out of seminary.

"I just . . . needed some holy water," I say plainly, not wanting to lie in church. "I hope that's okay."

"Of course it is. Whatever you need." He spreads his arms wide. "That's what we're here for."

"Thanks." I dip the bag in, then seal the sloshing-full Ziploc. I'll worry about transferring the water to the perfume bottle later.

He stretches his large hand out toward me. "I'm Massimo. Father Castellano."

I look at it, unsure what to do. What is wrong with me? I'm just not used to my priest being damn near a contemporary. I'm used to way-past-middle-aged Father Ludwig and his ten-yard comb-over that swirls around his head in a crop-circle effect, which you get a good gander at as he's bending down to hand out Communion wafers. This guy before me has short black hair, a firm jaw, and a bright white smile that could adorn the cover of any men's-fashion magazine.

"Please don't take this wrong, but you're not old enough to be a priest, are you?"

His laughter reverberates up to the beams of the church. "You flatter me. Let me assure you that I earned my degree many years ago, and Radisson is my third parish. I'm thirty-three."

Red tinges my face, and I feel like a total goober. "I'm sorry, Father. Geez. I mean . . ."

Shut up, Kendall.

He smiles again. This time with his eyes, like Tyra Banks is always telling the girls to do on *America's Next Top Model.* "You must be new to Radisson."

"I am," I say, fingering the Ziploc full of *agua.* "My family moved here a couple of weeks ago. We're still getting settled in, but we'll start coming to Holy Eucharist, I promise."

Father Castellano nods and then squints at me in recognition. "Oh. *You* must be Kendall Moorehead, then."

Hand to my chest, I ask, "You know me?"

"I know *of* you," he says. "Father Burt Ludwig from Chicago called me about your family." Following an elongated pause, he adds, "However, your mother called me about you."

There are absolutely no secrets in this town. What happens in Radisson is shared with Radisson.

"Great," I mutter. "Look, I don't know what she told you about me dabbling—"

The priest holds up a hand to stop my defense. "I'm not here to judge you, Kendall. I'm here to help. In any way. Please know that."

I scrunch my brows down in a "what 'choo talkin' 'bout, Willis" way—*What? I've seen reruns on TV Land*—and try to figure out Father Castellano's game plan. "You're not going to tell me that talking to spirits is evil, satanic, or demonic?"

"Are you talking to demonic spirits?"

"Not so far." Unless you count ghosts that lash out at people. "You can't be too careful, though." I hold up the little bag to show him. "That's why I need the holy water, so I can protect myself when dealing with the spirit dimension."

He steps forward. "Whatever strengthens your faith and trust in God."

Any minute now, the other shoe will drop. He'll tell me what a bad idea this ghost hunting is. How my abilities are a sin. That I should be spending my spare time at the church praying for my mortal soul or working with the Episcopal Communicators network—they're a group that focuses on helping young people deal with the stresses of just being a teen. *Oh, honey, how much time do you have for me?*

Surprise follows when he says, "I think it's wonderful that you and your friends are trying to help those who may need assistance crossing over to their final resting place with our Lord."

"You do? Y-y-you don't think we're crazy?"

"No. And in fact, that's what I told your mother when she came to see me. I told her that God has called you for a specific purpose and no one should stand in your way until His plan for you is revealed."

Whoa.

I swallow the ginormous lump in my throat. "I've never thought of it that way." I jump slightly when the church bells ring, signifying fifteen minutes until the hour. "Excuse me, Father Castellano, but I've got to get to school."

As I move to walk off, he places both hands on my shoulders to stop me, and then looks down into my eyes. "Just a moment, Kendall." He takes one hand from me to open the Ziploc. Dunking his thumb into the water, he then draws it across my forehead, making the sign of the cross.

"The Lord bless you and keep you—the Lord make His face shine upon you, and be gracious unto you; the Lord lift up His countenance upon you, and give you peace. Amen."

"Amen," I say. "Thank you, Father."

"I'm here anytime you need anything, Kendall."

I smile and wave. "I may take you up on that!" Then I bolt for school.

———

Where r u? JT

My heartbeat races like a tiny raft scuttling through white-water rapids as I look at the text message on my cell. *JT.* Jason. He's looking for me!

@ study hall

I click Send and squish the desire to giggle like Kaitlin watching old Olsen twins DVDs. I can't believe I made out with Jason like that. I mean, honestly! I can't believe he likes me. He does, doesn't he? Why else would he have kissed me like that? Especially after the rough start we had. It's hard enough being in a new town, trying to keep up with school-work, and on top of that, learning that I've been a dormant psychic who's now awakening to her abilities and hunting ghosts. And now I may have a boyfriend?

Ooo, another message from him.

Library? JT

Yep!

B there in a sec. JT

Becca Asiaf drops her heavily braceleted arm to the table. "Enough with the tap-tap-tap, beep-beep-beep, would you? I think I've found something major."

We're using our study-hall time to dig through old news-papers and scan microfiche to research city hall and what might be haunting it. Becca shoves a recent *Radisson Gazette* across the table to me and points. I stash my phone in my backpack and reach for the newspaper. "What am I looking at?"

Becca sighs. "It's an article about that development your dad's working on. The model that was destroyed at city hall, wasn't that about the new distribution center for Mega-Mart?"

I scrutinize the article a little more, scan-reading. "Oh, yeah. It's this massive two hundred fifty-seven acres on the outskirts of town where they're putting in the distribution center that'll cover a huge portion of the Southern chain stores for Mega-Mart. I heard Dad and Mr. Nichols talking about it in the backyard the other night."

Becca points at the paper. "It's a pretty aggressive project. They're adding affordable housing and a new elementary school to try and attract people to the Radisson area."

I keep reading. According to the reporter, the land originally belonged to a Mr. Charles Stogdon, who moved to Radisson from Buncombe County, North Carolina, in 1836. "Holy crap, 1836! That's a hell of a long time ago."

"Good, you got to that part. Keep reading."

My eyes dart right and left, taking in all of the words and loading them into my memory bank. Charles Stogdon was quite wealthy prior to the Civil War, and this land was part and parcel of a good chunk of the county that he owned. Somehow, the property came to be under the purview of the City of Radisson. Nothing's been done with the land—other than occasionally baling hay for local farmers—until this Mega-Mart venture.

The hairs on my arm stand at attention, alerting me to my psychic sense picking up on—*something*. In my mind's eye, I picture a stodgy older man with a handlebar mustache, a dark hat, and a dark coat. He appears to be irritated about something, raising his fist high. I blink at the vision, and just like that, it's gone. Gone, but not forgotten.

"I think we should look into this more. I mean, there's a connection to this project. Something tells me we'll find more of a link to this Charles Stogdon guy," I say.

"You're reading my thoughts exactly, Moorehead," Becca says. "Then again, you are psychic."

"Or so she says," I hear Jason say from behind me. This time, he punctuates it with a soft laugh and not his usual judgmental derision.

"Hey," I say a bit too breathily. This causes Becca to roll her eyes.

"What'chall doin'?" he asks, taking the seat next to me. He sits with his legs spread wide, so like a guy to take up as much space as he can, and the knee of his khakis touches mine. The sensation is almost more than I can stand.

While I attempt to wrestle my rampant teenage hormones, Becca fills him in on our latest discovery. I can barely pay attention. Even though Jason is supposedly listening to all that Becca's telling him, underneath the table, his fingers weave into mine and his thumb strokes the space between my thumb and forefinger—wreaking complete and total havoc on my central nervous system.

I don't move. I just surreptitiously hold his hand beneath the table as Becca finishes up the story of Charles Stogdon.

She points at both of us. "I think you're right, Kendall. This Stogdon dude has something to do with all of this."

Jason turns his head and shoots a grin my way. "We headed to city hall after school?"

"You bet. We'll get the evidence and then go over to Celia's to review it."

We. Yeah, I guess he's a part of this now.

"Anything?" I ask Celia impatiently.

She's seated at her desk, staring at the large computer monitor with four different camera angles displayed. Right after school she and Taylor retrieved the tapes from last night, and now we're all sitting around reviewing the evidence. Celia gnaws on a Twizzler and tugs the headphones off with one hand. "I told you, it takes time. Ghosts don't just perform on command."

"I know. Sorry," I say. "I'm just anxious."

Celia pats my leg. "'How poor are they that have not patience!'"

"Thanks, Iago," I say with a smirk. "Make a short shrift, would you?"

Celia threads her fingers through her hair. "Ah, but see, you've moved from *Othello* to *Richard III* and the transition isn't as you'd hoped. *Short shrift* is a confusing expression. Most people think it means 'quick work,' but in some reference sources, it means 'inadequate time.' Did you know that *shrift* really means 'confession'—like a priest shrives a person by taking confession and then giving them penance, like a Hail Mary or what have you? So, to literally 'make a short shrift,' you're making a confession."

Taylor, Becca, and I scream out in unison, "Celia!"

"Okay, okay. Geez. See if I try to educate you in the fine art of Shakespeare literature anymore." She takes another chaw off the Twizzler and then points at the screen in the upper left-hand corner. "I've seen a lot of orb activity and I'm noting the time on the footage. That tells me if there's something there, we're picking up its movement on the infrared cameras."

"Excellent!" I look over to where Taylor's slide-showing through the digital images she took. "Anything from you?"

"Some amazing digital photography, if I do say so myself," she says with complete confidence. She tosses her honey blond hair over her shoulder and purses her glossed lips. "Nothing substantial yet, but I still have a long way to go."

My eyes shift over to where Jason's listening in with Becca as she sorts through the sound recordings we made throughout the night. He winks privately at me, and my skin warms. I'm frustrated because all I can do is . . . watch. There's nothing for me to do at this point because everything is about the evidence we gathered. There are no assumptions or psychic feelings for me to conjure up that could help at this moment. I just have to wait until we can interpret the information that will help us once we go in for the full investigation on Friday night.

Becca pulls her earbuds out. "I have an EVP for you to listen to."

I stand over her as she cues up the .wav file. *"Oooooooffffffff muuuuuuuh lllllahhhnnn."*

Jason snickers. "You gotta be kidding me. That's nothing but a garbled mess."

"Shhhh!" Becca snaps.

"Play it again," Celia instructs.

"Oooooooffffffffff muuuuuuuh lllllahhhhhnnn."

Celia concentrates hard. "Can you slow it down, Becca?"

"Sure." Becca types in some strokes, ups the amplification, and plays it again.

"Oooooooffffffffff muuuuuuuh lllllahhhhhnnn."

I stare at Celia as she deliberates the syllables. "Well?"

She looks to Becca. "Are you hearing what I'm hearing? 'Off my land.'"

Becca claps her hands together. "Snap! Exactly what I thought."

"Off my land?" Jason asks. "What does it mean?"

Easy, I think. "There's a disembodied voice in city hall that wants someone off its land."

"Whooo-hoooo!" Taylor shouts, raising her fist up to the ceiling. "Damn, I'm good. I mean, really. I. Am. Good. Wait till y'all see what I got."

We all gather around her, shouldering one another to get a look at the laptop screen.

"What are we seeing?" Celia asks.

Taylor shows us an image of the courtroom that's on the

first floor in city hall. The yellowy paint of the room seems darker in the IR pictures. Two large tables with chairs are before the judge's bench. "I set the timer to record every ten seconds throughout the night. Mostly it's a bunch of nothing, until—"

She clicks on a frame that reads out "01:18:30 a.m." that shows the same empty courtroom.

"Now watch," she says. She taps the mouse on the arrow to go to the next photo, which reads "01:18:40 a.m." Ten seconds later. We all gasp in unison.

"Toldja. I'm good, aren't I?" she says with a bright smile.

Becca leans in more and bites her lip where her piercing is. "What the hell is that?"

"No way." Jason tilts his head. "It looks like a man."

"Phenomenal," Celia says and claps her hands.

"It can't be a man," Becca says. "What's that?" She points at what looks like a long suit coat.

"His clothes?" I ask.

"Wait," Taylor says. "It gets better." The next frame is "01:18:50 a.m." and what do you know: he's gone!

"It's trick photography," Jason says with a sneer.

Taylor reaches over and punches him hard on the top of his arm. "Right. Because I was sitting in city hall by *myself* at one-flippin'-o'clock in the morning dressed in a costume and messing with my own camera!"

Jason blocks her next blow. "I'm just saying—"

Taylor throws her hands up. "God, Jason!"

"You can't tell me that's not some sort of reflection or malfunction of the camera. That is the digital one Dad got you for Christmas two years ago, and it was cheap to begin with, so it probably has a scratch on the inside or something that caused that image."

"A scratch that looks like a man?" I interject.

"Ten seconds between frames is nothing. Anyone can run across the courtroom in under ten seconds," our skeptic continues.

Celia frowns. "You can be sure we'll test it to see if that's possible."

"It has to be," he says.

"Shuffle through those again," Celia instructs. When Taylor does, we all stare at the images. One minute the man's not there, the next he is, and then he's gone again.

"What are you thinking?" I ask Celia.

"That we need to try and debunk that tomorrow night when we're doing our investigation," I say. "We need to see if a person can cross the room in ten seconds, in order to determine whether someone was doing that to throw us off. If it can't be done, then we've definitely got proof of a full-body apparition."

"That's horseshit," Jason says with a snort.

Becca speaks up. "Could this be that Charles Stogdon guy we were reading about today?"

Celia squints. "Who?"

"Oh, right," I say, and then fill her in. Then I remember the image of the man I'd seen in my thoughts during study hall. That picture sort of, kind of looks the same.

Taylor enhances the picture to 200 percent to get a better look at our figure. "It looks like he's wearing a suit and has his fist raised."

"Nice 'stache," Jason says.

"Facial hair was very popular back then," Celia says in defense of our ghost.

"Back when?"

"He looks pissed," Becca notes, completely ignoring Jason's comment.

Right. I, too, bite my lip. "I wonder if this is who attacked my father."

Jason sits back and lets out a long sigh. "Okay, if you're gonna buy into this imaginary man, then I wonder if it's who attacked *you*."

Celia's eyes enlarge. "*What?* When? What happened?"

"Why didn't you tell us?" Taylor scowls.

Becca doesn't seem bothered that I covered this up.

I fill them in on how I almost took a header down the marble stairs but Jason had caught me.

"Thank God for that," Taylor says, her hand to her heart. "Oh! Celia, rewind all the way back to the beginning of camera three. That's the top of the stairs and it may have captured Kendall when this happened."

As I peer over Celia's shoulder, I realize that Taylor's video recording may have captured more than just my falling down. It may have documented the kiss. Cripes!

"There." Taylor points. "That's right after I set up the camera."

I watch as Jason and I climb the stairs together, stop, and then head off down the hallway. After a short while, we come back into view. "This was when Jason's temperature gauge registered a low reading and I was following this cool breeze down the hallway."

The video shows me padding along the hall and stopping at the top of the banister.

"Look!" Celia says. "On the back of your leg."

Sure enough, there's a large, dense orb trailing down my jeans. Then, without any warning, my feet are literally swept out from under me and I start to fall.

"Holy shit, Kendall!" Celia says. "There was something on you! Something did that to you."

"I *know!*" I say.

"Play it again," Taylor says. "See if you can zoom in on the orb."

Celia does, and the round white spherical figure seems to have a depth or bulkiness to it.

Jason leans his hand onto the desk and I see Celia taking note of his proximity. I hope she's not mad at me that I've let him join our group. I couldn't really stop him. And I didn't want to. She looks up at him as he asks, "Aren't orbs supposed to be dust or bugs?"

"Do you recall any giant moths or anything swooping around when we were walking down the hall?" I ask a bit snarkily.

"No. You're right. But still. That couldn't have just upended you like that. Maybe you tripped."

"The video doesn't show her tripping," Celia says.

I place my hands on my hips. "You were right there with me, Jason."

"I know. I can't believe that a globe of light did that. It makes no sense, and quite frankly, it seems asinine to even suggest it was responsible."

"So you're an expert now?" I ask.

"No, I'm just saying—"

Because we're arguing over what had or hadn't happened there at the top of the stairs, we fail to stop the videotape. I don't even think about it until I hear Celia nearly shriek.

I spin around. "What is it now?"

She points to the screen and her mouth falls open. Taylor's blue eyes dilate, and Becca just laughs. For on the screen is the very vivid image of Jason and me completely macking on each other.

I wince. "Oh, shit."

Chapter Seventeen

"THAT'S *HOT*," REBECCA SAYS, gazing at the tape of the kiss.

Celia seems like she's going to cry. "How could you?" Utter disappointment is painted in hi-def colors across her face. Or maybe I've just learned to read auras all of a sudden. Suffice it to say, she's *not* happy with me. "I thought you were serious about this, Kendall."

"I am!"

She points at the screen where Jason and I are now kissing on a loop. "Yeah, right. You can't be serious about your gifts and using them to ghost hunt if you're making out with a member of the team."

Jason stands to defend me. At least, I hope that's what he's doing. "Look, it just sort of happened, okay? You know how it goes."

Fixing her glare on him, Celia says, "No, *I* don't!"

Taylor's usually sunny disposition morphs into downright disgust. "You're just a big fake, Kendall Moorehead. You drummed all of this up to be friends with me so you could get at my brother." She lasers her eyes at Jason. "Ever since you and Courtney Langdon broke up, girls at school want to be buddy-buddy with me to get an in with you. Well, I'm not going to be a part of this anymore."

I'm confused beyond reason. "What? Taylor, you're out of your mind."

She gathers up her laptop and camera bag, slamming and jerking things around. "No, honey. *You're* out of your mind if you think I'm going to spend one more minute of my time on this tomfoolery you've cooked up. Psychic? Yeah, right. I bet your dad didn't even get attacked. You probably destroyed that model yourself." She harrumphs and storms out of Celia's room.

"That's not how it is at all!" I say in her wake. Turning to Jason, I say, "Is she frickin' kidding me?"

He starts after her. "Taylor, wait!"

"Piss off, Jason!" she screams out, halting him midstride in the doorway.

I sit on Celia's bed with my head in my hands. How could this have gone so wrong so fast? Peeking through my fingers, I see that Celia won't even look at me. She thinks I only did this to get a guy. No! Not at all. I can read her thoughts easily. *You used me* and *You betrayed me* ring out so clearly that I'm surprised that Becca and Jason can't pick up on this too.

Speaking of Becca, she winks at me and then gathers her things. "Well, I guess that's that, huh? It was real. And it was fun. But it wasn't real fun." As she walks past me, she pats me on the shoulder and whispers, "Don't sweat it, K."

After she leaves the room, the silence is so palpable and electric, it would make our EMF meters blaze off the charts.

Celia stares ahead at her computer screen. "I'd really like it if you both left now."

"Celia . . ."

"Now, please." The emphasis in her tone leaves nothing to discuss.

Even Seamus growls at me—and drools a little—from his L. L. Bean monogrammed cushion next to Celia's desk. Okay, Nichols family. I get the message.

"Come on, Kendall." Jason grabs his jacket and then steers me by the elbow out of Celia's room and down the stairs. Outside, I stand stupefied over what just happened. Taylor's nowhere to be seen and Becca's on her way down the street. I wonder if Celia will ever speak to me again. And why was kissing Jason a betrayal of *her?* You'd think a psychic could read between the lines, but I'm at a loss.

"Can I drive you home?" Jason asks.

I point across the street. "I live right there."

"Hop in," he says. "We'll drive around and get some air, then I'll drop you off."

Defeated, I scuff my sneakers on the gravel path that leads to the Nicholses' driveway and Jason's Jeep. "Might as well. You can't hunt ghosts without ghost hunters."

School totally sucked major ass today. Celia avoided me like the clichéd plague, and Taylor opted to not even come in at

all. Jason texted me and said she was having "female problems." Yeah, I'm the female and, apparently, the problem.

At least *he's* still talking to (or texting) me.

Having nothing better to do on a Friday afternoon—and
trying to not technically buck Mom's "don't go see Loreen"
edict—I slip over to Central Perk and order a chai latte. I
sweet-talked Kim, the daughter of the owner, Ruthanne, into
going down to Divining Woman with a note for Loreen to
come meet me here. If she seeks me out, then in theory, I'm
not being disobedient. Ten minutes later, my psychic friend
walks in with a worried look on her face.

She peels off a black sweater to reveal a blue and white T-
shirt that reads "Don't Squeeze the Shaman." I almost snort
chai latte out of my nose. It's the best feeling I've had all day.

"Loreen, *where* do you get these T-shirts of yours?"

She waves her hand about like she's swatting a fly. "Oh, you
know. Here and there."

"Nowhere I've been," I say with a laugh when all I really
want to do is cry.

Reaching across the small café table, Loreen takes my hand,
turns it over, and looks at my palm. She trails her short fingernail across one of the lines and frowns. It totally tickles, so I
pull my hand away and scratch it against my jeans.

"What's troubling you, Kendall? Something's not right."

I sip my chai. "You could put it that way."

Loreen places her hair behind her ears and squeezes her eyes
shut. "I could put it several ways, considering all the chattering

I'm hearing from you. So many thoughts and images. La-la-la-la . . . I don't want to hear," she sings out.

I swat at her. "Okay, okay, everything sucks. That about sums it up."

Ruthanne places a cup of hot black coffee in front of Loreen and winks at us. Without adding sugar or cream, Loreen scoops up the steaming cup and takes a hearty gulp. "Talk."

My eyes follow the motion of the coffee cup. "That is gross. How can you do that? Nas-tay."

Loreen snaps at me. "Kendall. Ignore the coffee. Focus. The 'everything sucks' part."

So, over our respective beverages, I tell her how everything has completely pooped the bed, from what happened at city hall to getting shoved, Jason catching me and us kissing like fools, to the review of the tapes at Celia's house and to my ghost-hunting team not talking to me anymore.

She thinks for a moment and then folds her hands together underneath her chin. "Let's put the teen drama aside for a moment and dwell on the paranormal aspect. You could be dealing with a residual haunting."

"Right." I nod. "Which means the haunting could be centered on moments of super-intense emotions that once occurred in city hall."

"Exactly. I'm especially curious about the timed photography your friend took that shows a man. Any clue to who he might be?"

I reach into my backpack, pull out my notebook, and tell

her all that Becca and I found in the newspapers. "We have an educated guess. His name might be Charles Stogdon, the man who used to own the land that my dad and the city are developing. You know, the new Mega-Mart project?"

"Oh. I see." She looks off as she thinks about this.

"What?"

Loreen studies the newspaper clip. "This is fascinating! If this Stogdon man is indeed residing at city hall, then you're dealing more with an intelligent haunting."

"Which means?" I ask.

"Well, first and foremost," she starts, "it means the spirit has free will and is making conscious decisions, like pushing people down the stairs, unlike the ghost in your house, who seems more curious and less combative. I think you need to concentrate all of your efforts on searching records at city hall for more information on him and his connection to all of this. It's there, I just know it."

I jot down notes with her suggestions and then straighten up. "Will you help me out?"

She pats my hand. "Nah, this is your project, Kendall."

"But I can't do this by myself. I need people with me, protecting me, watching my back. I mean, I even went to the church and got some holy water from the priest, who wasn't too shabby to look at, let me tell you."

"Which church?" she asks with piqued interest.

"Christ the Redeemer Episcopal. You know Father Castellano?"

Loreen fingers her strawberry blond hair behind her ears. "I think I've seen him around town. What did he say to you? Did he discourage you, like your mother?"

"No," I say. "In fact, he told me my abilities are a gift from God, and only God knows what the intentions are."

"That's right, Kendall. What do you think His intentions are?"

I stop and think for a moment, my pulse popping under my skin for some reason. "I'm supposed to help these spirits on to wherever it is they need to go. For some reason, I can hear and see and feel and smell them. If I don't help, then what good am I?"

A wide grin spreads across Loreen's face. "That's my girl." She tosses a five on the table to cover our drinks and slips her sweater back on. "I think you need to stay the course. You can handle Charles Stogdon, as long as you're protected."

"Geez, I haven't exactly handled things very well up to this point." Not with my mother, not with Celia and the others, and especially not with Jason. We can't get involved until this case is solved. I'm a ghost hunter. That's what I do. Boys have to come second.

Loreen looks at me, assuring, "You know what you have to do, Kendall."

I drain the last of the chai latte and slam the paper cup on the table. "Yep. It's time to go grovel to the rest of the ghost hunters and beg for forgiveness. We've got work to do."

Chapter Eighteen

Saturday morning, I'm greeted at the door of the Nicholses' mansion by their maid, Alice (how very *Brady Bunch* of them), and a snarling Seamus chewing on a rubber bone. I don't think the growl is necessarily for me, more like his annoyance at not being able to go outside and bury the toy unchaperoned.

"Hey, Alice. Is Celia home?"

The older lady frowns. "She's upstairs. Where else would she be? That girl never leaves her room. See if you can get her to go out and let the stink blow off of her."

I nod my head and smile. Seamus follows me up the staircase and then loses interest. He flops over in front of the antique secretary in the hallway and continues masticating the rubber treat. I plod down to Celia's room and knock softly.

"I said I didn't want any breakfast, Alice," she calls.

"It's not Alice," I say meekly as I open the door.

Celia's hair is a holy mess, looking like a bird's nest on top of her head. She peers over at me for one second through the chaotic strands of black bangs that hang in her eyes. Then she turns her gaze back to the computer screen.

"We need to talk, Celia."

I notice she's deeply engrossed in an online sudoku tournament; she's doing quite well. Her denim-colored henley shirt is unbuttoned at the top, and the sleeves are rolled up to her elbows. Her legs are folded up underneath her, giving her extra height to see the engrossing game before her—like she's not already a giant.

I watch as she fills in a 2, a 9, and a 4 in the middle box to complete the puzzle. Expert level, of course. The girl's a friggin' genius. And a good friend. The best one I have here. Anywhere, for that matter, since Marjorie kicked me to the curb in favor of Gretchen Lind and people who actually still live in Chicago and who don't see dead people. I need to mend the fence with Celia. ASAP.

"Cel—"

She clicks "Bring on the next puzzle!" and keeps inserting numbers into the appropriate squares, ignoring my presence. Breathing deeply, I focus on her and the pain that's now a barrier to our friendship. My eyes close and I envision her sitting in class drawing in her notebook. That silly sketch I've teased her about extensively. Then the clouded image in my head clears, and I vividly see just exactly *who* she's drawing. Now I know I really need to apologize.

"Cel, I'm so sorry. About everything. About Jason." I hold my breath to see if she looks my way. Not really, but she puts her game on pause. Continuing, I say, "I had no idea you had a crush on him. I swear, I didn't!"

She shoots up and runs a hand through her unruly hair. "How—? Who—? Oh, that's right. The whole psychic-abilities thing. Shit."

"Yeah. I promise you, Celia, I had no idea you had feelings for him until just this moment when I figured out it was Jason you were sketching that day in class. You've got to believe me. I don't have a vicious bone in my body."

Instead of answering, she trudges over to her messenger bag that's slung over the ladder-back chair in the corner. She pulls out her calculus notebook and comes to sit next to me on the bed. Celia turns to the end and thumbs a few pages until she reaches her doodles. There, in a beautifully sketched pencil drawing, is a perfect likeness of Jason Tillman. Down to the mole on his cheek and the dimple near his mouth. Wow, you've really gotta like someone a whole hell of a lot to get those details down pat.

"All this time, I thought you were drawing Clay Price," I say.

"Yeah, well. Now you know, okay?"

I take the notebook and admire her handiwork. "You're really good, Celia. You should do something with your art."

She toys with a wayward curl of hers that's fallen into her face. "There's not really a need for it in the scientific community."

Turning to face her, I say, "Oh, but there is! If I see a spirit and we can't capture it on film, then I can describe it to you and you can sketch it out. You know, like a police artist. Only, you'll be a spirit artist. Just another layer to our ghost hunting."

I see that familiar sparkle in her eyes over our joint project. However, it's quickly squelched when her gaze returns to the image of Jason. "Yeah, well, it would have been."

"Celia, please." I take her hand and squeeze. "I had *no* clue that you were interested in Jason. That kiss you saw just happened. I was scared shitless and had almost done a swan dive off the banister. He was there, and, well, it is what it is. I never planned it or intended for it—or him—to come between our friendship. Or Taylor's. You guys mean the world to me."

Tears fill my bottom lids, making Celia appear to be a bit wavy.

"Seriously?"

I blink and a salty drop falls. "Totally. I can't believe I didn't pick up on your feelings for him. Some psychic I am, huh?"

She half smiles and it appears she might cry too. God, we're such girls! "Don't apologize. I've had a crush on him since, like, forever. He'd never like a geek like me."

"You're not a geek, Celia."

She raises a brow at me and lifts a smile. "Just a tad?"

"Okay, a bit quirky and original, but definitely not a geek," I assure her. "If you quit hiding behind your bangs and your baggy boy clothes, guys would notice what a knockout you are."

She blushes. "Thanks, Kendall. I'm sorry I lost my shit over

this the other day. God! I'm sure Jason figured out that I liked
him too. How embarrassing!"

"No, don't worry," I say. "He's a guy. They don't notice anything."

A chuckle bubbles out of her. "Funny thing is, y'all make a
lot more sense than he and I ever would have. Besides, I'm too
tall for him." She stops and bites her bottom lip. "You like him,
don't you?"

Deep sigh. "I didn't think I did. He was such a jackass to
me at first. But he really grew on me. And he's interested in
our ghost hunting. Okay, yeah, I *really* like him. Is that okay?"

Celia swipes at a tear that never fell and wipes her hand on
her pajama pants. "Of course it's okay. Besides, I've got Clay,
right?" She bursts out laughing and I can't help but fling myself on her in a big bear hug. She hugs me back and we laugh
and cry like the silly females we are.

"Clay Price *is* a hottie," I say. "And he's definitely interested
in you. We need to use that credit card of yours to get you
some new clothes and do a fashion makeover. Then you need
to give him a second look and the time of day."

"What*ever*." She sits back and tosses her notebook across the
room. "Although I think I will take you up on the makeover."

"Thatta girl. And we'll get Taylor to help. She's so glam-
orous."

Celia laughs hard. "Not Becca, though. I don't think her
particular pierced-and-tattooed style would go over well with
the parentals."

Then we fall silent for a moment. I know she's thinking about our eclectic group.

"It really sucks that our ghost-hunting team fell apart," she says quietly. "We were starting to make some kick-ass progress."

"We still can," I say, wide-eyed and hopeful. I pull Dad's set of office keys out of my pocket. "Wanna come down to city hall with me to do some research?"

"Give me ten minutes to change!"

And we're back in the game.

"Bingo!" Celia raises her arms to signal touchdown. She's been sitting in front of the microfiche machine in the basement of city hall for the last two hours while I've been poring over the county record books.

I'm covered in dust and muck from this old room. "Pay dirt?"

She swivels in her chair and goes to the printer that's spitting out page after page. "It's all right here. Everything we need to fight this spirit. I know exactly what happened to Mr. Charles Stogdon. I know why he's here, why he's razzed off at your dad, and why all of this is happening."

She hands the stack of papers to me. I clutch them as I read the information as fast as I can. Moments later, I'm nearly winded from the facts, figures, and data. Thank goodness the City of Radisson has kept such awesome records. We totally have a break here in our investigation, and I can't wait to dish the 411 to everyone.

"We've got to reassemble the team," I say.

"Easier said than done."

I pout. "True." I wave the papers. "But this changes everything. You get in touch with Becca and I'll text Jason for him and Taylor to be here at six p.m. sharp."

"Time to go dark?" she asks.

"Tonight, we ghost hunt."

There's an unobtrusive thumping on my bedroom door. For a moment, I think it's Emily trying to make contact again. It's not her, but it is a near ghostly face.

"Mom? Are you okay?"

She purses her lips together and toys with a Kleenex she's clutching. Has she been crying? Am I the cause? Crap on a crutch.

"May I come in, Kendall?"

I don't exactly have a choice, since she's walking in and closing the door behind her. Not that I mind having her in here, but I sense great fear, angst, and concern from her. There's a small purple and white flyer in her hand, and I'm concerned that the nurse of the house is about to suggest some sort of intensive medication for her troubled teen.

"Mom, before you say anything, just let me say that I'm fine."

"You're not fine, sweetie."

I strongly inhale. "I know you're weirded out by all of this. How do you think I feel?"

Mom hasn't exactly had much time to adjust to the fact that her older child is a psychic who sees, hears, and talks to spirits. I suppose I'll be grappling with it for the rest of my life as well. However, there's nothing either of us can do about it. It's a calling, just like Father Castellano and Loreen said.

Mom steps toward me. "Your safety and well-being is my chief concern, Kendall. You speak of ghosts and spirits like they're neighbors come in for a glass of iced tea. Telling me you hear voices in machines and can use odd equipment to detect dead people . . . well, what am I supposed to think?"

We're back to square one. "That I'm involved in a cult." Right. Because east Georgia is a bastion of cult activity. I roll my eyes and sit on the end of my bed. My sneakers are clutched in my hands and I know I'm not joining Celia anytime soon at city hall.

Sitting next to me, Mom places one hand on my arm. She pauses and wets her lips, as if searching for the right way to say something. "I don't think this is satanic in nature, although I have spoken to our new priest about it."

"Yeah, Father Massimo. I've met him." Her eyes give away her astonishment. "See, Mom, I'm not the devil-worshiping heathen you think I am."

"I don't think that!" she snaps. "What normal sixteen-year-old wants to ghost hunt, though? What happened to hanging with your friends, going to high school football games, eating pizza, dating cute boys?"

I snap to attention. "Maybe I do all of that now. Celia and

Taylor are my best friends." I've yet to tell Mom about being ostracized by Marjorie. "Becca's cool too. We hang out at school and we have the ghost hunting in common. They get me and accept me for who—*and what*—I am. Jason Tillson likes me for who I am."

Her eye twitches a little. "Who's Jason Tillson?"

I begin smashing my socked feet into my sneakers. "Taylor's twin brother. He's gorgeous, and sweet, and he likes me. He doesn't think I'm a freak. Like you do."

"Kendall, I didn't say that."

Standing, I say, "You're thinking it, though."

Mom's gaze drops to the floor. "Your father and I disagree on allowing you the freedom to do this ghost hunting. I don't think it's right. Not with me or with God."

I nearly dive at her. "But Dad was *hurt,* Mom. Like, almost knocked down the staircase."

She shakes her head in clear denial. "Your father's always been a bit of a klutz. Remember that time at Taste of Chicago when we got to go on stage with Emeril Lagasse and he burned his hand on the grill?"

Feeling the frustration bubble to the surface, I cram my fingers into my hair and rub my head. "This isn't about Dad being accident-prone or anything. The guy in the city-planner position before him specifically left the job because he was attacked by the same entity. He was afraid, and that ghost succeeded in his mission of scaring that guy off."

Mom's on her feet in a heartbeat. She places her hands on

my shoulders and sternly looks into my eyes, not with the distress of a worried mother, but with the face of a medical professional. "Sweetie, you need help."

My first instinct is to vomit. Then burst into tears. Maybe both at the same time. Either way. My own mother thinks I'm a complete mental case.

"I-I-I don't need help, Mom. I need *understanding*."

She lifts my chin with her forefinger. "The only way I can understand is if you let me help you." She suddenly shifts from concerned mother to registered nurse. "We had a lovely young sales rep in the other day, and she highly recommends Zyprexa for our patients. Dr. Murphy and I talked about the symptoms you've been demonstrating. I'll bring you in so he can examine you, and after he does that, he and I will discuss the option of putting you on this for the time being until we can get you to Atlanta and see a psychotherapist." She hands me a pamphlet.

My world tilts slightly. At least she isn't committing me . . . yet.

I stare at the marketing material in my hand, dumbfounded, and then read out loud, "'Zyprexa is approved for the treatment of schizophrenia, acute manic, or mixed episodes of bipolar disorder, and maintenance treatment in bipolar disorder.'" I mean, I know a lot of kids today are on mood-altering drugs, and Mom's only being a concerned parent over my mental health. But how can she *really* think this about me? About her own flesh and blood? "Mom, I promise you I'm not bipolar or manic or schizo!"

She shakes her head. "Kendall, you might be suffering from a mild form of schizophrenia. If we can catch it when you're still young, we can halt the crippling effect it has on the brain."

Blood pulsates rapidly under my skin to the point where I believe my nerve endings are going to ignite. My brain is on fire. Searing thoughts, words, and reactions. My feet stay planted in one place, yet it's like my bedroom is spinning out of control. Like Dorothy's house in *The Wizard of Oz* as it tumbles and whirls through the tornado. What if Mom's right? She is a medical professional with a master's and tons of experience, after all. What if I really am losing my beans? It might actually make more sense than my being psychic.

It's not true, though. I *do* have this ability. And I *have* to use it to help these spirits that are trapped here.

Hot tears sting the corners of my eyes. I shove the flyer at my mother, when what I really want to do is rip it into ten thousand pieces and make confetti out of it. "No! I'm not going to start taking meds, Mom. This is who I am. You have to accept it."

"I can't!" she shrieks, fists curled by her side. "I won't!"

Dad's standing in my doorway, his eyes soft and sympathetic. "Sarah, we talked about this. Leave Kendall be."

"But David," Mom whimpers, "she's my baby. I have to help her."

Dad comes up behind me and wraps an arm around my waist. The warmth from him comforts and soothes me, ebbing my tears. "Sarah, we have to let her be who she is."

Mom sniffs. "I just want her to be happy and live a normal life."

"I think this is normal for me, Mom." I remember what Father Massimo said. "It's a gift that God's given me. I gotta use it."

"Maybe it is," she says softly. "But what if it isn't and I stood by doing nothing when I could have helped you?"

"Let her get to work, Sarah," Dad says. The bruise on his face is a little more purple than it was to begin with, but it will heal. A lot faster than a broken leg or a cracked spine would have if he'd gone down the stairs. I have to make sure it never happens again.

If Charles Stogdon is hanging around city hall, my friends and I need to bring peace to his existence so my dad will be safe from here on. From what Celia and I found earlier today, I just need the chance to connect with Charles, explain the circumstances to him, and straighten this out once and for all. "I can do something about what attacked Dad. I *know* I can. You've got to believe that." Then I throw Mom a bone. "If you insist, I'll go to a psychotherapist. But only to prove to you that I'm not crazy. You have to promise to get an appointment with someone who specializes in what I'm going through."

Mom sniffs. "I suppose I can do that."

"That's my girl," Dad says. "Both of my girls."

After wiping a tear away with her finger, Mom moves toward Dad and me. The three of us come together in a big ol' pile of Mooreheads—arms weaving around one another and hugging tightly. I know Mom loves me and is only protecting me. This is my calling, though.

When we break apart, Mom lays her palm against my cheek and then kisses me lightly. "I love you, Kendall. You're still my little girl."

Smiling into her touch, I say, "I always will be. But I'm a ghost huntress now."

Mom breaks free and excuses herself. Moments later, she returns with the small black velvet bag that holds my rose quartz pendulum. "If you're doing this," she starts, "you're going to need this, I suppose."

I palm the gift from Loreen and then hug Mom again. "Everything's going to be all right. I promise."

I hope I can live up to that vow.

Chapter Nineteen

Two hours later, at dusk Saturday night, we're ready to hunt.

"I sure hope this works." Celia braces for the protection I'm about to give her. She's outfitted in her special ghost-hunting flak jacket, complete with tools, equipment, extra batteries, and a small cross in one of the pockets.

"Loreen says we have to protect all of the equipment as well."

"Okay, Moorehead. Go for it." Celia stands with her arms and legs spread, like she's getting wanded by TSA at the Atlanta airport. I take the Clinique Happy bottle, now full of Episcopally blessed holy water, and I spray it all over her. "Hmm, salty."

"Stop that," I snap. "Don't be sacrilegious."

"Get the cameras and computers so the spirits won't suck the battery power dead," she says.

We spray the laptop—as much as you can—the temperature gauges, EMF meters, and basically everything else in a fine mist of the magical blend. I turn it on myself and spritz my face and my chest, and then I have Celia do my back. I also make the symbol of the cross on my forehead and do a good "in the name of the Father, Son, and Holy Spirit" up and down and sideways cross. Loreen e-mailed me earlier to remind me to dab some holy water at the base of my neck, behind each ear, and around my belly button. Something about protecting the body's chakras. I don't even want to know what that means . . . yet.

Celia seems confused. "I thought only Catholics crossed themselves like that."

"Everything's optional in the Episcopal Church."

She shrugs. "I'm Baptist—not that I go to church that much—but whatever works for you."

I tap her skull. "It only matters what you believe, Celia."

"Hey, y'all," Becca says as she runs into city hall dressed in a black turtleneck and black jeans, like she's going to rob a bank instead of track ghosts. "We doin' this?"

"We certainly are," I say.

Becca looks from me to Celia and then back. "You two okay now?"

"Everything's cool," Celia assures her. "We talked and—"

Holding her hand up, Becca interrupts. "I don't need the deets. Just tell me what I need to do."

"First off," Celia says, "you need protection."

"Why?" Becca asks. "Am I having sex with some hot century-old ghost?"

I cackle. "Hardly." Then I squirt her with the water. "Here, use this on your equipment too, so nothing goes wrong with it."

She stops me with her hand on my arm. "Look, K, I just wanted to let you know that I don't really give a shit—in a good way—about you and Jason. He's fine, so why shouldn't you go for it? What you do is your business."

"Thanks, Becca."

As we're setting up base camp in the front hallway, I pick up the familiar purring of Jason's Jeep outside. Excellent! He got my text message and is going to assist tonight. He's right about having a skeptic to keep us honest. It *is* a good thing. Whenever Celia gets too caught up in the science and I get too bowled over by the metaphysical, Jason can keep us both grounded.

The front door opens and he steps in, dressed in an RHS sweatshirt and baggy jeans. As happy as I am to see him, I slump a bit when I notice that Taylor's not following behind.

"Hey," I say tentatively.

"Hey yourself." He smiles and tugs me by the arm. "Can I see you over here for a sec?"

I gaze over my shoulder to see if Celia's upset with me. I don't want to rub this thing with Jason in her face. No worries, though. She's on her hands and knees under the folding table connecting some sort of cable to the computer monitor. Girl's in her element, let me tell you what, and I don't think she gives a rat's patootie about Jason and me right now.

I follow him around the grand staircase. There's a nook

underneath where they store extra folding chairs. Jason spins me around and pins me to the wall. Before I know it, we're locked in an amazing kiss. A. Maze. Ing. One that I feel in every electron, neutron, and proton in my body. His lips are soft and sweet, and deep down in my gut, I know this is the first meaningful kiss of many more to come. This is the reality of my many dreams about him.

Jason pulls back, but keeps his hands on my hips. "Look, Kendall. For the record, I'm *not* sorry about this thing that's happening between us."

My mouth falls open. "You're not?"

"No. Are you?"

"I, I, well, no." Honestly, when have I had time to think about it?

He scrubs the top of his short-cropped blond hair with one hand. "I can't explain what's going on here. It's like I can't help myself. I'm drawn to you, Kendall." He levels his eyes at me. "You didn't put some sort of spell on me, did you?"

I have to laugh. "I'm psychic, not a witch."

Moving in to kiss me again, he says, "I had to check."

As much as I'm enjoying frenching him right here, we need to get back to the others. "Later?" I say more than ask.

"You can count on it."

His intense blue eyes back up his words. I close my eyes to the toe-curling inside my Reeboks and the bolty sensations zipping up and down my spine. Without thinking too hard about the feeling sprinting through me, I kiss him firmly on the lips to let him know that I'd love to pick this up at a future date.

"Kendall, where are you? We need to do a sweep," Celia calls out.

Jason and I giggle at the thought of being caught again. Instead of continuing, we check our hair and clothes—*Step away from the cute guy!*—and join Celia and Becca. "I'm here to help," he announces.

"Good. 'Cause we can use some brute strength to kick a little ghostly ass." Becca smiles and sticks out her tongue in fun, revealing a silver stud in the middle of the pink flesh.

Celia hooks her hands in her vest pockets. "We don't actually beat up the ghosts or spirits, Becca."

Becca cracks the knuckles on her hands and then screws up her face. "Whatever. I pack one hell of a left hook if we need it."

Is that how she won all of those beauty pageants?

I turn to Jason. "Is Taylor with you?"

The lead investigator, Celia, takes charge. "We really need her, Jason."

I hang my head and toy with the crystal drop of Grandma Ethel's that hangs around my neck. I also have a cross necklace of hers in my pocket. I didn't want to leave my protection up to just a fine mist of holy water. It's also going to take some divine intervention for Taylor to forgive me, I suppose. "She's still pissed at me, isn't she?"

"We had a long talk today," Jason says. "Mostly, she's too embarrassed to come in."

"Are you serious?" I scoff.

Celia perks up. "Come in? As in, she's outside?"

"Sitting in my Jeep."

Waving her arms, Celia shouts at him, "Go get her!"

"Let me," I say. "It's my mess. I've got to make it right."

I buzz out the building, down the front steps, and over to Jason's Jeep. It's parked at a meter in front of the Confederate-soldier statue. As I approach, I see Taylor's got her head down. My heart rate trips up a notch and I can sense her unease over this whole stupid situation. I don't want to upset her or make her more uncomfortable. It's important—particularly because of all the other things going on in Taylor's home life with her parents—to make it crystal clear that she isn't just coming along as a package deal with her brother. We want *her* in the group because of who *she* is and what she brings to the team.

I tap on the window, startling her. She rolls it down and quietly says, "Hey, Kendall."

I rest my hands on the door frame. "Hey, you. Coming in?"

She lowers her lashes. "I didn't know if you'd want my assistance after all the terribly mean and hateful things I said to you. *J'ai honte de me.*"

"Huh?"

"I'm ashamed," she says with a sigh.

I love when she expresses her true feelings through another language.

"Oh, please! I'm sure I'll get called a lot worse than that." Especially as more people find out about my gift. There are plenty of cruel names that will surely be tossed in my face. *Freak. Liar. Exaggerator.* Or according to my mother—who reluctantly allowed me to pursue this case—a potential paranoid schizophrenic. But I won't think of that now. Focus on the job ahead. There'll be time in the future to prepare for life's possible societal shunning. I snort a little and smile at Taylor. "When we're old, like forty, and remembering this, we'll laugh our butts off."

"I'm sorry I said—"

"Look, Taylor, when we formed this whole group, Celia and I handpicked you because of your talent with a camera. But you have that and so much more. I like you because you're you and not because I wanted your brother. I didn't exactly like Jason when we first met." Although I *do* want him now. "What can I say, though? We were just pulled together. I can't explain it." And that's the truth, nothing but the truth, so help me God. "Besides, you're fun and friendly and you've made me feel at home in a strange town."

"I've tried. You're really cool, Kendall."

My turn to blush. "You know, when I saw you in homeroom that first day at school, I picked up right away that you were a standout person. But I felt like you'd be too popular and pretty to ever be friends with the new girl in town. I was totally wrong. You're one of my best friends, Taylor."

Her eyebrow dances up. "I am?"

"Yeah. I'm really sorry."

"Mee tooo, Kendall!"

She rolls the window back up and then flies out of the Jeep. She hugs me like we're long-lost sisters. Relief washes over me like a morning shower. With people like Taylor and Celia in my corner, I'm going to be okay in Radisson.

"I swear I didn't use you, Taylor."

She's about to cry. "I know, Kendall. I'm sorry. I just didn't want to lose Jason too. It's been hard with my daddy leaving. Jason's all I've got now."

Squeezing her tight. "No, hon, you've got us too."

Right then, Jason ventures down the front steps of city hall. From his shifting back and forth from one foot to the other, I read his nervousness loud and clear. "I think we need to go put him out of his misery."

She giggles. "Nah, let him suffer a little more. He has been an outlandish boor up until recently."

Jason shouts out, "Everything okay over there?"

Taylor and I break apart. "It's great," she says. Then she dabs her eyes, her perfect waterproof makeup not daring to run at all.

"You're a phenomenal photographer and we are going to need your talent tonight."

"You can count on me, Kendall."

We link up with Jason and the three of us head back inside. Time to get serious about what's ahead for us tonight. In the front lobby of city hall, the equipment is set up, the cameras are in place, and everything looks ready to go. I hope my sensitivity is in tune with the surroundings and that I'll be able to make contact with Charles Stogdon, if that's truly who's been haunting this building. Whoever it is, I have a bone to pick with them. *Try to knock my dad down the stairs* . . . If it is Charles Stogdon, I need to straighten him out on exactly what's going on here in Radisson. If at all possible, I need to help him find the white light and move on to a more peaceful realm.

"Are we ready, Celia?"

She wipes sweat off her forehead with the sleeve of her shirt. "This place is wired. If anything's here, we'll get it."

"Excellent." I reach into my pocket and pull out the pendulum that Mom saw fit to return to me, for whatever reasons. I clutch the silver chain and feel the coolness of the stones under my fingers. The slick texture of the quartz is heavy in my palm. I squeeze its sturdiness and take a deep breath. Since this is my first time doing this, I guess I'm as ready as I'll ever be.

Becca steps up, holding a crude drawing of the floor plan of the first and second floors of city hall. "While y'all were outside, Celia and I did a quick sweep of the building with the EMF meters to pick up on the hot spots."

"Hot spots?" Jason asks.

"Yeah, like power sources, wires, circuits, stuff like that which would set the meters off," Celia explains. "Meaning that if the meters go off in areas that aren't marked as energy sources, the likelihood is that it's a spirit trying to manifest itself through another energy source that's not connected to the building. Like the batteries in our cameras, or even us."

Jason's eyes narrow. "You really believe that?"

Celia spreads her hands wide. "There are literally thousands of ghost-hunting groups throughout the world who do it this way and swear by it. This isn't just some new fad. People are pros at this. If it ain't broke, why fix it?"

"Just because other people do it, doesn't mean it's legit," he says. "I still say it's all a bunch of bullshit."

"Skeptic," she mutters.

"Damn right."

I step away from the group and am pulled toward the bottom of the staircase. After several seconds, I know for a fact that despite what Jason thinks, we're not alone here. There's an immense, thick wall of energy directly in front of me. Is it Charles Stogdon? I don't see anything. Not yet.

Turning back to the group, I say, "Everyone's had some of the holy water?"

Taylor holds out her equipment. "Here, bless my camera and my mini-recorder."

Jason rolls his eyes, but sprays the water on himself to make me happy.

Everyone gathers around and I nod to Celia that I'm going to begin. "Now, before we start, let's stand in a circle and hold hands." I want to feel their energy before going into this battle.

Jason takes my hand and then reaches for Taylor's. She nabs Becca's and then she and Celia make the circle complete. A cohesive front. A single unit. A sole purpose: to find what's lingering here and stop it from hurting anyone again, particularly my dad. Celia squeezes my hand for reassurance, even though I sense a small tremor in hers. I guess it's nerve-racking to be doing this for the first time.

"Let's all take some deep breaths." A few moments of silence later, I repeat what Loreen instructed me to say. "I want everyone to imagine a soothing light surrounding you. To yourself, say, 'I am protected by a warm circle of light. God's light that protects me from harm and evil and keeps me safe.'"

"Amen," Taylor says.

"She's not a minister, Taylor," Jason says with a snicker.

"Shhhh," I say.

Celia clicks on the flashlight and points her EMF meter my way. "Are we ready?"

I pack away my qualms into the bottom of my stomach and grasp my crystal pendulum. "As ready as I'll ever be."

"Okay, Becca," Celia instructs. "Hit the lights. We're going dark."

CHAPTER TWENTY

I LOOK AT MY WATCH; the second hand is barely moving, it seems. "Are you as freaking bored as I am?"

"It takes time," Celia says, playing with the EMF meter, trying to make it register *anything*.

I stretch my legs out in front of me to get the circulation flowing again. We've been at the base of the staircase waiting, and it seems like a monumental waste of time. "Should we go to another location?"

Celia shines the flashlight on her face in an eerie "telling spooky stories at camp" way. "You said you were feeling something here."

"Dude, that was *two hours* ago."

She ignores me for the most part and fiddles with the temperature gauge.

"I think I'm going to fall asleep," I say. Nothing. No psychic headache. No tingles. No sensation of broken bones, nauseated stomach, or old-age heart problems. "Either that or I'm going to start doing jumping jacks to get some exercise."

Celia squints her eyes at me. "Did you know that it's a documented fact that you burn more calories sleeping than you do watching television?"

"So?"

"I'm just saying."

I sigh hard. "I'd rather be doing either right now."

Celia shines the flashlight on me. "We have to be patient, Kendall. Ghosts aren't just standing over there in the corner waiting for us to wave at them and point a camera and say, 'Hey, Mr. Ghost, pose and say cheese!'"

I block the light with my forearm. "All right already."

Five minutes later, I break the silence again when I hear a thud. "What was that?"

Celia cranes her neck to the left, but dismisses the noise. "It came from the courtroom. Jason and Taylor are trying to replicate the time-lapse pictures we got the other night. They're running from different sections of the courtroom to see if they can stop and pose between frames."

"Oh." Disappointed, I try to concentrate on my surroundings, tuning in my alleged psychic antenna to anything that might be out there. "Are there any spirits here who have something to say?" After a moment, I hear, *It's not going to work.*

"It's not?" I ask.

Celia quirks her mouth. "Huh?"

"What? Didn't you say it wasn't going to work?"

"No. That wasn't me."

"Was that a spirit?" I ask. Deafening silence reverbs at me. I did hear that, didn't I? "Never mind." Maybe Mom's right and I am going insane.

Something pinches my arm and I let out a yelp. I smack my hand down and feel something gooey under my fingers. Did a ghost do that?

"What happened?" Celia swings the flashlight my way again.

"A mosquito. Bleck!" I wipe the bloody mess onto my jeans and try not to be skeeved out. "If I'd known there were bugs in here, I would have put on some Deep Woods Off."

"Mosquito repellents don't repel," Celia informs me. "They simply block the mosquitoes' sensors so they don't know you're even there."

"Thank you, Mr. Science." I snicker. "You're a plethora of fun facts this evening, aren't you?"

Celia leans in. "Why, yes, I am. Did you know that Venus is the only planet that rotates clockwise? Apples have more caffeine than coffee. Oh, and the plastic things on your shoelaces? They're called *aglets*. Bet you didn't know that. On top of that, most of the dust in your house is from dead skin—seriously *dead,* in your case—and I bet you didn't know this, but it was rumored that Marilyn Monroe had six toes on one of her feet."

I jump to *my* feet. "Oh. My. God. I can't take this anymore. You're killing me, Celia."

"I'm just saying."

I shout at the top of my lungs, "This is *the most* boring ghost hunt in the history of ghost hunting. It's embarrassing.

Thank God we're not on television or anything. The TAPS guys on *Ghost Hunters* don't have these problems."

Celia stands next to me. "It's 'cause they edit out all of the tedious parts of the show. This is reality, kids."

Just then Taylor pops out of the courtroom. "What's all the yelling?"

Blinding her with the flashlight, Celia says, "Just Kendall venting her frustration."

"Do you blame me?"

To Taylor, Celia asks, "Are y'all getting anything in there?"

Taylor motions us forward. "You should come in here. This is pretty fascinating, what's going on."

I perk up. "Evidence?"

Taylor turns, easing into a smile. "Well, something."

I nearly start to run. "Jackpot, baby!"

"Yo, Asiaf." Celia calls upstairs to where Becca's been doing some EVP work. "We're all meeting in the courtroom."

"I'll be right there."

As we walk toward the courtroom, my head begins to hurt in a crazy mixture of fear and anxiety. I must squash the emotions. Loreen says a spirit can pick up on things like that. Especially if it's an entity with an ax to grind. Even if I am dealing with Charles Stogdon, I know nothing about how he was in life. All the research shows that if a person was an asshole in life, they're one on the other side as well. Is that what's causing my head to want to explode? 'Cause it does. A searing hot burn coupled with a tribal pounding. I smell the pungent odor of alcohol in the air. I slide my fingers to my forehead and massage my skull. This must be what it's like to have a wicked-bad hangover. My temples vibrate under the skin and it seems like my eyes are going to cross from the pain. "Someone associated with this room liked his liquor," I say. "A lot."

"Are you getting Charles?"

"I don't know. My head really hurts, though."

Becca pipes up. "I read there was a judge back in the 1870s who was known around the area for selling moonshine from his home stills."

"That's got to be what I'm picking up," I surmise.

"What does that have to do with Charles, though?" Taylor asks.

"It all blends together." I concentrate hard on steadying my erratic pulse. "The judge . . . and Charles . . . they're connected." A calendar page flashes in my mind. "It has something to do with the month of September."

"No shit!" Becca shouts out. "Are you kidding me? Man, you're good, Moorehead."

"Why's that?"

Flipping through a small notepad, Becca says, "That's the judge. His name was Nathaniel P. September, and he presided over the court in the 1870s."

Taylor looks at me with smug delight. "So it's his name?"

"I don't believe it," Jason adds.

I block him out, though. I block them all out. Something is

here with us. I snap my fingers and point in front of me to alert Celia. She follows alongside of me with her EMF meter as I slowly move through the courtroom. Immediately, her temperature measurer begins registering in the low sixties. "Fifty-nine, fifty-six, the temp's dropping," she says.

Even though the musty room is quite dark, I can make out the outline of the judge's bench, the witness stand, and the tables where the lawyers make their cases.

"And it's back up to sixty-nine," Celia says.

My stomach moans, half in frustration and half in continued anticipation.

"We've been trying to recreate those still shots I got," Taylor says. "You know, where we saw the man in the coat?"

I squelch my aggravation at missing whatever was just here and then quickly moved along. "Any luck?"

Jason approaches from one of the rows of benches. "None. There's no possible way anyone could run from any point in this room, pause in front of that table, and then run back out of the picture in the time the camera took the pictures. Unless it was tampered with. You know, someone messed with the timer."

"Who would have done that, Jason?" Taylor asks, her lips flat.

"Come on. It's the only answer. Either that, or the photo isn't real," he qualifies.

Taylor stabs her fists to her waist. "How else do you explain it, Mr. Smarty-Pants? You think I Photoshopped it or something?"

He raises his voice at her. "I didn't say that, Taylor. Quit putting words in my mouth."

Becca stops next to me. "They're at it again."

"Guys, it's okay," I say, trying to stop the sibling bickering.

Celia stretches her hand out in front of her. "Y'all, I'm definitely feeling a cold spot again. Here. Try it."

Jason puts his hand forward and then pulls it back. "Whoa! That's just weird. The air conditioner must be on."

"Nuh-uh," Becca says. "We had the custodian turn off the system for the weekend while we're here."

"It must have come on by itself then," our skeptic says.

I shake my head, sure that again we're not alone. It's the same sensation I felt when we had the misty images in my bedroom and made contact with Emily. Poor, forgotten Emily. I guess I owe her an apology for thinking *she* was the one who was going to hurt my dad. First things first. We have to cleanse this building and make it safe for Dad and his coworkers. "There's no A/C on, Jason. Deal with it."

He opens his mouth to counter, but then stops.

Taylor clicks her digital camera several times and begins looking through the photos on the readout. "There are some orbs here, but they could just be bugs."

The EMF meter flashes orangey red and is registering up to eight, which is, like, really high for an energy field.

Coinciding with that, my hand starts trembling, a bit spaz-like. My hands feel aged and itchy. I breathe in a few quick, shallow gulps of air.

"Something's here," Celia says as she watches me.

I center my thoughts on the area in front of us—the cold spot. I definitely sense not only what I think is Charles Stogdon, but also the former judge who worked here and had a massive drinking problem, although I don't think he has any interest in our ghost hunt. My head throbs and my throat seems to be tightly knotted.

"What's going on with you, Kendall?" Celia asks.

Words don't come easily. I force them out. "My head hurts."

"You've already said that."

Irritated, I say, "I know, but it still hurts."

She blows her hair out of her eyes. "Can't you think of anything else to say?"

I shake my head and bend over at the waist, hoping to alleviate the considerable ache. "No, because that's what's going on. My head hurts."

"Isn't there another way to describe it?" she asks.

"My *friggin'* head hurts?"

Jason pulls her away from me. "Come on, Celia. Give her a break."

Just as he touches me, I hear that whispered voice in my ear again.

"Off my land!"

"What did you say?" I ask him.

There's enough light to see that his blue eyes are dilated in the dark room. "I didn't say anything."

"But I just heard—"

"Off. My. Land!"

It's like someone's standing an inch away from me speaking low in my ear. Excitement surges through me. I stand and then spin to each side. "Charles? Is that you?"

"I just got something on the recorder," Becca pipes up.

She rewinds and hits Play. "You can hear us talking, and then in the background, there's a garbledy whooshing sound. Like clothing moving.

"Uuuuuuuuuuuffffffff muhhhhhhhhhhhh lahhhhhnnnnnd."

Becca's eyes meet mine. "'Off my land'? Is that what it says?"

"That's what I heard," I agree, my heart slamming away in excitement.

"No way," Jason says. "I didn't hear anything. Where did that come from?"

I unfurl my pendulum from my fist and look over at Celia. "I can't believe we wasted so much time at the staircase when we should have been in here."

She motions me over with her hands. "Sorry, but maybe you were where you needed to be, for some reason. Should we try and make contact?"

"Yeah, I'm going to dowse to back up all of the sensations going on inside of me."

Jason touches my back. "Are you okay to do this?"

I drown for a moment in those clear eyes of his. "I *have* to do this, Jason."

His eyes carry concern. "You don't have to do anything that's gonna hurt you just to prove yourself."

"I'm not trying to," I say with a smile. "Just watch. We'll make a believer out of you yet."

He winks. "I highly doubt that. But I am here for you, Kendall."

Lump. In. Throat. Not the time to swoon.

We gather in a circle where the frigid air surrounds us. It feels as if some sort of cloud or weather system engulfs me, passes through me. I'm chilled, but not like a normal cold. Like the air has substance to it.

I secure my pendulum the way Loreen taught me that day in her shop. "Are there any spirits here?" I ask, already knowing the response. We all watch as the chain and stone begin moving.

"That's a *yes* for her," Celia says, beaming. "May I ask the questions?"

I nod slightly.

Celia clears her throat and then says, "Are you Charles Stogdon?"

"Yes," I say, watching the pendulum.

"Can you make a sound for us, Charles, to let us know you're here?"

Taylor shifts and her shoe scuffs on the floor. "Sorry. That was me."

Celia continues, "Can *you* make a noise, Charles?"

Suddenly, in the balcony of the courtroom, there's a knock.

Jason jumps. "What the hell was that?"

"I'm on it!" Becca turns and heads up the stairs leading to the balcony.

Celia winks at me. "That girl is fearless."

Still dowsing, I agree. "We all have to be."

"Can you please knock twice, Charles?" Celia asks politely.

Knock. Knock.

"I don't believe this," Jason hisses.

"Shhh" comes from Taylor.

Adrenaline is flowing through my body like an intravenous drug. This is a high like I've never experienced—not that I've ever done drugs or anything, but you know what I mean. "Can you show yourself to me, Charles?"

The pendulum changes directions, swinging from left to right.

"No," Celia notes.

"I feel him," I say. "He's here. I know it."

Taylor snaps several pictures, nearly blinding me with the horrendously intense flash.

"Anything up there, Becca?" Celia shouts.

Becca hangs over the railing. "The recorder's picking things up, but I don't see anything. I definitely heard that friggin' knocking."

"Look," Taylor exclaims. She passes her digital camera over and points to the screen. "Right there. On the left."

Sure enough, there's a bit of a mist, like the pictures of Emily in my bedroom. And something of a shadow.

"Holy shit," Jason mutters.

I nearly cry in relief. "It's him." To the room, I say, "I know it's you, Charles. Please come talk to us. We mean you no harm or disrespect. We're here to help. To lend a hand with what-ever's keeping you here. To stop you from scaring the workers here and hurting them. And we can help you find peace if you'll just let us."

A window bangs in the balcony, followed by a cold breeze that whooshes by my arms.

My pendulum is spinning like crazy.

"Are you pleased that we're here?" Celia asks.

The back-and-forth motion clearly says *no*.

"Not at all," I say. "He's irritated. I can hear him growling in my ear."

Becca returns from the balcony and holds the digital recorder up. "There's a disembodied voice on here, but the EVP isn't clear." She plays it for us several times. To the rest of the group, it probably sounds like gobbledygook. However, I hear Charles's comment plainly next to me.

"You're meddling with my land."

"No, Charles, I'm not meddling."

Jason looks at me and then back at Taylor. "Who's she talking to?"

Taylor smacks him on the arm. "The ghost, you moron."

Then again. *You're meddling with my land.* So clear, it's like someone's in my head. I place my hands over my ears and back away two steps. There's no one physically there, but I know what I heard.

Celia knows something's going on. "Is he talking to you, Kendall?"

"Yeah, he thinks I'm messing with his land. And he's making my head hurt like blue-blazing bullshit." I bite down on my bottom lip to stop from crying out. Charles won't relent, though, and the pressure in my brain keeps building and building until I collapse to my knees. Tears ooze out the corners of my eyes, and I don't know if I can go on like this.

I reach a weak hand out to her and beg, "Celia . . ."

Seeing my severe pain, she reacts on my behalf. "It's not your goddamned land anymore, Charles," Celia tells him. "So leave Kendall alone! *You've been dead over one hundred and fifty years!*"

She did *not* just go there.

Before we realize anything's happening, two large windows in the back of the room slam open. Celia seemingly loses her balance and falls backwards. She lands—*bam!*—flat on her ass on the hardwood floor.

"Son of a bitch!" she screams out. "That hurt, Charles!"

Jason and I help her up, and she rubs her backside for emphasis.

"Well, that pisses me off," Becca says. "Sure you don't want me to sucker punch him?"

"You guys. We can't antagonize him," I beg.

Taylor pulls her camera away and has a heartbroken look on her face. "That's right. Sure, he's dead, but he can't move on, y'all. We have to help him."

I toss her a sympathetic glance and then step forward to where I think Charles is standing. I can't see him, but I sense company. "Tell you what, Charles. I'm going to give it to you straight. Once you hear the whole story, if you want us to help you, we will. If you don't, then we'll pack up our equipment, say a prayer of blessing to protect this building, and leave you be. But if after I tell you everything, you understand we're just here to help, I want you to leave this place. Deal?"

Becca holds her recorder out. Celia points the thermometer. Taylor clicks away on her camera. Jason stands behind me.

In my ear, *"Deal."*

"He's game." I take a deep breath and send a quick prayer to heaven. I'm ready to tell Charles everything that Celia and I discovered in our research. I must keep an even, assuaging tone if we're going to get him to pass into the light.

"Charles Stogdon. We know all about you," I say. "You were a wealthy landowner in Radisson in the 1830s after you moved here from North Carolina. Following the War Between the States"—I say that, not the Civil War, out of respect for him—"you freed your slaves, which was the right and honorable thing to do. You also promised some of those freed slaves that you'd deed part of your land to them so they'd be able to set up their own farms and houses."

"That's pretty righteous of him," Becca says.

I continue. "Right, Becca. But in the early 1870s, some people here in the community weren't exactly happy with the outcome of the war, or with Mr. Stogdon's generosity to his former slaves." I pause for a minute and hear a creaking sound behind me. Celia moves around, and the EMF meter continues to flash impressively. "You know this story, Charles. You know it because it's real and it happened. You were there. You know all about the false deed to your property, trumped up by one of your neighbors, that said you didn't own the land. Because you were an outsider from North Carolina, there were enough townsfolk to side with your neighbor in calling you a thief. Your neighbors all insisted you were mad. Especially because of your wanting to give land to freed slaves. No one did that."

Becca whispers, "I'm picking up all kinds of EVPs now. You're getting to him, Kendall."

In my head, I ask the pendulum to point to where Charles is standing. It swings heavily to the right, so I follow. "The city court got involved in the ruckus about the deed in a very public, heated trial. Judge September presided over it. He may have enjoyed his spirits—and I mean of the alcoholic kind—but he was still a Confederate and no pushover for someone who wanted to do the right thing for freed slaves. It all happened. The mob. The judge. The hearing."

"Here in this very courtroom," Celia adds.

I close my eyes to the images flashing before me, just like the ones I'd read about on the microfiche. "You stood before them and begged for your land, Charles. I can see you. You stood tall against your opponents. You screamed and fought for your rights, but there were too many people trying to silence you. They pushed you to the brink of sanity, and then you did become mad." I wince at the scene in my mind's eye. My pulse accelerates to match what Charles must have been feeling at the time. What he's probably feeling now. "They drove you out of the courtroom and chased you through the building. You were screaming and waving your arms, telling them it was your land! But someone got too aggressive when you reached the top of the stairs, and you fell to your death."

I gasp hard, trying to catch a lungful of air against the agony I'm feeling from the ghost. The broken neck, the shattered knees, the punctured lung. Death was instantaneous. Heaven was not. "Shit, Charles. This is horrible. No one to listen to you or stand up for you. Only to have things end the way they did." My breathing is ragged as I try to finish.

Jason's hand is on my arm. "Kendall, are you okay? Your face is red and your voice sounds weird."

I shake him off. I have to concentrate on what's going on.

"You, you, you . . . had no heirs, Charles. So the land reverted to the city's trust, where it's been ever since. So, legally, it's theirs to do with as they please." One more strong inhalation. "It's not your land anymore."

With that, I collapse back against Jason, like I've just run the Chicago Marathon with cement in my sneakers. Jason holds me steady. However, nothing can prepare me for what happens next.

In the blink of an eye, Charles Stogdon appears before me—only me—as clear as any living human being I've ever seen. He twitches his handlebar-mustached mouth and says in a booming voice, "Like hell it's not my land."

Chapter Twenty-one

IT'S AS IF CHUCK NORRIS has just roundhouse-kicked me in the chest.

Charles Stogdon stands before me in a black frock coat made of fine wool, a little worse for the wear after these past hundred or so years of haunting. Underneath is a pinstriped suit with a smart cravat—I think that's what they called them way back then—at the neck. A gold watch chain hangs from one of the buttons of his vest and tucks neatly into a side pocket. He's holding a black hat in his clenched fists, and in his expression I read anger and defiance. His thick mustache frames his mouth with strands of black and gray, showing either his advanced age or his wear and tear from the horrendous times of the Civil War. Dark circles color the skin underneath his weary brown eyes. Eyes that must have known happiness at one point in his life. Eyes now icy over what I've said to him.

I reach out toward him, not knowing what I'll feel if I make physical contact. "Charles? Is that you?"

He worries his hands together, mashing up his hat. "Young lady, you have no right saying that land isn't mine."

I look to the left at Celia, then to the right at Taylor. Then I turn to gaze at Becca. "You see him, right?"

"See what?" Jason asks, his dimple showing—which means he's trying not to laugh.

"I'm serious as a heart attack. Charles Stogdon is standing right here." I point to his booted feet in front of me.

"Why are you here?" Charles asks. "You're disturbing me. Just like that man with the coffee."

Coffee? Oh, right. Charles broke Dad's coffee mug. "That's my father," I say.

"What's your father?" Taylor asks.

"Don't y'all understand?" Celia says with excitement. "She *sees* him and they're communicating."

"Get the hell out of town," Jason says.

Celia pushes him out of the way and stands next to me. "There's a massive cold spot right here."

"That's where Charles is," I confirm. Leaning in to whisper, I say to her, "Look, let me talk to him and I'll report what's going on. We have to stay calm."

Her dark hair brushes my cheek. "Are you staying calm?"

I murmur back, "I'm about to throw up."

She hugs me. "You can do it, Kendall."

Facing Charles again and ignoring Becca's recordings, Celia's readings, and Taylor's photos, I concentrate on only him. "Why are you hurting people, Charles? Why did you hurt my dad?"

He scowls. "No one on my land."

"It's not your land anymore. It belongs to the city, no matter how they got it."

I listen to Charles as he explains to me, very passionately, the intention for the land, which we already know. "That land is for my freed slaves to start a new life. For them to plant vegetables and cotton and peanuts. Crops they can take to market and get a good price for. All of this reconstruction after the war. People need supplies, and that land will give the opportunities they deserve. They worked for it!"

I pay attention as Charles reveals more details. I gulp down the lump in my throat and repeat what I've learned to everyone. "Charles promised the land to a man named Thomas, who was his foreman. It was going to be a whole new life for him and his family."

"I want my land. For Thomas. Off my land!"

Holding my hands out, I say, "It's okay, Charles. Just stay calm. Thomas isn't here. He's been gone for a long time. Just like you. Do you understand that?" I wait for his answer. He just stares at me. I tell my friends, "He won't acknowledge that he's dead. He wants to know what they're doing with the land."

Celia nudges me with her elbow. "Tell him about the distribution center and all the jobs and stuff."

I run my fingers through my hair and adjust my stance.

Man, talking to a ghost can really wear you out. It's like my internal battery is wearing down to nothing. My skin is sticky, and every nerve end is electrified. "Okay, Charles, see, Celia's dad owns Mega-Mart—which you wouldn't really get since you didn't have, like, malls or big stores or what have you back in your time—but the city has donated the land to Mega-Mart and other developers to build this amazing distribution center."

From the glassy look in his eyes, I assume he doesn't understand anything I'm saying. I have to put it in terms he'll comprehend. "Remember that paper model you destroyed in Dad's office?"

"I do," he says, his voice quite authoritative. "It was a travesty of epic proportions. Building such a monstrosity on my land."

"It's not a monstrosity, Charles. It's really quite innovative. The development will provide affordable housing and will bring many, many jobs to Radisson for all people. White, black, you name it, it's equal opportunity. That's how we do things now. Everyone—including the community—will benefit."

"I don't believe you!" And with that, he turns and kicks one of the tables.

"Shit!" Becca screams, and Jason jumps as the furniture goes flying.

Taylor doesn't seem fazed, just continues videotaping.

"That was fabulous," Celia says. "Get him to do it again."

I glare at her. "I will not. He's not listening to me. He's

pissed." I spin back to him, but he's not there. "Charles? Charles! Where are you?" To Celia, I say, "He's gone."

"Gone? Where?"

The five of us rush out of the courtroom and back to the foyer. The EMFs are going off and I'm completely unsettled, aggravated, and excited all in one hard rock candy that seems to be stuck in my throat. In my head, I ask my pendulum where Charles has gone. It begins moving to the left, taking me to the front staircase. Then the direction alters to point forward.

"He's upstairs."

Taylor's right next to me. "Is he reenacting his death or something?"

"No clue."

We take the steps two at a time, following the creaks and footsteps we all can now hear above us. I hear Charles's gruff, derisive laughter.

Pointing, Becca says, "Look, the door to your dad's office is open. It was closed earlier."

Leading the pack, I follow my senses down the hallway where Charles's presence is pulling me again. Only this time, it's like a weight is on my chest. Not like someone's suffocating me or anything. Rather, it's a melancholy heaviness. A deep, deep sadness that permeates the entire office. The laughter is gone, replaced with a somberness.

"Charles? Why are you so sad now?"

"I want my land."

"I know. You can't have it, though. This is the twenty-first century. Time has passed. Things have changed. People have changed. The city is taking huge measures—and a lot of money—to turn your beautiful land into something beneficial for the greater good."

Charles is sitting in Dad's chair, looking down at the blue-print plans of the development. "Thomas wants to use the land."

Thinking quickly, I ask, "Did you give Thomas your last name when you freed him?"

Taylor speaks up. "I remember that from history class."

"No, he wouldn't take it," he says faintly. He's starting to fade.

"What was it?" I nearly shout out.

I hold my hand up to stop Taylor from saying more because I have to concentrate on what Charles is relaying to me. His voice has weakened a bit. However, he's showing me an image.

"Egg?"

Becca looks at me like I've finally gone off the deep end. "Huh?"

I try and explain. "Loreen said sometimes a spirit will show you an item or object when they're unable to manifest themselves further to you. I see . . . an egg. What kind of name comes from that? Eggbert? Eglington? Eg—"

Celia lowers her EMF meter and has a spark of knowledge in her eyes. "Ask him if it's Edgars."

I don't have to. "Yes. Thomas Edgars," Charles mutters.

"Your former slave was Thomas Edgars," I say. "Where did the name come from?"

I hear what seems to be a long sigh from Charles. "It was my dearly departed Ella's maiden name. Ella Edgars Stogdon. She was so good to Thomas."

"That's it," I say exuberantly. "Someone have a BlackBerry we can look that up on?"

"I do," Jason says without playing Doubting Thomas for once.

What a guy!

"We don't have to look it up," Celia says. "Dawson Edgars is the vice president for distribution at Mega-Mart. It was his original idea to build this development. He and my dad went to RHS and played basketball together. Daw's a cool guy. His daughter, Melanie, is a cheerleader."

"Oh, I know her," Taylor says. "She's a sweetheart. She helped with the Valentine's dance last year. Do you think she may be a descendant of Thomas?"

"It ain't impossible," Becca says.

Before I can repeat all of this, Charles sits up and takes notice. Obviously, he can hear my friends. "Children of my Thomas?"

"Right, Charles. Thomas has got to be their ancestor. We can Google it or something and find out, but sure."

As much as a ghost can glower, Charles does so over the word *Google*.

"Umm, I just mean we can research it and make sure."

"So, my Thomas will be involved in the land after all?" he asks.

"It looks that way. Well, not Thomas directly, but his great-great-great-great-grandson, possibly." I'm quite sure in my heart that Dawson Edgars *is* from Thomas's lineage.

Celia speaks out in the direction of Charles. "Your original intentions are technically going to be met—only in a more modern way, Mr. Stogdon."

"It seems so," he tells me.

"He understands that," I share.

Becca says, "Maybe they could, like, name a street in the development after Charles or something, you know?"

"What a fab idea!" Taylor says. "Maybe even a monument or statue of him?"

Charles straightens. "The city would do that for me?"

"We can ask them to, Charles," I say with my best and brightest smile. "I mean, with my and Celia's dads both involved, we've sort of got strings to pull."

Next to my ear, I hear him whisper, *"What an honor."*

The air around Charles shifts, changes, and I'm picking up his acceptance to the situation now. I step around the desk, leaving my fellow ghost hunters, and squat in front of him where he's sitting. If I thought I could take his hand, I would. But I don't dare try.

"So, did I live up to my end of the deal?"

There's a disorientation in his eyes, but how could there not be, under the circumstances? "We had a deal," he says, relenting.

"It's time for you to find some peace now, Charles. No more haunting. Go find your way."

He just looks at me with those large brown eyes of his. He seems so real. So alive. He's not, though. He's a ghost. A lost spirit who needs to find his way home. To his eternal resting place and God's loving arms. I've seen enough movies and TV shows to know there's supposedly a white light that he needs to go into. Can he see it?

"You can rest now, Charles."

"I know, child."

"You've got to go into the light now."

A smile dances out underneath his heavy mustache. "It's glorious. God's own hand reaching down and inviting me to join my loved ones. Is that Ella I see?"

I suck in a good breath. "Go to her, Charles."

There's the soft, feathery sensation of a kiss on my cheek. And then, Charles Stogdon just . . . disappears.

"Is he gone?" Celia asks.

Before I can answer, all of the energy I've been operating off of—perhaps what Charles had been using from me to manifest himself—completely drains out of me. My legs are rubbery and my toes sting something fierce. The connection with him has sucked every ounce of oomph from me. The shock of the total and complete exhaustion catches me full force. I collapse to the floor.

"Kendall!" Jason and Taylor both fly at me; Celia and Becca follow.

"Shit, Kendall," Celia says. "You look like death on a cracker."

I snicker and then laugh harder until I start to cry for no reason. I succumb to the gripping sobs that shake me. Jason sits and pulls me against him for strength. I don't want to cling desperately to him like some sort of weak woman, but let's just say my energy well is refilling, thanks to his warmth and concern. Taylor winks and takes a picture of us together.

"Oh, great," I say with exasperation. "Take a candid of us when I look like—death on a what? A slice of bread?"

"A cracker," Celia says with a smile. It's all I need to know that she's okay with this whole thing between Jason and me.

"I don't have any freakin' clue what just happened, but I'm glad you're okay," Jason says.

A dot of sweat rolls down my back and into the waistband of my jeans. I'm totally drenched after this, although mentally, I'm stoked. "Believe that I can talk to spirits now?"

The corner of his mouth hitches. "You were talking to something. Whether it was a spirit or just something in your imagination, I don't know. Is it really for me to say?"

Becca looks around. "Where's the ghost dude?"

I wipe the perspiration off my forehead and try to steady my rapid breathing. "He's gone."

"Back down to the courtroom?" Taylor asks.

"No, he's not there either. I think he's crossed over." I crane my head around and gaze into Jason's eyes that are analyzing me so intensely, so sweetly. He places a chaste kiss on the top of my head. Nuzzling into the safety of his strong chest, I let out a long sigh and close my eyes. "In the words of Lady Macbeth, 'What's done, is done.'"

It seems like I slept a millennium, but in reality, it was only what was left of Saturday night and most of Sunday.

I wake up and stretch my limbs under the covers as far as they'll go. My right foot hits something. Or someone.

"Kaitlin?"

She's holding my brown bear, Sonoma, and looks genuinely concerned. "Are you okay, Kendall?"

Sitting up against my pillows, I say, "I think so. Although I feel like I was hit by an eighteen-wheeler."

Kaitlin smiles faintly. "Mom said you were really sick. Like, 'might have to see a special doctor or something' sick."

I reach forward and snag Kaitlin's fingers to weave through mine. "I'm not going anywhere. I just had a long night and needed to . . . sleep it off."

"Oh. Okay. 'Cause I don't want, like, anything to happen to you," she says with her eyes down.

Awww . . . what an adorable non-brat, I think with a chuckle. "Come here, you."

She crawls up the bed and plops down next to me. I wrap my arm around her and Sonoma and we just lie there for a while, listening to nothing. The little sis comforting the big one.

When I decide to make my appearance in the kitchen downstairs, around three in the afternoon, Mom quietly puts a plate in front of me with a fried chicken breast, a waffle, and a side of homemade mac 'n' cheese. I think it's a bit odd, but she tells me the Nicholses' maid, the gray-haired Alice, brought it over for me. Apparently, it's a soul food tradition, called, aptly enough, chicken and waffle, that comes from the original jazz days back in Harlem when musicians would play all night and then show up at a restaurant in the wee morning hours. They didn't know whether to feed them breakfast or dinner, so they served both. Works for me! As does the salty chicken and the maple-sweet waffle. The mac 'n' cheese is to *die* for!

As I sit here wolfing down food like I've never eaten before, Mom doesn't hassle me too much about not getting up for Holy Eucharist. In fact, she doesn't really say much at all, other than telling me that Father Massimo called this morning to check on the success of our ghost hunt. Damn, word sure does spread fast in this town. Then again, I already knew that.

Around three thirty, I take a ridiculously long, hot shower

that probably drains the water heater of its supply, and then get dressed in jeans and my Bobby Hull Blackhawks jersey.

When I reappear downstairs, Mom's Pledging our living room furniture. "Your father is over at the Nicholses' and would like for you to come over as soon as you're dressed."

I spread my arms wide to indicate my outfit. "Is this appropriate?"

"I'm sure it is," she says, not looking up from her task.

Buckley's sitting on the couch with one leg hiked up straight into the air, cleaning himself. I don't see Natalie and Eleanor around, but I sense that they're near.

"Are we okay, Mom?" I ask delicately.

"Just go to your father, Kendall."

Walking into the living room, I take away the dust rag she's using and then I sit on the arm of the chair. Buckley stops washing and jumps off the couch to come over to me. He hops up into my lap and starts purring. "Look, Mom, I know you're not happy with me. I don't completely understand what's going on with me either, but you've just got to give me some time to figure it all out. Okay?"

Mom nods, and her thoughts aren't masked at all.

I stroke Buckley's gray and white head. "You're a mother. You want to protect me. You want to keep me from harm. I understand all of that. I'm okay, Mom."

She lets out a sigh so long I wonder if it'll ever end. "You slept for twelve hours, Kendall. You were worn out."

"I still am," I say.

"Dr. Murphy came over earlier because he'd heard about your ordeal. He thinks it would be a good idea for you to come into the office for a full physical exam."

"I don't need that. It's the psychic energy, Mom. And dealing with the ghost of Charles Stogdon."

Hurriedly, she reaches for the dust rag and begins cleaning again with great fervor. "Your father explained what happened at city hall last night. I can't say I believe it, though you obviously do."

"I do." I wish I could make her understand.

Her eyes meet mine and I can see a sheen of tears just above her bottom lids. "I know you're growing up. I'm going to have to accept that sooner or later. You'll always be my little girl, though. I will *never* quit worrying about you or stop trying to protect you. And I'm still going to do all I can to understand what's going on with you."

I fling my arms around her waist and hug her tightly, jostling a still-purring Buckley in the process. Mom combs her hands through my freshly washed and dried hair. We stay like that for a few moments until Kaitlin bursts from the den to the front door to let in Penny Carmickle. Moments later, we hear Guitar Hero roar to life in the other room, and we both laugh.

"You know, I think *she's* the one who'll end up in therapy," I say.

Mom swipes the cloth at me. "Go see your father."

I scoop up Buckley, kiss him on the head, and then place him on the floor.

"Love ya! Mean it!"

I walk out through our backyard and over to Celia's house. She answers the door and pulls me in by the arm before I can even say hello.

"We're in here." She tugs me through the massive front corridor into a large dining room. There sit Becca and Taylor on one side of the table and my dad, Mr. Nichols, and an African American man I don't know on the other. Between them is a computer monitor and Celia's laptop.

"What's going on?" I ask.

Celia ushers me toward the empty chair next to Taylor. "We didn't want to bother you since you were, like, passed out and stuff. We've been going through the tapes and pictures from last night all day, analyzing everything. Now we're de-briefing our clients."

I snicker at the thought of my dad being a "client."

"Dad, you know Kendall," Celia says to her father.

Mr. Nichols stands. "Sure, sure. Have a seat, Kendall. Are you feeling better?"

I step over a stretched-out—and snoring—Seamus to take a chair. I scoot it up closer to the table. "Yes, sir. Sleep was the best thing for me to get my energy back."

"Good to know," he says. He gestures to the man sitting next to him. "I want you to meet my friend and associate Dawson Edgars."

"Kendall." The man smiles and extends a hand across the table to me.

"Nice to meet you, Mr. Edgars."

"Call me Daw. Mr. Edgars was my father."

We chuckle together. Then I realize *this* is Thomas Edgars's descendant. "It's you!"

He cocks his head at me. "It is?"

"Charles told us all about your ancestors. How cool that you and your family still live here in Radisson?"

He folds his hands together. "Celia, Taylor, and Rebecca have been telling us all about your investigation last night and I'm just amazed at the information. The fact that you knew my ancestor's name and that he was once a slave of Mr. Charles Stogdon—that's phenomenal."

"Thanks Mr., err . . . Daw."

Daw continues. "My grandmother has long been the keeper of our family history and she gave me this scrapbook." He hefts a big red book up onto the table. There's gold embossing on the cover that reads "Edgars." He turns to the front and then spins it around to me. "This is the only picture our family has of Charles Stogdon. It's not really a photo at all but something called a ferrotype or a tintype."

I reach my hand out and pull the book toward me. Sure enough, there's a metallic sheet with a black-and-white etching of Charles Stogdon. He's wearing an outfit quite similar to what he had on when he appeared to me last night. "That's exactly who I saw at city hall."

Daw looks to Dad and Mr. Nichols. "Fascinating."

"That's my girl." Dad grins proudly at me. "Your team got a lot of interesting sound clips and photos last night."

Taylor points at the screen. "I got some great shots, Kendall, when you were talking to Charles. None of us could see him. However, if you look here," she says, "you'll see the outline of a shadow."

"Pretty cool," I say. "That's definitely where he was."

Celia winks at me. "The EVPs indicate that Charles Stogdon indeed wanted everyone off his land. Temperature readings correlate with the timing of his apparition and appearance to you, with the digital readings sloping down into the mid-forties."

Becca sees my look of wonder and adds, "Don't worry, K. We've already told them about the terminology."

"Oh, okay."

Daw speaks out. "We've agreed that as a result of your findings, it would be a wonderful idea to honor the memory of Charles Stogdon in the Mega-Mart development."

"We're going to name the main street into the distribution center Thomas Edgars Boulevard," Dad says. "And the whole development area is going to be referred to as Stogdon Landing."

A smile breaks wide on my face. "That would mean a lot to him." I *know* it would.

Dad pulls off his glasses and flicks at a spot of dust. "I'll admit this idea of ghost hunting sounded a bit off the charts,

Kendall; that is, until I was assaulted. You girls have worked hard and researched and brought this entity under control. Seems you've got a good team together and you're serious about what you're doing."

"We are, Dad."

"Are you going to continue?" he asks.

I know what the right thing to say is. "Only if you and Mom approve."

He sets his glasses back on his nose. "I can't speak for your mother, but I'm all for it. You have an ability that you need to use. Although I swear you didn't get it from me. Don't worry, I'll work on Mom."

I get up and go around the table to hug Dad.

Mr. Nichols laughs. "So *this* is what you spend all of my hard-earned money on, Celia? Equipment and computers and software?"

"Umm, yeah." She tosses her bangs out of her face. "A girl's gotta have a hobby."

Taylor folds her hands in front of her. "Let me just say that I'm honored to have been chosen to join this group. I can only hope that my photography can help us bridge a gap to the other side."

Celia and I exchange smiles. "She's really into this," Celia says.

"We all are," I add. "Especially if it helped make Dad's office safe and allowed Charles to move on."

Daw stands. "For all of your work, I want to invite you

ladies to the groundbreaking at Stogdon Landing. I'll let David know the details, and you can all come out for it. Maybe even help with the ribbon cutting."

"We'd love that, Daw," Taylor sings out.

I wink at Celia, who says, "We done good here."

"It's just the beginning."

Boooooooorrrrrrr! Even Seamus barks out his agreement.

I can barely concentrate through my morning classes on Monday because *everyone* is talking about our successful ghost hunting.

Celia's wearing a pair of smart black pants and a fitted sweater that complements her not-so-developed chestal area. Taylor and I dug it out of the depths of her closet and swore to her that we'd burn her graphic tees if she didn't show off her figure. Her hair is fluffy and styled with some of the hair products that Taylor left with her last night. The hint of mascara on the tips of her lashes really brings out her eyes, and the faint lip-gloss gives her totally kissable-looking lips. Not like *I'd* want to kiss her—*hello!*

Taylor rushes up to Celia and me as we're about to head to our lockers after calculus. Her hair is perfectly coifed, as per usual, and she looks no worse for the wear after the weekend ghost hunting. "Y'all are never going to believe what happened!"

"Are you okay?" I ask, trying to reach out to her with my psychic abilities.

"Ryan MacKenzie asked me to study with him!"

I blink in confusion. "What's a Ryan MacKenzie?"

Celia smacks me hard on the arm. "He's only one of *the* cutest guys in school. Running back for the football team. Shaggy blond hair. He's always reading *Catcher in the Rye*."

I've seen him around school. "Oh, cool!" This is apparently a big deal for Taylor, who definitely needs some positive male attention in her life.

Taylor talks a million words a minute. "He said he heard about our ghost hunting and how we'd made contact and how everyone's talking about it and how we could literally start a franchise and clean out every house in Radisson from the spirits left here for so long and that we should study together and he can help me out with biology if I help him out with history and—"

My head's going to detonate from Taylor's excitement. But I'm happy for her. She deserves it.

Taylor stops and snaps her fingers in front of Celia. "Girlfriend, you are *très* chic today. Simply gorgeous."

I look at Celia and tease her. "See what happens when you bathe?"

As she's about to tomboy punch me, someone calls out to her.

"Hey, Celia! You forgot this!"

We turn to see Clay Price trotting down the hall after us and waving a notebook over his head. Yikes! It's the one with Celia's drawings of Jason.

Slightly out of breath, Clay says, "You left this in calculus. You might need it tonight . . . you know, to do your home-work."

Celia snags the notebook and her cheeks stain. "How did you know it was mine?"

Clay simply smiles. "Easy. I saw the illustrations in the back and I know you like to sketch, so I put two and two together." He steps closer. "That's a cool drawing you've got in the back."

I see Celia swallow noticeably, and I feel bad for her. It was hard enough for her to show me her picture of Jason. Now Clay's seen it?

Bravely though, Celia flips the spiral book open to share with him. I peer over her shoulder and gasp when I see, not the drawing of Jason, but one of Clay sitting in class listening to the teacher.

"What can I say?" Celia starts. "I was bored in class and you were in my line of sight."

Clay grins widely at her. "Glad you finally see me."

Taylor grabs my arm and mouths, *Awww*.

Clay continues. "You look great today, Celia. Did you change your hair?"

She ducks her chin a little. "Yeah. Thanks." Celia shifts her weight from one foot to the other. I can sense her hesitation, mixed with some uncharacteristic boldness. "Maybe you can come over after school and see our ghost-hunting equipment. You know, how we do everything. I can show you the evi-dence we got this weekend."

"That'd be cool," he says. "We can run over to Chick-fil-A afterward, you know . . . if you want."

"Sure. Great."

After Clay's gone, Taylor and I both start squealing like sixth grade girls. "I knew you liked him!" I say.

Celia smirks and tries to shrug it off. "Yeah, whatever."

I can see right through her, though. Her features are so animated, it's like a Disney character about to burst forth in an Elton John song. Her eyes have an adorable twinkle to them as she takes an over-the-shoulder peek at Clay's retreating form. Ah yes . . . gone is her crush on Jason Tillson. In my mind, I see her in her room, tearing the page of him out of her notebook, wadding it up, tossing it in the garbage can. Ironically, behind that page are other sketches of Clay, so he was in her thoughts all along too.

"Did I call that one or what?" I say, not caring that I'm gloating.

"Hey, bitches," Becca calls out. "On your way to the caf?"

"Yep!" Taylor says with a bubbly joy in her voice. "You wanna come sit with us today or do you have to spin?"

I lift my brow. "Put a CD on and come hang."

Becca thinks for a moment. No longer are we the Barbies who bother her. We're teammates in an honorable venture. She's one of us now. "Sure," she says with a smile. "Y'all a'ight, you know?"

I put my arm around her and hug her whether she likes it or not.

We buzz through the cafeteria line—a cheeseburger and fries for Becca, Celia, and me; a salad with no dressing and a hard-boiled egg for Taylor, who wants to look her best for her study date with Ryan MacKenzie—and head straight to our table. I feel the eyes of Courtney Langdon and her flock of followers on my back as we pass by. I've got bigger fish to fry than the likes of a junior girl so insecure in herself that she has to resort to bulimia. Course, once she finds out Jason and I are an item—*we are, aren't we?*—she'll totally hate me. I'll deal with that whenever we get to that bridge.

Speak of the devil! Jason is waiting at our table for us, a mischievous look in his eyes. He takes my tray and sets it down next to his. "Where've you been all day?"

"Duh. Class."

We all sit, and before I can attack my ooey-gooey cheese-burger that's calling out to me, Jason snags my hand under the table and weaves his fingers through mine. "I've been worried about you. Your mom wouldn't let me see you yesterday."

"I was in a low-grade coma."

His mouth curves into an infectious grin. "You're okay now, though?"

I smile back and squeeze his hand for reassurance. "Thanks for being there the other night for me. I know you don't to-tally believe what we're doing—"

"I'm starting to come around after everything I witnessed. Don't get me wrong. I'm still a skeptic to the core, but I am interested in what you do and what you think you see."

"Well, good. Because that wasn't our only ghost hunt. I have to keep doing it."

He grips my hand tighter. "Then you're going to have me around."

I knit my brows together. "For protection? Jason, I don't need—"

"—a protector, I know." His eyes move over my face. "No, it's because I just want to be where you are."

I hear Taylor clear her throat, so I glance over. Again, she mouths, *Awww.*

Becca takes a ginormous bite of her cheeseburger and talks with her mouth full. "You two need to get a room or something."

We all laugh and attack our lunches. We talk about the weekend and our success at city hall and what to do to move forward. Can't just ghost hunt once and be done with it. There's still the issue of Emily, the floaty lady, in my house. Celia's going to make us a website, www.ghosthuntress.com, where we can document all of our cases—and where people can contact us if they want us to come help them out. (And no, we won't take money because that would just be unethical. We're doing this because we have to.) Becca's going to keep recording files of all of our EVPs on her laptop and even mix some of the sounds into her DJing. How freaky-cool is that? Taylor's going to post some of our images on various websites, like Ghost Village and Darkness Radio, so others can share in our experiences and leave comments. Jason promises to continue to be our skeptic, but not be so forceful in his disbelief.

Me? Well, I'm going over to Loreen's after school to tell her all about the ghost hunt and to keep learning about my awakened psychic abilities. I'm fortunate to have her guidance in my life, and my mom will just have to get over it or get used to it. That's what I have to do.

I glance around at our table: Celia, the geek-turned-swan rich girl; Taylor, the ebullient beauty; Jason, her popular and gorgeous brother; Becca, the Goth DJ; and me, the girl from Chicago who's found some good friends who accept me the way I am. What a crazy group we make, the five of us. But we're on a mission to help the spirits of Radisson. Something tells me we're going to be very busy once word gets out.

Jason drains his Coke and wipes his mouth with a napkin. "I've gotta go. Playing hoops next period with some of the guys. You got a sec?" He motions with his head for me to come with him.

"Yeah, sure." I follow him as he buses his tray.

To my amazement, I can't pick up his thoughts right now. Not like I've heard his thoughts before, like I have Celia's or others'. A warm glow passes through me as I anticipate what he might say.

He turns, and those amazing blue eyes shine down on me. "Listen, I know ghost hunting is important to you. I just hope you'll make time for me. You know, only you and me. Like, going out on dates and stuff."

I like the "and stuff" part if that means making out with him some more. I smile so hard, I think my jaw might snap. "Jason Tillson! Are you asking me out on a real date?"

"Not just one, Kendall. A lot of dates. Starting Friday night. I'll pick you up at eight."

And with that, he heads off toward the gym.

I return to the table where three sets of very inquisitive eyes examine me with concentrated scrutiny. Taylor breaks the silence, asking what they all want to know. "What was that all about?"

I can't contain my squeal. "Jason just asked me out for Friday! Can you believe it? Holy crap! What will I wear?"

Celia rolls her eyes. "Oh my God. You are *such* a girlic girl."

To an outsider just trying to make her way and fit in, this is the nicest thing anyone's ever said to me. I'm gonna do just fine here in Radisson.

Epilogue

After church on Sunday—Father Castellano was delighted to see me—I walk over to the cemetery to visit Charles Stogdon's grave. The sky above is brilliantly blue and bright, and there's a sense of peace and serenity in the air. The sun sleeks through the tree branches, painting the freshly cut grass with golden light and shadows. A cool breeze touches my arms and I know that autumn is definitely in full swing.

I never thought of a graveyard as a beautiful place, but as I look around now, I realize it's quite amazing. The final resting place for loved ones. Epitaphs of praise, appreciation, and sorrow. Obelisks that reach to the heavens. Simple stones that mark forgotten souls. Each magnificent and special in its own way.

I cross the small footbridge over the water that flows through the burial ground. No sounds of marching Union soldiers today, just birds twittering overhead in the trees. The babble of the brook adds to the tranquillity of the fall day; a few leaves lazily float down the stream.

Back in the farthest corner of the cemetery, I find a small

wrought-iron fence around a simple white marble headstone that reads "Stogdon." I climb over the enclosure and bend down to clean some of the ivy and stray weeds off the marker. I lay down the small bundle of Shasta daisies and spray roses that I picked up at the grocery store for five bucks. It's the thought that counts, right?

"Charles? Are you here?"

I listen to the whistle of the wind, trying to get a sense of whether Charles Stogdon is here or not. I certainly hope he isn't, after all we went through the other night. I pause and listen for anything that tickles my psychicness. Silence in my mind. I don't pick up on him at all. He's at peace now, thanks to my group. And I helped him move on to the next realm, where he can hopefully rejoin treasured family members and his friend Thomas Edgars.

"Nope. You're not here, Charles." I cross myself and say a quick prayer of thanks.

I'm about to go when I determine I'm not alone.

The air is suddenly thick with the aroma of lilacs. Leaves shuffle behind me and I'm sure I'll see the caretaker—who'll want to know what I'm doing—when I turn around.

I take a deep, sharp breath and stare at the face before me in utter astonishment. Is my mouth hanging open? 'Cause it feels like it is. "Emily?"

Is the woman standing before me in a white gown seriously the spirit I've seen and experienced in my room? Only she seems to be in human form now.

"Is it you?"

A smile crosses her ethereal face. "Yes, Kendall. It's me. I'm glad you recognize me."

Do I? I mean, I've seen misty images of her in my room and in the infrared shots Taylor got as Emily took off in a bolt of energy. I don't think I've ever seen her in my life, like, this up close and personal. I inspect her appearance a little more. She's quite pretty. Young. Can't be much older than I am. Maybe nineteen, tops. Soft green eyes are surrounded by charcoal black eyelashes. Her cheeks are pale, but then again, she's dead . . . *hello!* Her white dress seems to be of the hospital-gown variety, although she wears it better than most. (No opening in the back that I can tell from here.) There's something vaguely familiar about her.

"Have we met before?" I ask.

Emily steps toward me, no longer merely floating. "I've been with you your whole life, Kendall."

I'm barely able to restrain my shock and surprise. "How? When?"

"You used to see me when you were a tiny little girl. We played with your dolls and stuffed animals. I helped you name most of your teddy bears, since you were calling them Bear, The Other Bear, Big Bear. I think we named the white polar bear Carlton and the brown one, oh, what was it . . . Sonoma?"

I begin to shake. "T-t-that's right. I still have Sonoma sitting in a rocking chair in my room. I remember Mom always wondered how I would know how to name a bear after a very grown-up place in California."

Emily moves her long brown hair over her shoulder. "It's where I was born. Remember? We talked about it. We used to play a lot together. And we would sing songs all the time."

I squeeze my eyes shut and try to access the memories she's referring to that must be locked in my psyche. This all sounds so familiar. Didn't Dad say I used to have an imaginary friend? That I'd sing tunes they'd never heard before. I don't know. I was just a little kid. I do remember naming all of my stuffed animals and not knowing where the names came from. I thought it had merely been my creative imagination. Could it really have been Emily's help?

"Yes, Kendall. It was me."

I muster up all the energy I can and dive deep into my memory. There's a crib with a comforter that has pink and yellow lambs on it. A baby monitor sits on the polished dresser. The overhead mobile cranks out "Twinkle, Twinkle, Little Star." And there's a young woman sitting in my rocking chair, holding Sonoma the bear, telling me about the rolling hills and grape fields in northern California. The recollections rush back in wordless wonder.

"I *do* remember you. I called you E."

She nods and smiles again.

My chest constricts with a warmth I haven't experienced . . . ever. "Why did you go away?"

"Your parents told you that you couldn't have an imaginary friend anymore. So you quit talking to me. You ignored me for the most part, and soon, I just faded away. It was best that you obeyed your parents. You were a good girl. So full of life and spirit and spunk. I never left you, though, Kendall. I've been with you every day of your life, whether you could see me or not. When you broke your arm. When you had measles, followed by chicken pox. Your first day of school. Your first kiss." Her eyes tease me. "Your last kiss."

I flush all over, thinking about the make-out session with Jason last night in his Jeep. We totally steamed up the windows, let me tell you what!

Putting thoughts of Jason aside, I ask Emily, "Do you have something to do with my awakening?"

"I simply reached out to you again."

"So, with this awakening of my psychic abilities—which I must have had when I was little 'cause I could see you—you've decided to come back into my life?"

Emily places a hand on the fence surrounding Charles's grave. "You're open to seeing me again. Your friend Loreen was right. In the silence of this small town, you were able to sense me again. It's an amazing gift that you have. My mother had the gift, you know?"

I get a closer look at her. "Are you Resurrection Mary? You know, the lady in white that everyone sees in Chicago's Resurrection Cemetery?"

She giggles like a teenager. Like me, almost. "No, not at all. Although I know her and she's a lovely woman."

"Then why are you here?" I nearly beg. "Why me? Why now?"

Shaking her head, she says, "Too many questions at once, Kendall. It's not my place to tell you. All I can say is we're cosmically connected. Like you and Loreen. You'll have to find the rest out on your own."

"You're damn right I will. I'm an excellent researcher." Although I don't have the first freaking clue who Emily is, why she's my imaginary friend, or why I can see her again.

"I will tell you," Emily says. "What you're doing with your friends is quite admirable. There are a lot of beings and spirits wandering around—who are stuck and need your help."

"Are you stuck, Emily?" Shouldn't she be the next ghost we should help?

"Yes and no. I know I'm not alive, but I'm not ready to fully pass on into the light. I'll know when the time is right. There are entities that need your help more right now."

I swallow the dry lump in my throat. "I know."

"We can help them together, Kendall. You, me, your ghost huntresses—and your cute ghost hunter, Jason. You just have to know where to look," she tells me.

"Where?"

She spreads her arms wide. "They're everywhere. And they see your beacon of knowledge shining out to them."

I gaze out over the landscape of the cemetery and unexpectedly connect with an assortment of spirits I hadn't seen earlier. Over by the footbridge are the Union soldiers, camped out, it seems. To the left, there's a Native American woman in full tribal garb, holding a little boy by the hand. And up on the far hill, there's a young black girl in a ragged outfit climbing a tree. Certainly like nothing I've seen today. My mind speedily deciphers that she's the ghost of a slave. A girl who lived over a hundred and fifty years ago and died during the Civil War.

"They're all caught here?"

"For one reason or another," Emily says. "But you'll help them."

Looking at the many spirits around me, I let out a pent-up sigh. "Wow. I've certainly got my work cut out for me. Good thing I've got two years of high school left!"

To be continued . . .

DISCLAIMER

The thoughts and feelings described by the character of Kendall are typical of those experienced by young people awakening to sensitive or psychic abilities.

Many of the events and situations encountered by Kendall and her team of paranormal investigators are based on events reported by real ghost hunters. Also, the equipment described in the book is standard in the field.

However, if you are a young person experiencing psychic phenomena, you should talk to an adult. And although real paranormal investigation is an exciting, interesting field, it is also a serious, sometimes even dangerous undertaking. While I hope you are entertained by Ghost Huntress, please know that it's recommended that young people not attempt the investigative techniques described here without proper adult supervision.

BIBLIOGRAPHY

Terminology and descriptions pertaining to Kendall's psychic awakening, skills, and abilities from Maureen Wood, psychic/intuitive/sensitive/healer/Reiki master.

Kendall's LifeSounds 440® white-noise sound machine product information from Marsona and www.luxevivant.com.

EMF Meter descriptions and definition from en.wikipedia .org/wiki/EMF_Meter.

Celia's Lead in Hair Products experiment—from the University of Sydney, Australia, *Chemistry Demonstrations and Experiments on the Internet*: alex.edfac.usyd.edu.au/methods/science/Internet-chem-dems-expts.htm.

Definition of "Residual Haunting" from en.wikipedia.org/wiki/Residual_haunting.

Ghost hunting terms and definitions from various sources including author's firsthand knowledge and experience, The New England Ghost Project (www.neghostproject.com),

Darkness Radio (www.darknessradio.com), Ghost Village (www.ghostvillage.com), TV shows *Ghost Hunters, Dead Famous, Most Haunted,* and *Paranormal State,* and www.Wikipedia.com.

Prayer to Saint Michael from en.wikipedia.org/wiki/Prayer_to_Saint_Michael.

Shakespearean Quotes from www.enotes.com/shakespeare-quotes.

Zyprexa® product information from www.zyprexa.com.

Kendall Moorehead's world has just been blown wide open. Don't miss what happens next in

BOOK 2

GHOST HUNTRESS
the guidance

Let me tell you what: it's been a busy couple of months for me, Kendall Moorehead. Once word got out about how my team of ghost huntresses helped a 150-year-old spirit that was trapped at city hall pass into the light, well, everyone and their brother has stopped us with a ghost story or two to tell. Being official ghost huntresses has made me and my friends—Celia, Taylor, and Becca—the talk of town, and we've garnered a ton of attention. (Not all of it is positive . . . especially the dirty looks and ill treatment from school beeyotch Courtney Langdon and her flock of followers. However, I think that has more to do with the fact that I'm now dating her ex-boyfriend—and Taylor's twin brother—Jason Tillson.)

It's sort of hard to have a boyfriend when all of your weekends are filled with visits to Radisson's most historical—and often haunted—locations, the mustiest and dustiest of basements, and the homes of some lonely and weird townspeople. Like right now.

I shift on the antique couch and clear my throat to ease the tension in my tight chest. I don't think that Mrs. Lockhart is one of those weirdos we've been running into lately—the kind who wear tinfoil hats and sleep in their bathtubs for fear that something is watching them—because she was a kindergarten teacher in Radisson for years and schooled all three of my friends. However, the woman is definitely brokenhearted and forlorn. The sadness radiating from her is palpable, and I can feel it in the fibers of my being like the heat from a well-stoked fireplace.

I nudge Celia in the ribs with my elbow, and she knows that I'm ready to get down to business.

"So, Mrs. Lockhart, can you tell us again everything that happened with your husband?" Celia says in a very grown-up, professional manner. She flips open her notepad and twirls her Bic between her long fingers.

Becca clicks the digital recorder on and places it on the marble coffee table. She's our sound expert on the team, trying to capture EVPs, electronic voice phenomena. EVPs are the coolest thing ever. I mean, I can hear the spirits' voices in my head, but the digital recorder can actually pick up disembodied voices that will answer questions or make statements during our investigations. That way, if we capture anything, it totally backs up what I'm saying. Taylor nods at me and then moves over to where she has the video recorder set up. She's a whiz-bang at anything photography related. That's why she's on the team. Some of the pictures she's captured with the infrared camera and the night vision are a-freakin-mazing!

Sitting forward, I fold my hands together and listen as Mrs. Lockhart explains why we're here. The older woman dabs her wrinkled eyes with the corner of a lace handkerchief. She sniffs hard and then takes a deep breath.

"Delaney and I went out to Scottsdale last week to visit with our youngest daughter, Veronica—our older girl, Evelyn, lives next door to us—and her boys. They're such good boys, those grandsons of mine. Derrick is on the soccer team and Spencer has learned to ride his bike—"

"Yes, ma'am. Now, about Mr. Lockhart, please," I say, trying not to be rude.

"Certainly. As I was saying, we were having a ball at Veronica's. Even to the point where Delaney said he would consider moving out there, much to Evelyn's chagrin. I never thought he'd want to leave Georgia. But the weather out in Arizona is simply amazing." Mrs. Lockhart moves behind her ear a stray lock of salt-and-pepper-colored hair that escaped the tight bun at the base of her neck. I feel a tension at the back of my own neck and wonder if it's empathy from what she's going through or if I slept wrong last night.

She continues. "Delaney loved the putting greens and courses out there and was spending most afternoons golfing and relaxing. He's been so stressed lately, what with the economy and all and watching our retirement accounts dwindling. But on Saturday he didn't come back from his tee time and Veronica and I got worried. Someone from the country club called and told us that he'd had a . . . a . . ." She trails off a moment and then begins to cry. My heart goes out to her, knowing she's lost the love of her life. I mean, literally lost him.

"It's okay, Mrs. Lockhart," I say, hoping it sounds soothing. It would probably be a good thing for me to get up and go sit with her. Taylor nods at me from across the room as if she's reading my mind. I slide off the couch and move to our client's side, taking her frail hand. Immediately with the connection of skin to skin, I'm stung with grief and pain and a deep, deep loneliness. In my mind's eye I see Millicent and Delaney as a young couple, walking hand in hand down by the Spry River here in Radisson. So much in love, with the rest of their lives ahead of them. Children . . . two girls and a boy. Years flash before me like shuffling cards until I see her weeping in her daughter's arms. "Can you finish the story you told Celia on the phone?"

Mrs. Lockhart fists her free hand against her mouth and nods. "He . . . he had a h-h-heart attack on the eleventh hole and was more than likely taken straight to Jesus with no pain or suffering." She blots under her eye again to catch a wayward tear. "The man he was playing with said he'd just gotten a hole in one," she adds with a slight laugh.

"Man, golf's a rough sport," Becca mutters. Taylor immediately gives her a nasty look.

Celia jumps in to cover Becca's comment. "Tell Kendall the part with the airlines, Mrs. L." Celia looks at me. "This is the most important part."

The woman keeps going. "Oh, very well. It seems that Southeastern Airlines kind of—well, how do I say this—misplaced my Delaney."

"They what?" I ask incredulously.

She tugs a piece of paper out of the pocket of her housedress and passes it over to me. It's got a barcode with a number and is marked "ATL," the airline code for Atlanta's Hartsfield-Jackson International Airport.

"Is this a claim ticket?"

"For his coffin," she says.

Holy crap!

"Just a second. You're telling me . . ." I begin.

Celia finishes. ". . . that she checked him into Baggage in Phoenix, but when Mrs. Lockhart landed in Atlanta and went to claim him, Delaney was missing."

Mrs. Lockhart sniffs into her handkerchief. "I was so distraught; I didn't know what to do. Evelyn had to drive over and talk to the supervisor. Poor child was grief-stricken herself, losing her father, and she had to go though all of the airport's bureaucratic red tape."

"What can we do, though, Celia?" I raise my brow and bite my bottom lip as I consider what it is exactly that I—that we—can do to help locate the body. Not really the type of investigation we're used to.

Mrs. Lockhart grips my hand tightly in hers. "You've got to use your powers to find him."

"I don't really have powers." I'm not a comic book or movie character like Superman, Ironman, or Wonder Woman. "I locate *spirits* of the deceased, not the deceased themselves."

"Have you talked to the local coroner?" Becca asks.

"He was no help. But y'all will be, right?"

"I-I-I don't know—" What exactly can I do?

Her eyes light up. "Oh, but that's just it. I feel Delaney here in the house. Evelyn said she's sure he's around, too. She's even felt him over at her house. Surely you can try to contact him. He would know where his body is, wouldn't he?"

Celia shrugs. "I suppose."

Taylor lets out a long sigh and says, "*Une telle tragédie.* Such a tragedy."

So, let me get this straight. I'm to make contact here in the house with Delaney and he's going to tell me where we can find his body so Mrs. Lockhart can get him home for the funeral he deserves to have. A final resting place. As ludicrous as it sounds, I guess we can help out with that. Honestly, I don't think the *Ghost Hunters* have ever had a case like this one.

I release the older woman's hand and drag my palms down the sides of my jeans as I stand up, not sure which one of us has let off the nervous sweat. "I'll give it a try."

She's on her feet, too. Gratitude paints its way across her wrinkled face.

"I'm going to need assistance, though," I say to my posse.

"We're here, Kendall," Taylor pipes up.

"Ditto" from Becca.

Celia nods and smiles.

I push my wavy brown hair behind my ears and then rub my hands together. "I appreciate that you guys are here, but I'm going to need even more help."

"Emily?" Celia asks.

My turn to nod.

And just like that, my spirit guide, Emily—who first came to me as a voice in the white-noise machine in my new bedroom—is with me, ready to give assistance. She's only visible to me at certain times, and I mostly just talk to her in my head. Yeah, I know . . . throw a net over me. That's what my mom's threatening to do anyway.

I walk through the expansive old house, trying to get a sense of who Delaney Lockhart was before he passed. Since I've only lived in Radisson a couple of months, I don't know everyone's business like most people in town seem to have a talent for. Taylor told me that Mr. Lockhart had worked at the First National Bank and Celia knew him to be an avid lake fisherman who always shared his catch of the day with people down at the Methodist church. Now, as I sit in the worn Barcalounger in the den, I'm seeing a slide show of images in my head. Delaney was tall. He'd lost his hair. He cut his fingernails in this spot while watching TV. (Eww!) He was a stern father but loved to spoil his grandchildren. He snuck Swisher Sweets cigars out in the backyard for the last twenty years. I'm sure that must have had something to do with his heart problems.

Focus your energies to the right, Kendall . . .

Emily directs my attention over toward a door. "Where does this go?" I ask.

"To the basement," Mrs. Lockhart answers. "The laundry room is down there. Other than that, we mostly use it to store extra belongings from when we moved out of the main house when Evelyn got married, and we let them have it."

"That's okay. We're not here to rifle through your things," I assure her.

"It's a mess. I don't think you girls should go down there. Especially if you have allergies."

Hmm . . . and me without my Claritin.

I hear Emily whisper, *Goooo* . . .

If she says so, then I must.

"I have to go down there." I turn the handle and immediately the smell of dust and mold and dampness attacks my nostrils. Celia flicks the cord of the light dangling in the doorway.

"This doesn't look very good," Taylor says.

Becca snickers. "Don't be such a girl, Tillson." And then she passes all of us and heads downstairs.

"I'll stay up here," our hostess says.

It's probably better that way.

Emily whispers to me. *Laundry room.*

The four of us pick our way through boxes of Christmas ornaments, winter clothes, and toys for the grandchildren to get back to where the washer and dryer sit. My chest begins to tighten in a deep ache under my lungs. The atmosphere is dense in this section and I'm finding it hard to get a good breath of air. It's like I want to pant but there's nothing to suck into my lungs.

"Are there any spirits here with us?" Becca asks as she holds her digital recorder out in front of her. "Is the spirit of Delaney Lockhart present? I have a recording device in my hand that is able to pick up your voice if you have the energy to speak to us. We can play it back and see what you had to say and try to help out."

While Becca's doing her EVP work, my chest continues to throb. My heartbeat accelerates to *Speed Racer* levels and I try to tell myself that this isn't really happening to me, per se—it's just that I'm empathetic and can oftentimes feel what the spirit might have experienced.

I hear Emily plainly in my head. *He's here . . .*

"Play back your recorder, Becca," Celia says before I can.

After a quick rewind, we hear Becca's question and then a garbled swooshing into a voice that says, *"Leeeeeeeeeeeeffffffff be-hind."*

"Did you hear that?" Becca says with excitement. "Score!" She loves getting EVPs, and I must admit I get a real rush out of it, as well.

Then, a little further into the recording, we hear, *"Miiiillllllie."*

He called her that, Emily tells me.

I take out my rose quartz pendulum that I use for dowsing. It's really cool because I can ask it yes-or-no questions and can have a two-way conversation with a spirit. I'm absolutely sensing a presence here in this basement. However, I have to make sure it's Delaney Lockhart. We've run into so many street ghosts in our investigations lately—random spirits that inhabit Radisson, people who lived a long time ago, before the interstate to Atlanta cut through or the town was wired for cable.

As I hear Taylor clicking away in the background with her digital camera, I'm still experiencing the emotional choke of extreme heart pain. Is this from Delaney's cardiac attack? It feels more like . . . a broken heart than blocked arteries. Not that I'm a doctor or anything. There just isn't that sense of blood stopping and not filling the chambers of the heart. I'm picking up something much more forlorn.

"Are you Delaney Lockhart?"

I watch as the pendulum dangles from my thumb and forefinger and swings from left to right. This is how I get the answer no.

Hmm. "Are you a female spirit?"

The pendulum confirms another no.

"Are you a male spirit?"

"Duh," Becca says with a snicker.

"You know we have to explore all options," Celia snaps.

My pendulum begins to swing clockwise, which signifies a yes answer.

"Check this out!" Taylor shouts out. "I just took a series of pictures of that corner."

Sure enough, there's a mist in the bottom-right corner that continues to get larger in each frame until it takes on a shape. A very distinct human shape.

Taylor points. "That looks like a soldier's cap. Like someone from the Civil War."

We do have a lot of Civil War history in this town. Local legend has it that General Sherman visited Radisson on his infamous March to the Sea. He and his men were so enamored by a townswoman that they didn't burn the place, leaving many historic antebellum houses in their original condition, much like the mansion that Celia and her parents live in on the street behind my house.

Turning to Celia, I ask, "Did Mrs. Lockhart say anything about a ghost in her house before Delaney's death?"

She shakes her head, tossing her short black bob back and forth. "Never before, although she claims her daughter Evelyn's house is haunted. That was one of the reasons she and Mr. Lockhart gave it to her and moved out here into the carriage house."

"You're some kind of street ghost, aren't you?" I call out. "You sensed what was going on here, that we were looking for a spirit, and you butted your nose in. If you are, you need to leave, please. You don't belong here. Go back to where you were or let me help you cross into the light."

Before I can say another word, I clamp my hands over my ears to stop the piercing pain. All I hear reverberating through my head is this wicked, evil laughter. Sinister, almost, echoing off my cerebral matter. I scream inside, telling him to bugger off. He's not wanted. I clutch my chest and then I feel an insane twinge in my head.

He's trouble . . .

Like I need Emily to tell me that.

I fall to my knees due to the intense throbbing in my temple. Taylor drops next to me. "Jason should have come with us tonight," she says. "He's going to be inconsolable if anything happens to you."

Yeah, my boyfriend still doesn't exactly like that I do this on a regular basis.

You'll be fine. Ride it out, Kendall.

I reach for Taylor's hand and hold on tightly as the pain begins to subside. I just wish the soldier would stop it with the evil laugh, like he's taking pleasure seeing me this way.

Suddenly a man appears before me in plaid shorts, a white Titleist shirt, and a Nike visor. Oh, this has *got* to be Delaney Lockhart. He glances down at me and smiles. Then he tosses a glower to the corner where the soldier is standing. Inside my head, I hear him tell the other man to be gone and to leave me alone and to "go back to Evelyn's." Great, we're going to have to come back and clean out her house, as well.

The soldier disappears just like that.

Celia and Taylor help me up. I cock my head to the left. Celia's EMF detector lights up like a state trooper's sirens. EMF stands for electromagnetic field detector. It reads levels of energies. It's widely thought in the paranormal community— *yes, we're a community*—that spirits use energy to manifest. And since everything in the world is basically made of energy, you never know where a ghost may appear or how they'll do it. Let me tell you what: I've got a manifestation, all right.

"Mr. Lockhart?" I ask out loud.

Celia and Taylor spin in the direction of my voice. Becca follows along behind me.

I hear him plain as day, as if he's really standing before me. Well, he *is* standing before me. Only no one can see him but me.

Mr. Lockhart smiles at me. "I'm sorry about that soldier. He's been nosing around here trying to get attention and cause trouble. Are you okay, dear?"

"Yes, sir," I say, catching my breath. All of my physical symptoms have eased. "You know why I'm here, right?"

Becca lifts a dark brow at me and then positions the digital recorder in the direction of where I'm speaking. Taylor snaps away on the camera, and Celia stands by taking all sorts of measurements. They've all seen this before and know just to go with the flow and not freak out that I'm seeing an entity . . . and having a conversation with it.

"They left me behind," he says. "Those idiots at the airline. I sat on a conveyer belt for at least two days. Good thing I was embalmed before they put me in the casket. Otherwise"—he waves his hand in front of his nose— "that would be a horrific smell, don'tcha think?"

I snicker at the ghost's joke about his own demise. I have to be serious, though, since I don't know how long Delaney will be able to manipulate the energy around for me to see and hear him. "Where are you?"

He takes off his visor and scratches his head. "I don't rightly know."

My body sags and I exhale noisily. "You have to remember something. A detail? A sound? A smell?"

"Nope. The formaldehyde sort of masks everything else."

"Ask him about the airplane," Celia instructs. "Is there anything he can remember about it? Particularly the color?"

"Sure, sure," he says, hearing Celia's question himself. "I remember going into this big ole gold plane."

"Gold," I say to Celia. "He says it was gold."

She runs her hands through the top of her hair and I can almost hear the wheels of thought turning. "Mrs. Lockhart said she was on Southeastern Airlines. Their planes are blue and silver. The luggage handlers must have loaded him onto the wrong flight."

"Who has gold planes?" Becca asks.

Of course Celia, knower of all things trivial and seemingly unimportant—seriously, the girl could win the adult *Jeopardy!* tournament—snaps her fingers. "Journey Airlines has gold planes. I've seen their ads on television."

"Do they fly into Atlanta?" Taylor asks.

Celia indicates no. "Their hub is Memphis."

The energy shifts in the room and becomes almost staticky. My own oomph is starting to fade, as I know Delaney's been pulling off my psychic abilities to talk to me. He smiles and waves and blows a kiss. "We'll get you home," I say in my head.

You did well . . . Emily notes to me.

We rush upstairs to tell Mrs. Lockhart. Well, I don't. Becca has to help me up the stairs and over to a couch to regain my strength. Man, connecting with spirits like that just wears me the hell out. I need a massive nap now.

Celia dials up Journey's toll-free number on her cell phone and gets the proper customer service person to help out. We listen to the one-sided conversation as she relays the information. Mrs. Lockhart stands holding Taylor's hand as she awaits the verdict.

"Yes, she's right here and can give you all of the information." Celia breaks into a wide grin. She passes her cell phone to Mrs. Lockhart. "They have your husband."

"Thank you, Jesus!" she sings out. "And you girls! Thank you, thank you! This wouldn't have happened without you. Now my Delaney can come home for a proper burial. Evelyn and Veronica will be so relieved." She puts the phone to her ear and begins giving her personal information.

"Yep, just another typical day for the ghost huntresses," I say with a contented sigh. Taylor and Becca high-five and Celia leans over for a fist bump.

Why am I still feeling a bit kerfuffled, though?

You haven't seen the last of that soldier . . .

And along with Emily's sweet voice, the sinister laugh is back.

Yeah, I have a feeling our paths will cross again.